Crazy Love

Praise for Tom Lennon's first novel,
When Love Comes to Town

'An important book...sensitive, sincere. Full of real people struggling with real emotions.'

Books Ireland

'Those who will [read it] will gain a heart-rending insight into the traumas of those who seek love and affection in a society where gay relationships are not accepted. A worthwhile read, which gets its message across very effectively.'

The Evening Press

'*When Love Comes to Town*...is a brave attempt at putting into fictional form the difficulties facing the gay man. The story is told honestly, with no gratuitous descriptions of sex, and the characters are drawn well and in no way stereotyped. All right-thinking people should read it and if a few wrong-thinking ones did the same, it might help to change their views.'

Vincent Banville, The Sunday Press

With thanks to all at The O'Brien Press,
especially my editor, Susan Houlden.

Published 1999 by The O'Brien Press Ltd.,
20 Victoria Road, Dublin 6, Ireland.
Tel. +353 1 4923333; Fax. +353 1 4922777
e-mail: books@obrien.ie
Website: http:/// www.obrien.ie

ISBN: 0-86278-560-X

British Library Cataloguing-in-publication Data
A catalogue reference for this title is available
from the British Library

   1 2 3 4 5 6 7 8 9 10
  99 00 01 02 03 04 05 06 07

The O'Brien Press receives
assistance from

The Arts Council
An Chomhairle Ealaíon

Colour Separations: C&A Print Services
Printing: Cox & Wyman Ltd.

Crazy Love

Tom Lennon

THE O'BRIEN PRESS
DUBLIN

For my family

Chapter One

It's Thursday evening, the pub is crowded, the air is smoky and, by the minute, the conversation is becoming increasingly more inane. You don't want to be here, but you are. It's office etiquette. An appearance has to be made, same as a funeral. If you narrow your eyes into slits, the bar looks like the insides of a beehive. Everyone seems to be crawling over one another. Another few drinks and there's no doubting that it will resemble the hectic frenzy of a disturbed nest.

There's a group of secretaries huddled together over by the window and you know only too well that they're trading opinions on the real story behind Eileen's departure. The crowd from design are also out in force; the boys with their ponytails, the girls with their shaved heads. Everything about them reminds you of those ridiculous postures of adolescence. Fashion terrorists on the march, uniform in their difference, speaking their own peculiar language and keeping their heads at a perfect tilt, always ready for that camera flash.

You are stuck with a gathering of the executive staff. Sophie, the boss man's secretary, decides that Ronnie Burke is too far gone to give the introductory chit-chat. And as though to prove this, Ronnie Burke bumps into an immovable object and there's something of a skirmish to avoid the spray of gin and tonic. Ronnie is one of the company's directors, and he has a stomach to prove that he has done more than his fair share of client entertainment. A replacement for Ronnie is being sought, the faces are being scanned, but there really is only one nominee, there really is only one person who would want such a dubious honour. And as expected, Kevin Daniels offers his services and no one says anything for a moment.

"Okay Kevin, go for it," Sophie says eventually. She is amazed. Kevin claps his hands together and calls for a bit of hush. Thirty years old, he could still pass for eighteen. His slight frame suggests that he was the one whose mother gave him the sick-note for PE classes, and something about his milky-coloured baby face always conjures up the unsettling image of his wife snuggling him up to her breast for feeding.

"Peoples, we are gathered here to pay tribute to Eileen."

The juggernaut of pub chatter grinds to an abrupt halt. Airbrakes hiss, tyres screech, then silence. Even the distorted background music has been lowered. People are eyeing Kevin Daniels in an amused, almost quizzical manner. They suspect this might be a joke but they're not quite sure.

"As you all know, Eileen has been the cornerstone of the computer department for the past...God knows how many years, and I for one am deeply grateful to her for her sterling work."

There are audible gasps of disbelief. Even by Kevin Daniels's standards, this is quite something. Balls of steel, they call it. This is why people have him earmarked as top-brass material.

"C'mon Eileen, get them off you!", Ronnie Burke's heady roar ends the moment.

Disdainful glances are exchanged. Sniggers emanate from the drunks. Some people look around at Ronnie, but the majority pretend not to have heard the comment.

"And now peoples, without any further fuss, I'd like to hand you over to our esteemed managing director, who will perform the presentation...Mr Jim Carney." Kevin Daniels's arm-waving style of introduction puts you in mind of Kermit the Frog.

This is the signal for Carney to roll his way up onto the hastily-assembled rostrum to say the standard few words of praise before he performs the presentation. And good old Eileen continues the ritual by pecking Carney on the cheek, admiring the crystal bowl, and telling everyone how much she has enjoyed working in the computer department for the past, "God knows how many years". Unknown to her, the crystal bowl was hastily acquired in a last-minute lunchtime purchase. But it's obvious she realises that most people present either know, or else have made a fair guess, that her departure is not the voluntary move she claims it to be. You just stand there, sipping your flat beer, marvelling at the pretence all around.

However, her audience's attention perks up noticeably when Eileen begins to name names. She's thanking people, including your good self, but as anticipated by the crowd in the tearoom, she makes a point of omitting Kevin Daniels's name. He's her immediate boss, the one responsible for her getting the old heave-ho. She becomes breathless, overcome with the almost guilty excitement of a child calling a teacher a rude name to their face, and you realise that this is her little moment of revenge, a petty snub which will be blown out of all proportion in the tearoom tomorrow morning.

But Kevin Daniels is clapping away with such gusto any objective observer might be led to believe that Eileen had just been presented with the Nobel Prize for Retirement Speeches. People are casting incredulous glances in his direction. Talk about pulling the rug out from under poor old Eileen's feet. A few of the secretaries have their tongues out, performing a licking motion. Eileen is staring at him, her bottom lip quivering, looking as though she's on the verge of using the crystal bowl to reshape his head.

Possibly sensing this imminent danger, Kevin Daniels moves to your side and says, "No blood spilled. Could've been much, much worse."

You nod, uncomfortable at being implicated like this.

"Will we have another?", he's pointing at your drink.

"No thanks, Kevin, I've had my quota."

He takes a quick look around before he whispers,

"We have heard a certain rumour that you might be getting your new assistant now."

You raise your eyebrows. Across the bar people have gathered around Eileen to admire the crystal bowl, towards which you contributed a tenner.

"Why, did he say something to you?"

Kevin Daniels touches his nose and contorts his face into that smarmy smile of his, and not for the first time you picture yourself crouched down in a dark alleyway, your crazed eyes staring out through balaclava slits, your sweaty palms clutching a baseball bat. Daniels skips around the corner and you crack his eggshell skull open with one neat blow.

But you say nothing. The faintest of smiles gives him the impression that you approve of his methods. You are the ultimate in presenting the right face. Control is your middle name. Two pints is the limit for office socials. No unguarded comments must slip out.

And fittingly, the Phantom glides into your line of vision and immediately sets about regaling a group of secretaries. Judging by their reactions, he's telling his latest crop of jokes, jokes which are usually of a decent standard, but he must suspect that the secretaries he's talking to all think that he's a nutcase. And for good reason too. Everyone knows that he's only here to sip on one measly bottle of Guinness for a half-hour or so and then it's back to the office with him. The night-watchman gives a daily update on what time he finishes up at. It keeps everyone amused. Seven am is the record. On occasions, the same night-watchman catches him in the gents toilet performing domestic chores such as shaving himself, washing his armpits, washing his hair, even scrubbing his socks. It's sad, but sometimes sad things can be so amusing. Everyone agrees that he will one day haunt the building. A forty-five year old bachelor, the Phantom is the creative director, Head of design, and it's the likes of him who make you realise that there are positive aspects to marriage.

Outside the pub at closing-time Ronnie Burke is rolling on his back on the damp pavement. He puts you in mind of a stranded tortoise. A group of passing college students stop to assist this respectably attired middle-aged man to manoeuvre himself into an all-fours position. "I'm fine," you hear Ronnie slur, "just something I ate." The students laugh in an exaggerated manner, but Ronnie knows that they're eyeing him sadly, resolving never to end up a pathetic case like him. The bould Ronnie clambers to his feet, steadies himself, and in classic Burke fashion he thanks them for being so helpful, but as soon as they're ten yards away, feeling good with themselves, he fires insult after insult after them. You hear him toss out words like sluts, dole spongers, parasites and, of course, homosexuals, before he stumbles away, car keys in hand, through the swimming light of the side-street.

Misty rain drifts into the windscreen, the wipers go swish-swish, the blurred oncoming lights blind you, and you worry about encountering Ronnie Burke's tank of a Mercedes. Finally, you ease your way out on to the relative safety of the main road that takes you all the way out to Legoland. You are in control, you tell yourself, pressing your foot down on the accelerator. The smooth engine of the powerful 520i springs into action. Even with two pints spread over three hours you are a different man behind the wheel. Power is a fast car. Up ahead, the red tail-lights merge into a long skipping rope. Across the bay, beyond the intermittent sweep of a lighthouse beam, the lights of Howth flicker and dance like thousands of fans holding up lighters at a rock concert. With the radio up loud, something is tempting you to shut your eyes and see how far you can drive without causing a major pile-up. A press of a button opens the electric window. The blast of chilly night air clears the head. Everything is under control. You push your foot to the floor. A group of pedestrians watch you speed past, no doubt thinking, There's a thoroughbred hotshot if ever I saw one.

It's a relief to find Anne asleep in the spare bed in the baby's room. A hassle-free sleep is always welcome. Obviously Her Ladyship has refused to sleep in her cot once again. It makes you smile to imagine the rumpus she kicked up. You stand by the bedside and watch them. Curled up, facing one another, they make you feel like a stranger. Some impulse tempts you to wake Anne up, talk to her; hug the baby and hear her squeal with delight when you touch your bristling stubble against her soft skin. But you need sleep, hours and hours of it.

A half an hour of lying in the darkness with a jumbled version of the day's events playing themselves back in your head is enough. Fearing the onset of insomnia you roll out of the bed and head downstairs. There's an open bottle of wine in the fridge. A glass will help you to unwind. One of Anne's magazines is lying open on the problem page. It's *Dear Lucy, my breasts are too big*, and *Dear Lucy, my husband's penis is too small*, and *Dear Lucy, I achieved a multiple orgasm while out horse-riding*. You wonder how many, if any, are genuine. It's easy to picture the fun the magazine's employees must have in their attempts to outdo one another with their ingenious letters. But one thing is certain, it's mind-boggling to think of the letter Anne could potentially write to *Dear Lucy* about you.

Then you do something you haven't done in a long time. You go into the living-room, take the wedding album down off the top shelf and browse through the pictorial record of the day of Great Pretence. This was the day you delivered the Oscar-winning performance. Liam Neeson and the boys could've learned a thing or two from you that day. Even now, three years on, the memory still churns your stomach. Time froze that day. It was like you were swimming underwater amid a blur of smiling faces. That day of pomp and ceremony when you felt that the groom was someone else and you were watching him, delighted by his apparent joy. A day of great pretence when even the weather was ambiguous, with blustery April showers drifting down in the glaring bright sunshine. There were flowers and music, the antique Rolls Royce, rows and rows of fashionable hats, dresses, suits and tails; family and friends, speeches, smiles, food, drink and dancing; and you were sure you heard the muffled cries of future babies that would one day prove you to be a real man.

And the groom went through it all without missing a beat. Anyone could see that he was caught up in the swing of it all, that he wasn't different after all. Razzmatazz wasn't the word for it. You seemed to be watching yourself during that rip-roaring speech, a speech which was peppered with hilarity, but which also touched those important notes of sincerity. Everybody loves a bit of sincerity on these special occasions. How you pulled it off, you'll never know. The "I do" bit in the church was child's play compared to the sincerity speech; the "I am so deeply in love with Anne, she is the most wonderful person I have every met" bit. That still leaves you cold. Then thanking her parents, her father posthumously, "for making you the happiest man alive". These were exactly the words a good friend had used at his own wedding months before, but no doubt, for him, they were heartfelt. And to keep the sham going this graceful groom danced with every female in the place, from Anne's octogenarian great grandaunt to the little flower girls. Everyone said that he was walking on air, while he was really walking deeper and deeper into the mire. Leading his wife on a merry dance if the truth be known.

The group photo is the one. Particularly the people towards the back, college friends and the like, people you haven't seen in years. Some of the faces flicker a memory, but their names elude you. The ones nearer to the front are the immediate families and the friends who kept in touch. All of these friends are married now, living in their own exorbitantly priced Legoland houses, tacitly competing with one another from everything to building that new conservatory to having that second child. It's a race to see who's first to pop it, and of course, out of all of this, it's the crèche-owners who are the high-rollers.

* * * *

Watching the baby awaken is definitely one of the highlights of your day. If she's still snoozing you make sure to nudge against her cot, just so you'll see that look of utter amazement when she first opens her eyes to greet the day. Everything is brand new. Her arms and legs jiggle with sheer joy when she sees you reach into the cot. She's so excited she almost forgets to breathe. Her eyes are saying, There's Dada, there's Mama, there's Dolly, there's Teddy, you're all here around me; I had the most wonderful adventures in dreamland. A part of her passion is transferred to you. This is the true meaning of morning glory.

On the way down the stairs, she jerks her finger out, says, "Wah's sat?", and points to the objects you have to name for her. This is the game. You say the word and she repeats it in her own special way. You could happily spend the entire day with her, but success demands that you get ahead of the posse, that your rubber tyres have to be among the first to grip the concrete artery which leads into the heart of the throbbing city.

And nine hours later, at four o'clock that afternoon, you're at your desk, checking through the monthly budget figures for the umpteenth time, when Jim Carney phones and asks you to drop up to his office. Ominously, amid the paper jungle, there's a half-empty bottle of whiskey and two glasses sitting on the mahogany desk. He signals to you to take a seat, and when you do he leans forward, his hands joined, his glazed eyes fixed on you.

"D'you know something, we have more computing power here than the Yanks used to send Apollo Nine to the moon. Makes you wonder, doesn't it? Makes you wonder what the hell that shower down in the computer room are up to." His hands are held aloft in a gesture of despair.

"Hmmmm." You avert your gaze and permit yourself a silent yelp of jubilation. Kevin Daniels is the computer man. But you know it's also Carney's way of glossing over Eileen's dismissal.

"Paul, it's no great secret that I'm very pleased with the work you're doing here."

You lower your head modestly. Carney's pupils are dilated, his cheeks ruddy; it's no great mystery where the half-bottle has disappeared to. But, weighing in at nineteen stone, he has the constitution of the proverbial horse and, as people have discovered to their detriment, he also has an amazing capacity to remember everything that is said in the midst of an alcoholic haze.

"In fact, I'd go so far as to say that you've become indispensable to the company."

"Thanks, Mr Carney." The word 'indispensable' pleases you. But you already know this. If people have a problem, they come to you. You thrive on this. It's such a deep-seated need to succeed, a desire to show any potential detractors that you're not going to be the failure they might have expected you to be.

"And in view of your excellent performance, I'm pleased to tell you that I've sanctioned a rise of five grand for you this year."

"Thanks, that's very generous of you."

"It's well deserved."

Carney points to the bottle of whiskey. "Pour us a drop there in celebration."

You pour him a glass.

"What's this?" He holds the glass up and inspects it as though it was laced with poison.

"Paddy."

"You better fetch me a magnifying glass."

Like a good sycophant, you are searching for a magnifying glass before the irony dawns on you.

"There's no drought," he says, snatching the bottle from your grasp and filling his glass up to the brim. He swallows it back in two gulps. His rubbery lips seem to clasp the glass like a vice-grip.

"What age are you now, Paul?"

"Twenty-eight."

He nods as if you've just told him your innermost secret, and this action causes his many chins to open and close like an accordion.

"I had five kids when I was twenty-eight."

Tough, you want to say, but you don't. Instead you emit a polite laugh to convey a hearty respect for his virility.

"You know, we men spend most of our twenties looking for love and romance, that sort of thing; but as thirty approaches, the career becomes all important. Whatever level you reach in the company ladder during your thirties is as high as you're ever going to reach. Did you know that?"

You open your eyes wide to give the impression that this is the most fascinating snippet of information you've heard in a long time.

"And I'll tell you, once someone gets into the higher management echelons, it's difficult to budge them. Look at Ronnie Burke, for God's sake. The man's incompetent and he's a bloody director."

You utter a stonewalling laugh. He's testing you.

"It'd cost more than it's worth to get rid of him now." Carney points to the bottle of whiskey. "Pour one for yourself."

You do this because he won't let you out of the room without having at least one.

And as soon as you do, Carney rambles into the story of how, as a fourteen-year-old messenger boy, he cycled the streets of

Limerick on a rickety old bicycle which he had to back-pedal to operate the brakes. You half-listen to the much-repeated tale of how such humble origins gradually evolved into Carney Textiles, manufacturers of exclusive ladies and gents clothing, with a turn-over in excess of ten million and a staff of one hundred and fifty. (One hundred and forty-nine since Eileen's departure.) You raise the glass to your lips to give the right impression. The taste of the whiskey causes your eyes to water. If he starts on about how he spotted a niche in the clothing market, how he's catering for the new tastes of the *nouveau riche*, the remainder of your drink might end up in his eye. But he doesn't; one thing about Carney, he's aware of audience thresholds.

In typical fashion, he swivels around, displaying surprising dexterity for a man of his bulk, and switches the topic of conversation.

"Paul, I've authorised my secretary to put an ad in the papers for a new assistant for you."

He doesn't believe in wasting time. Eileen's seat must still be warm. But it irritates you that Kevin Daniels got wind of this before you.

"I want to free you up for more important matters."

Is this a poor reflection on you, you wonder. Is it because you're unable to handle the work? This causes a moment's uneasiness. How could you explain that you work late to avoid going home, that things in the merry nest aren't all they might appear to be. If it was though, he'd hardly have given you the payrise. But maybe it's like a football manager getting that dreaded vote of confidence.

"In fact, I'm going to put your name forward for the board."

You look at him politely, pretending that you are unsure of what he's saying.

"Paul Cullen, Financial Director, how does that grab you?"

Before you have time to finish your grovelling thank yous, Carney has heaved his massive frame up out of his chair and edged his way, crab-like, towards the french doors. It's easy to see how he earned the affectionate nickname of Jimmy Joe Fat from the crowd in the tearoom. He pushes the doors open and steps out onto the small balcony which is littered with his prized collection of potted plants. Down below, a tour-guide has to compete with the blare of a car alarm to make herself heard to her group of eager Japanese tourists. They are probably Joycean scholars in the city of plenty. Boom City, nightclub capital of the Milky Way, cultural centre of the Universe. Again, displaying remarkable agility, Carney bends over to flick a tiny insect off a yellow flower. His jacket tails lift up to expose his extraordinarily large backside, which, office rumour has it, necessitated the extra-large toilet seat in his office's *en suite* bathroom which, rumour also has it, had to be lifted in by crane.

"Rather pleasant odour, haven't they?"

"They have," you mutter, thinking that just the slightest of nudges would send the Fat Man plunging over the low balcony railing and give the tourists down below something really juicy to tell their friends back in Tokyo.

"I'm still just a big country boy at heart." Carney stands upright, holds his hands on his hips while he catches his breath. After a few wheezes, he slips his inhaler out of his pocket and sprays two blasts into his mouth. "Jaysus, I need a little refreshment after all that exertion."

You step back into the lavish office where Carney plonks himself down into his swivel chair, points to his drinks cabinet and asks you to pour him a different whiskey.

"Which type?" you ask, somewhat taken aback by the array of bottles.

"Surprise me."

You pour a measure of Scotch and hand it to him. At his insistence you pour yourself a refill and sit down, while he prepares himself for the arduous task of putting his unforgeable scrawl of a signature to a mound of cheques.

Availing of this distraction, you empty the contents of your glass into a nearby flower pot and then raise the empty glass to your lips and make a big deal out of swallowing air. Thinking of the effect the whiskey might have on the plant amuses you. Will it kill it stone dead, or will it cause it to grow up into a swaying red-nosed flower?

"I hear Eileen used to do a bit of scribbling."

The mention of Eileen causes an uncomfortable sensation. Is there anything that doesn't eventually reach the Fat Man's ears through his well-established network of spies, which reach all sections of the office like the veins on a plant leaf? But he's definitely on a guilt-trip over Eileen. Probably because she thanked him so profusely in her parting speech.

"Really?"

"Short stories if you don't mind."

For some reason, this belatedly heightens your opinion of Eileen. You wish you had known this earlier. Artistic people fascinate you.

"I used to do a bit of scribbling meself."

"Did you?" It's proving a struggle to give the impression that you are interested.

"Poetry, if you don't mind." Carney lowers a sizeable mouthful of whiskey, and his subsequent guffaw sprays droplets on to the dubious supporting documentation of the top cheque. "Written for some young one I wanted to get into the sack." This is followed by another guffaw and more spray. "The things we lads will do for a rub of the relic."

Carney goes into convulsions, his mammoth frame shakes; he wheezes, gulps, gags, unable to catch his breath. It's the look of fear in his eyes that makes you realise that he isn't in fact laughing, but that he is in the throes of an asthma attack. It's an awkward moment. He could conceivably pass away right in front of your eyes. You could be the office hero, or you could be hit with a charge of accessory to manslaughter. So what did you do when Mr Carney was clearly in distress? Nothing, Your Honour, I simply sat there and watched him pass away. Haven't you ever heard of the Heimlich manoeuvre? No, Your Honour, I have never read the *Kama Sutra*. That'd get the courtroom buzzing and those shorthand pens scratching.

His face has turned a shade of blue, and he hasn't drawn breath for at least thirty seconds. You probably should alert his secretary, but you would look very foolish if he had recovered by the time help had arrived. Maybe you should thump his back and risk a charge of assault. The moment ends when he manages to produce an inhaler from somewhere and a prolonged spray steadies his breathing. Moments later, he polishes off what's left of his whiskey. The man has a constitution which defies medical science.

* * * *

Every artery leading out of the city is clogged and, of course, you are convinced that the road you have chosen is the most clogged of all. It's high blood pressure time. The cars nudge forward, centimetre by centimetre. Exhaust fumes shimmer in the heat, hazy scenes spin past in window reflections. The clear blue sky appears green through the tinted glass. Fingers drum on tin-can roofs. Tempers are frayed. The lights at Donnybrook go from red to green three times and not one car budges an inch. That elusive freedom is up ahead, but like in a nightmare, your feet are stuck in three feet of glue. Your stress gauges are rising, moving perilously close to the danger mark. A flick through the FM waveband locates a traffic reporter, she relates a story about some poor schmuck of a motorist who took three hours to get to the street from the fourth floor of St Stephen's Green Shopping Centre car park. There's a definite hint of glee in the reporter's voice. Every other station seems to be playing chart music, which does nothing except pump the stress levels up still further.

You open the sunroof and try to think comforting thoughts. Fifty-five K and a brand new 520i with alloy wheels and tinted windows at the age of twenty-eight. That's success. A house in Legoland that's jumping in value daily, and those gilt-edged stocks, share options, the non-contributory pension, the tax-free offshore account into which twenty per cent of the salary is paid, and the miscellaneous investments that only move up. That's success. Poverty, ill health and insanity are what you fear. Otherwise, you can cope. But this traffic jam better clear soon or you'll begin to hyperventilate, and who knows what that will lead to. The possibility of spontaneous combustion enters your thoughts.

The five grand rise doesn't lift your spirits the way it would have done in former times. Slowly, you're discovering that the filthy lucre isn't all it's cracked up to be. There's only so many things you can buy, and so little time in which to buy them. The conflicting messages you received are funny though; at school, you were given the impression that too much money was a bad thing. At college, you were told that making money was all that mattered. The poets and musicians jeer at people like you who pile up the loot, but if the truth be known, it's usually precisely what they want themselves, but it wouldn't say much for their artistic credentials if they were to admit this.

Off to the west, the early summer sun is casting its orange glow across the sky. What are you doing stuck in your car on a beautiful day like this? If you didn't hold yourself back, you probably could've become something else, maybe even a stand-up comedian. Would you not be better off cashing it all in and buying a little grocery shop, or maybe a small farm, or maybe live on social welfare and spend your days out in the open air? Some sort of New Age traveller with permanent dirt beneath the fingernails. Or even a window cleaner. Or maybe you should hitchhike your way across Europe into Asia, and live it up in Kathmandu or somewhere. Or better still, catch a plane to a South Sea Isle and become lord of the island. These are questions which wash against your sanity defence-wall.

But the stress levels plummet when a handsome cyclist stops his bicycle and waits for the lights to change. A cooling fan has been aimed at the source of your hyperventilation. What the other drivers don't realise is that you are mentally divesting the cyclist of his colourful kit, stripping him down to the bare essentials, and tantalisingly applying soothing hot oils to his aching muscles, which you would gently rub in without showing any hint of rushing to get down to the nitty gritty.

The lights change, the traffic moves forward and you have to shift in the seat to get your rock-hard stiffy to sit comfortably. It'd take an ice-pack to tame this one. Sometimes, when Anne's in the car, she notices your eyes wandering to take in male pedestrians and cyclists, and you often feel obliged to pretend that you know them from somewhere. *I used to work with him. I know him from college. I played football with him.* A feast of lies. There's a world going on out there, a subterranean world. You've seen those men who duck into public toilets and fail to re-emerge. At indoor soccer in the public leisure centre you've seen those guys, on their own, who seem to linger in the changing-rooms for an eternity. And then there's those other ones who are regularly popping into the sauna or the steamroom, even in the height of summer, and they haven't a pick of fat to sweat off. They've caught you looking, they've given you the eye, but the fear of exposure prevented you from waiting behind and maybe initiating proceedings. What if you were wrong? What if they came back the following week, pointed you out in front of all your football companions and said, Hey lads, wait till I tell you about this fellow here. What if, what if, what if? Your whole life is a series of what ifs. The secret is to bury yourself in your work and not think about missed opportunities. In any case, it's all too sleazy for your liking. That's what you like to believe anyway. And in some strange way, you feel that people will approve of you for not doing what they disapprove of.

Through the arch at the entrance to the private estate you go, and you're on the last furlong. The fake neo-Georgian façades of Legoland, the windows with their criss-cross patterns, the manicured lawns; everything is resplendent in the dying evening sun. A haven of detached red-bricked residences, separated from one another, in some cases, by a mere three feet. This is security town. Timer-lights which can be triggered from a hundred yards, dogs that could swallow a child in one gulp, and residents who dream of ringing the entire estate with an electric fence, and who fantasise of arriving home one day to be greeted by a flashing neon sign which reads, ARMED RESPONSE. It's also Alarmsville. Alarms on houses, alarms on cars, alarms on lawn mowers, and rumour has it that one innovative youngster has installed an alarm on his bicycle. How long before they're planting antipersonnel mines in their gardens? This is what your loot pays for. This is where you live, a safety-first sub-urban graveyard inhabited by video hermits.

You drive slowly around the green where the children are at play. Someone has altered the 10 miles an hour speed-limit sign to 100 miles per hour. The group of gawky teenagers gathered in the laneway at the top of the estate are the prime suspects. Their cans of lager glint in the sunlight. Most of them are already as tall as you, making you glad that you didn't succumb to the lure of the bigger garden that went with the house beside the laneway. You return the exaggerated waves of the tracksuited couple from down the road. They're jogging around the peripheries of the green with their neighbourhood watch antennae on constant red-alert. They don't have children, yet they're the ones who, in their quest for happiness, consider mid-November a suitable time to mount an illuminated Santa Claus and a merry troop of reindeers up on their garage roof, and they drape Christmas lights on the solitary palm tree which has somehow managed to squeeze its way out of the soil and survive a wretched existence in their postage stamp front garden. How did you end up here, you wonder, as you turn the car into the narrow driveway of your overpriced house which already has warped doors, leaky taps and an uneven kitchen floor.

Anne is at the top of the kitchen slope, at the cooker, her back turned to you. The baby is strapped into her high chair, splashing her food around with a red plastic spoon.

"Now look, Dada's home." Anne turns around and wipes her hands in her apron. She speaks to you through the baby and who could blame her.

"Hello Baba."

"Dada! Dada!" she squeals, dropping her spoon and gleefully wiping her messy hands against her bib in anticipation. She is your hope and joy. You place your face to hers and experience a warm glow inside when she wraps her tiny hands around your neck and rubs her cheeks against your stubble.

"How was your day?" Smiling, Anne hesitates, not knowing whether to kiss you or not.

"Got a rise out of the Fat Man."

"Did you! That's great!"

"Mat's mate!"

You turn to tickle the child and the moment is gone. The kiss is avoided. Anne plucks the baby out of her high chair. "Who's a messy little girl? Who's a messy little girl? Lia is. Lia's a messy little girl." The mention of her name has Lia shrieking with delight. Anne holds the grinning child at arm's length and carries her over to the sink.

"I'll tell you though Paul, no one deserves a raise more than you do. You work far too hard if you ask me."

"Tass meeee," the baby squeals.

You decide not to mention the nomination for director. Like so many other things, it's not really important anymore. It feels like you're assembling the prettiest roof in the neighbourhood before you've put down the foundations.

"And it's good that your efforts are being rewarded."

"Poo, poo."

"Oh no, not again."

"Poo, poo." The baby chortles with delight. Poo poo is the latest buzz word among her set at the childminder's.

"Ignore her," Anne says.

"How was school?"

"Oh, you remember that little fellow Aaron Butler I was telling you about?"

You nod, your thoughts drifting.

"D'you know what he told me this morning? He said his mammy was sleeping in his bed last night and that his daddy came into the room and gave his mammy a box in the mouth."

You click your tongue in dismay.

"Poo, poo."

"Moo moo?" You ask the baby.

"No, poo poo." She tilts her head as though she is the parent and you are the child. She is wonderful.

"I didn't know what to say to the poor little fellow."

"Yeah." You furrow your brow into a concerned frown.

"Imagine what he's going to be like when he's older."

A primary school teacher who's just turned twenty-three, Anne seems to be still in love with you. In awe might be a better description, almost like she's under your spell. She listens to the music you like, reads the books you read, and she's even grown to prefer the company of your friends to her own. But all it takes to break a spell is a click of the fingers. And what happens when she begins to assert herself and sees things as they really are? What happens if she finds out that you only became an early weekend riser since you got married? How could you explain that going to bed with her is almost bearable, but waking up in the morning with her is unbearable? That it's something emotional. It's like you exist in a parallel universe and she doesn't even suspect this. As a result, you are reluctant to allow your conversations to stray below the surface, into the world of real feelings and emotions. Conflict is avoided, trivia is all the rage. Like a car that's permanently stuck in second gear, you never allow yourself to open up. More than likely, Anne has deluded herself into believing that this is normal fare between spouses. She loses herself in big novels, magazines and, of course, the baby. In a way, you're like two flatmates with a little treasure of a baby.

Your mother often used to say that some people should never get married, and you used to wonder if it was a veiled comment directed at you. Mothers know their children. But then, your mother was partially responsible for the rushing rapids you got caught up in. You were washed along, you couldn't resist. There were no rocks or overhanging branches to cling on to. Everything was flowing inexorably towards a Christmas ring, the notice in *The Irish Times* social and personal column, a drinks party to celebrate, a flurry of firm handshakes and wispy air-kisses, a mad stag party down in Temple Bar and a spring wedding. Everyone else you knew was doing it so why shouldn't you? While you were dating, Anne gave you a little gift every Saturday and so, in a perfunctory manner, you did the same. But it meant so little to you. There was no passion on your side, but the old sea of pretence was tossing you about and in some respects you did convince yourself that there was. Don't let this one get away, your mother often joked. And in some way, you did it to satisfy your parents and now, three years later, both of them have passed on and you're left swimming in the mire.

And during the first few weeks of your marriage, Anne used to leave little notes around the house, saying things like, "Sweetie Pie, my feet are cold!!!" and "Peekaboo, I'm waiting in the bedroom!!!". No doubt she considered them to be cute and seductive, but little did she know that they used to cause you to be almost physically ill. For some reason, it was the exclamation marks that used to irritate you beyond belief. But you knew that if it were someone you were really in love with who was leaving these notes, you would have kept and treasured every last one of them instead of tossing them on the fire. And even during the "heart-to-heart" chats of those early days, it was like somebody else was doing the talking for you. It was like some frequency in your brain had been altered, like you were split in two, like you were looking in a distorted mirror in which one half was fat, the other half thin. But whatever way Anne looked into the same mirror, all she seemed to see was this caring, thoughtful and considerate old hubby of hers.

What would she say if she knew about the depraved images which frequently waylay your thoughts, like a dog that rushes off into a sewer-pipe and drags out the dirtiest and most publicly-embarrassing item? Sometimes you think that it might all be easier if she just keeled over and died suddenly. People would say that he was so grief-stricken he couldn't look at another woman, so he turned to men instead. *Dear Lucy, do you think I should murder my wife?* But then, there is no doubting that you are quite fond of her in some peculiar way. In many ways, she's like a sister. There's familiarity, and nuances, and memories between you. You understand one another. Besides, you don't want to end up alone out there in that uncertain world. You need her, but you wish you could be more honest with her. And sometimes you almost delude yourself into believing this.

In the living-room after dinner, she points at the TV and says, "Oh, this looks interesting," and she ups the volume. A prize-winning author is talking about his travels. Asia, America, Africa, this fellow's been everywhere and he's not much older than you. He says he doesn't know how anyone can settle in one place. "You rot if you stay too long in one place. Everybody needs change," he proclaims, with the type of superior look you'd expect from a former smoker when offered a cigarette. Then he announces that as far as we know, this life thing ain't no rehearsal, that this is the real McCoy, and with that he paints a picture of Judgement Day. "So what did you do with your life? Well, I trimmed my hedges and kept my net curtains free of fingerprints. I drove into my office every day for forty years and did my work. Then, just this morning, I felt this pain in my chest and the rest is history."

He needs head-butting.

The programme goes into an aerial span of oriental country-side. The helicopter's rotor-blades are visible.

Anne says, "Wouldn't it be just brilliant to be able to travel like that."

"Oh yeah, wonderful," you say, "it must be great fun arriving in strange cities with a rucksack full of dirty clothes and nowhere to stay."

An uncomfortable silence descends between you. All it takes is for you to speak again, to pretend that there was no awkward moment between you, but you don't. It's like you want to provoke her into saying something to you. Anything.

The programme goes into an ad break and Anne is off channel-hopping. On BBC2, they're showing a nature programme about animals eating one another. On Sky News, they're reporting on humans killing one another. Anne keeps zapping and you feel a flush rise to your cheeks – on three separate channels, they are showing programmes of gay interest. It's like the major networks have colluded and decided to make it their business to embarrass you. On BBC1, there's a discussion about gay clergy, on Channel 4 they're showing the madcap capers of a group of gay theatrical men whose parents must wonder what they've reared, and on RTÉ1 there's a studio discussion about being gay in Ireland. Anne leaves it on the studio discussion. You watch her closely. She's angry now, and if there's ever going to be a sign that she suspects, this is the time.

The charged atmosphere moves into overdrive when a man on the panel admits that he's a married gay man with teenage children. That's all you hear, the rest is a blur of how much happier he is now that he's "come out", and how his wife sort of suspected for years anyway, and how they're best of mates now. Blood rushes up to your head with such force you're sure Anne's going to hear a thump, and she'll look around to find you stretched out on the floor, victim to an untimely implosion of the brain. Is this the moment when everything is suddenly going to slot into place for her? Will she turn her head slowly to look at you, the realisation dawning upon her in one great wave and gasp, That's what you are, isn't it? That would certainly put you on the spot.

You silently urge her to switch channels, while at the same time you want to hear what this geezer has to say. Your lifestyle starves you of these juicy details. You have an in-built radar for instantly picking out words like "homosexual" from a full broadsheet page of a newspaper, but this is the real thing.

"God, can you imagine if your father was gay!" she says, almost matter-of-factly.

You feel a constriction in your throat. Her tone was neutral, you decide. Nothing to worry about. How would a regular hubby respond? She's going to look around in a moment and catch you with your beetroot red face. And all you can think of is appearing on some tacky game-show and being introduced as the man with the in-built gay-radar, and of an American-style TV audience whooping and clapping as you point to the one relevant word out of thousands within seconds of the blindfold being removed. *Go Paulie, go Paulie*, you hear them cheer.

Inevitably, the panel move on to the subject of the big A and, like deft strokes of a painter's brush, the stories you've absorbed over the years enter your thoughts. The hairdresser who worked on a cruise-liner. Whisper, whisper. The banker who took holidays alone in Morocco. Whisper, whisper. The schoolteacher who lived in Paris throughout the 1970s. Whisper, whisper. The builders' labourer who listened to classical music.

Say no more. You store up all these stories, neat as a magpie. And in some obscure way, they justify your duplicity for you.

The newspaper comes to the rescue. You slide it up in front of you without as much as a rustle and when she glances around, you're engrossed in reading about some diet doctor who has died from obesity. Duplicity is in the air.

Why did you marry her? So many times prior to the marriage you had psyched yourself up to end the relationship, but you always somehow managed to convince yourself that it was probably only a phase you were going through, that you would wake up one morning and discover that you no longer had this thing for men. And then there was your family and friends and all those social occasions where you had to have a girlfriend in tow; graduations, football club functions, work functions, Christmas, anniversaries, family barbecues, weddings and, of course, the dreaded circuit of paired dinner parties. They just kept trundling along like traffic on a busy motorway. And then, your contemporaries began to walk up the aisle. The pressure was on. In the end, the easy option seemed to be to take the dive.

Chapter Two

Kevin Daniels and the Phantom are elected to carry out the interviews with you. The first five applicants are too highly qualified and much too zealous for your liking. They make it sound like it's only a matter of time before they'll be doing your job and you'll be out on the street with your hastily-purchased crystal bowl. But, one by one, Kevin Daniels picks them off with his quick one-two. The first question lures them into saying something off their prepared script, the follow-up sucker punch gets them to elaborate.

And then the sixth applicant walks into the room and your mood alters. Something happens between you and him at that first moment of eye contact. Something inexplicable. And when he speaks, a chorus of trumpets seem to sound in your head; instantly, everything seems to change colour and smell differently; you don't need to be told that something strange is happening here, something too strong even for you to fight against. This is a face you would pick out across a crowded room. You have never seen eyes so blue. They cause the words to stumble from your mouth in a haphazard manner, so much so, your fellow interviewers cast glances in your direction, probably wondering if you have lost possession of your senses. It's like some sort of magical potion has been slyly secreted through the air vents. And you thought love at first sight was the preserve of romance magazines and pop songs, just another invention of the marketing people.

His name is Johnny Lyons and there is no doubt that you are going to pore over every last tiny detail of his CV at the first available opportunity. Address, family details, hobbies, birthday, star sign, , every little crumb is going to be devoured. And he seems to sense this too, because throughout the interview he hardly takes his eyes off you. Your fellow interviewers might as well be basking themselves outside in the sunshine for all the attention he pays them. But then, you think, he's probably realised he has a sympathetic ear, or else he just senses that he has an admirer, an easy ticket to a job.

"So where do we see ourselves five years from now?" Kevin Daniels asks, and Johnny looks around him the way people do when they suspect that they're being addressed by an escapee from a lunatic asylum.

"Oh, you mean like, what will I be doing?"

"Yes," Kevin Daniels says, like he's talking to a dimwit.

You smile to let Johnny know you're on his side. For his part, Johnny smirks, shrugs and opens his mouth to display an endearing hint of dental protrusion. "Dunno, hadn't really thought about it."

This is the wrong answer. Kevin Daniels folds his arms and stares him into elaboration, a tactic he uses successfully to allow candidates to strangle themselves with their own words.

"Probably surfing the information superhighway on my bicycle."

An involuntary snort of laughter escapes from the Phantom. This smart-alec comment refers back to something the Phantom said earlier in the interview.

"Aim high and we'll end up high." Kevin Daniels's voice is distinctly lacking in mirth.

"Ah no, I see myself...probably in management or something."

"Or something?"

"You know."

"I do?"

A flush rises to Johnny's cheeks and you feel as though you're tumbling headlong. It's excruciating to watch him squirm, but you can't think of what to say.

The Phantom comes to his rescue with a pithy comment about bicycle lanes on the internet or something equally bizarre. He's a good man for deflating these situations. After this, Johnny speaks about his college results, his work experience, and it doesn't take a lot of cop-on to realise that he's applying the touch of gloss candidates tend to apply at interviews. As far as you're concerned, it doesn't matter what he says, just the sound of his voice has your foot jiggling uncontrollably under the desk.

"Well, I think I've asked all the questions I need to ask for now," Kevin Daniels says eventually, his expression clearly saying that he has no more time to waste on this candidate.

Both the Phantom and yourself agree that as far as you are concerned the interview is over, although there are so many questions you would like to ask this particular candidate, except that they are hardly suitable questions to pose in these circumstances.

* * * *

After an undignified scramble for the seats closest to the biscuits, the conversation in the circular tearoom soon focuses on the subject of murder. One of the secretaries from design elaborates on her plan to dispose of Ronnie Burke. She says she's going to stroll into his office wearing the shortest miniskirt in Dublin, "with slits up the sides", and while he's distracted she'll pop him with a few peremptory shots into the gut with a large staple-gun. Then, while he's struggling for breath, she'll finish him off with a few blows of the fire-extinguisher, and pluck his eyes and his tongue out with a staple-remover. "See no evil, speak no evil," she says, folding her arms.

Doreen, another secretary, holds a pair of scissors up and performs a snipping action. "And guess what we could use these for? Snip, snip, snip."

There are gasps of imagined agony from the men and howls of mirth from the women.

Then someone asks for a show of hands as to who would attend Ronnie Burke's funeral.

"Depends on whether we get a day off," the murderous secretary replies and her friends, who are perched on the long seat like a line of crows, cackle with laughter.

"Jaysis, yis are always in great form of a Monday," Tom, the handyman, says, rubbing his hands together, his dazzling set of false teeth glinting under the fluorescent light. He's a regular newshound. People are always saying that there are three major forms of communication; telephone, telegram and tell-a-Tom.

"There won't be a funeral if they can't find the body," Doreen says, before she explains how she would pop the body into one of the very large black plastic bags and leave him out for the bin-men.

Boredom sparks their imaginations. The tearoom theatre keeps everyone sane. One of the privileges of being a director is that your tea is brought to your desk, and you're thinking of how you'll miss the fun of the tearoom when the door opens and the room lapses into silence. Your heart seems to stop beating. It's Johnny who has stuck his head around the door. The tearoom performance comes to a standstill. Everyone is looking at him. A stranger in a suit always brings out the paranoid streaks.

"Is Mr Cullen here?" he addresses the question to Doreen who's sitting closest to the door.

"No Mr Cullen here, sorry."

He's about to leave and you stand up, very nearly knocking a table over in the process.

"Oh, you mean Jack the Lad Cullen."

You point your finger at Doreen in a mock-threatening gesture.

Outside in the corridor, you can't help smiling when he hands you a page of his CV and tells you in a guilty whisper that it was missing from the CV he submitted. His incompetence is appealing to *you*, the master of competence, the man who likes everything to be precise and correct. He's got to be one of the luckiest job interviewees alive. For some reason, you are conscious of other people passing by. You imagine that they will guess how you feel about him. After all, they spotted the Phantom's alleged romance, didn't they. So you beckon him aside and whisper that, in your opinion, he was the strongest candidate.

"Really!" He's delighted, and all the more handsome for it.

"Yeah, your relaxed manner won the day." You say this in case he makes a hasty decision and accepts another job he may have applied for. Every angle has to be covered.

"You thought I was relaxed!" he gasps.

"Cool as a cucumber." He wants to be adored and there's no

better man than your good self. There are years and years of unused flattery and adoration stored up inside you.

The moment is shattered when three shrieking secretaries come racing around the corner and sprint in your direction. Their expressions tell you that it isn't a fire or a flood that they are running from. Johnny is bemused. And just as you decipher their shrieks as, "Get lost, Ronnie!" and "Ronnie, will you buzz off!", their red-faced tormentor rounds the corner, swinging off the doorpost, and lowering his head with bullish intent, he charges in your direction, displaying a remarkable turn of speed for a non-sober man of his years. A high-heel skids on the varnished floor, one of the secretaries careers away from the pack, struggling to keep her balance. Ronnie the lion is quick to pounce. King of the jungle. He grabs the isolated secretary around the waist with one hand, lets his other hand drop to her backside. She shrieks and flails wildly, but this only has the effect of stoking up Ronnie's frenzy.

"Love's young dream," you whisper to Johnny.

"Love me for a reason and let the reason be love," he sings in a whisper, and you experience a dizzy sensation.

Seemingly oblivious to watching eyes, Ronnie Burke's hands go on something of an orienteering course over the contours of the secretary's body. It's then you notice the pair of silk camiknickers in his hand, which he appears to be attempting to hold up against the secretary to measure for size.

"Ronnie, I'll tell my father on you!" the young secretary squeals and this has enough of a dampening effect on Ronnie's libido to enable her to escape his grip.

Then comes the embarrassing moment. Ronnie lifts his head and sees you. His eyes loll in their sockets and you can almost hear his brain clicking over in its search for something suitable to say. Booze hounds like Ronnie detest sensible, sober people like you.

"Michelle, will you ever leave Mr Burke alone," you say to the secretary, and the way she glares at you makes you instantly regret the comment.

But Ronnie has got all the encouragement he needs. "All I

wanted her to do was try on our latest design," he says, waving the pair of camiknickers in Michelle's direction. "It's not like I was trying to get the knickers off her or anything." He guffaws, and then proceeds to make a fresh attempt to paw Michelle.

"I'll tell Irene on you," she says.

"I'll leave her if you say you'll marry me."

Michelle is shocked. "Ronnie!"

The sharpness of her tone jolts Ronnie's busy hands into a reluctant retreat.

"I'll sue you for sexual harassment."

"Ah, you don't even know the meaning of the word."

"Oh yes I do." Michelle wags her finger at him before she heads into the tearoom.

"Michelle my belle."

Ronnie focuses, becomes aware that he's in the presence of a stranger and, with what appears to be embarrassment, he stuffs the camiknickers into his jacket pocket. After you introduce them, he pats Johnny on the back and promises he'll do everything to make sure he gets the job. Then he grabs you by the arm and says he heard a good one. "This fellow goes into the doctor right, and he says, doctor, doctor, my dick is shaped like a rocket." He sways, then steadies himself. Each word takes an immense effort to articulate. "And what does your wife think? Well, she's over the moon."

You laugh, despite the fact that you first heard this joke as a ten-year-old. Ronnie is a drunken buffoon and what's more, he knows that you think he's a sad case.

Before he goes, Ronnie tells Johnny five times that he hopes he gets the job, even though he must realise that you know that he couldn't give a tuppenny damn who gets the job.

"I think I want to work here," Johnny says, while you're walking with him to the reception area with the distinct impression that you are walking on clouds. You have never felt so alive. It's true what they say: love can step in the door at any time. The trick is to be there waiting.

* * * *

There's no prizes for guessing who you want in the job, and you fight your corner with more than customary zeal. If it were possible, you would travel back in time, through the galaxies, and alter the future to get your way on this one. The other two are fussing over the relative abilities of the various candidates, and you rejoin them, sit down, and tell them that it's a one-horse race. The Phantom is easy to win over because he's basically not too bothered and feels he's wasted enough time as it is. He's got work to do. He's always got work to do. *Work, work, work,* as Andy so often says during his demented tearoom impersonations of the Phantom.

But Kevin Daniels is a different matter entirely. He's quite startled by your assessment. He has often told you that you are one of the most logical people he knows, and he finds it unsettling that the two of you should be at polar opposites on this matter. With his hand placed to his forehead in deep thought, he looks like a chess player trying to figure out an opponent's unusual move. In his book, Johnny was possibly the third or fourth strongest candidate, and you know he's right in this assessment; but you can't see reason. The blinkers are on. He's trying to figure out the mystery factor. Could he possibly guess the ulterior motive, you wonder? Not a chance. And if by some remote chance it did enter his permutation of possibilities, he would never say it.

"I'm the one he's going to be working with, and I just know that he's the one who'll be easiest to get on with." It's difficult to keep the blushes under control.

The Phantom nods. "That is an important consideration."

"But he's failed prelim. exam twice now!" Daniels is exasperated. He senses the decision is sliding inexorably towards Johnny.

"To be honest, Kevin, that's another reason why I'd select him above the others."

Daniels now suspects that you are possibly a secret substance abuser. Ronnie Burke mark two.

"Well, they're mostly qualified, they're not going to stay in an assistant accountant post."

This registers with Daniels.

"I mean, I don't want to spend time showing someone the ropes and just when they've grasped everything they decide it's too limiting for them and they up and leave."

"We take your point, but really, we wonder if the candidate in question knows how to count to ten."

Now you sense victory. "He has got a university degree."

Kevin Daniels is reeling. He's the only member of the company's executive staff without a university degree and it's an extremely touchy subject with him. Like Carney, he comes from an economically underprivileged background, and while you admire his climb up the ladder and his amazing dedication to self-education, you just can't resist getting this little dig in. This is a time to fight dirty.

"That doesn't mean he can count to ten," the Phantom says, and both of you laugh like members of an exclusive club.

"So be it, but let the record show that we had severe reservations about this particular choice." Kevin Daniels packs his briefcase, and the manner in which he slips out the door puts you in mind of an eel slithering through rocks.

It dawns upon you that the Phantom and yourself have a lot in common really. And he's smiling, like he understands your predicament. *Is he or is he not?* the secretaries used to say during the time the Phantom appeared to have a crush on Marcus, a young upstart who used to work in design. It was embarrassing being in his company back then. He never let up talking about him. Obsession wasn't the word for it. It was Marcus this, Marcus that, Marcus three bags full please; he even gave the little twerp credit for one of his most famous designs. Marcus inspired me, he was famously heard to remark, and now you realise that Marcus probably did inspire him. Everyone just assumed that something was going on, but the Phantom comes from a generation who would consider it better to be dead than to be called a queer and so, after Marcus moved to Germany, the two of them kept in touch, and the Phantom took an extraordinarily perverse pleasure in telling everyone about Marcus's subsequent engagement. In his eyes, it cleared him of all suspicion. But not in other people's eyes. They just thought it was kind of sad.

* * * *

There are days that change your life, and this is definitely one of those days. The world has turned a somersault, you feel like you are someone else. Your senses are touching a heightened state. Nothing looks or smells or even tastes the same. You float around like you're on some sort of hallucinogenic drug. You've never felt so alive. A powerful love for the world has gripped you. The evening light falling upon the city has a poetic quality to it, the long line of traffic up ahead has artistic merit, and for the first time since adolescence you feel inspired to attempt a poem. That raw nerve has been touched. This day needs to be perpetuated.

For so long, you have been the example of calm and control. From school to college to profession, all your life has gone to plan. But now, something is happening which you can't control. Even Legoland looks like one of Dublin's most desirable locations, as the brochures boasted.

"You're in great form tonight," Anne says after you land a big smacker on her lips.

"You're looking at a future director."

She shrieks with joy, kisses you, and for the first time in ages you're happy that she's happy. Let's go upstairs, she says, and you follow her up, and her exaggerated butt-wiggling causes you none of the usual irritation. And throughout the sweaty lovemaking you keep your eyes shut tight and think of Johnny. And as you lie there, in post-coital exhaustion, there's none of the usual repulsion, the nausea, the urge to get away from her. Instead, you tell her all about your new assistant. In a controlled, casual sort of way, but you know you're speaking the exact same way the Phantom used to speak about Marcus. It's Johnny this, Johnny that, Johnny three bags full please. If you were an objective viewer of yourself, you would click your tongue and think, Has he got the hots or has he got the hots. A cold shiver passes through you. Maybe Anne does realise. Maybe she's just lying there thinking, What sort of tosspot am I married to? Maybe in your passion, you're letting your guard down. It's time to make an exit.

In the bathroom, you position the shaving-mirror directly above your head and experience a dull sense of shock when you see the extent to which the hair on your crown has thinned. In your youth, hours were spent looking at every new haircut from different angles, while different situations were conjured up; a rock concert and you were anyone from Bruce Springsteen to George Michael, a film première and you were the latest Irish hunk, stepping out of the limo into a hail of exploding flash-bulbs, adored by mobs of screaming young women, who, upon closer inspection, turned out to be young men.

But now, you don't look. You know what's up there waiting for you. You've caught people sneaking those glances while they're talking to you. Those glances that say, Wow, he's really losing it. How long before the erosion has your scalp resembling a vast expanse of the Gobi Desert? And worse still, the lost hairs seem to have relocated themselves on your back, your shoulders, up your nose, in your ears. Clumps of it sprout from the oddest and most undesirable of places. A clip with a scissors will do for the moment, but a dose of electrolysis does have a certain appeal. You could pay for the treatment in used notes and no one would be any the wiser. And your pulse quickens when you consider the possibility of a hair-transplant. Techniques have improved. They're nothing like the rugs of yesteryear. All is not lost. Those years could yet be turned back.

The next problem is the stomach. It's lost its firmness. When you breathe out it's definitely paunchy. There have been warning signs. The last time you bought jeans there was the shock discovery that 32 was no longer your waist size. Of course, you led yourself to believe that it was the method of measurement that had changed, not you. And then there's the dental decay. Those ever-widening gaps which necessitate constant flossing. You urgently need two crowns but you know you won't get them until the pain comes. Is it any wonder you have those teeth-falling-out dreams? This inexorable decline is something you have tried to ignore for years, and in some respects it didn't bother you in that you sensed it made you less attractive to Anne. But why couldn't you have met him years earlier, at the height of your physical prowess? You'll have to bring in photos of yourself taken during the glory years. The thought of sticking these photos under his nose and saying, Look here, Johnny Boy, I was once a handsome lad, is crazy, but not, in the spell you're under, beyond the bounds of possibility. Nothing is anymore, and that's what makes it all so frightening, and so exhilarating.

Anne walks into the bedroom while you're in the middle of the series of sit-ups which are set to become part of your daily exercise schedule. She calls you a tiger, and you ask her if she thinks you are losing the hair because you know she'll say no, you're not, and what's more, she'll say it like she really means it. She goes even one better than that; she rubs your head and gives you the impression that you have the fulsome hairline of a seventeen-year-old. What quirk of fate threw you into her life?

*　*　*　*

A week passes, and during that week you remain under his spell. Weak-kneed, giddy, light-headed, all you can think about is him. You see his face everywhere, you hear his voice, you see jackets like his, people who walk like him, people who talk like him. And then you realise that you can't remember what he really looks like. People tell you that you're looking well, and you want to tell them that it's because you're in love. It's making you blossom. There's a song played constantly on the radio that reminds you of him, and in particular one lyric which goes, *You've got the most stumbling blue eyes I've ever seen.* It's the type of soppy love song you'd normally sneer at, but not now; now you've got to find out who the female singer is and buy that record. Through all of this though, somewhere in the back of your mind, you're petrified that it might all fall flat when you do meet again.

His first day on the job is a Friday, and on that day you take more care with your appearance than you did on your wedding day. Vanity is your middle name. After shaving, you clip the fresh hairs sprouting from the ears and the nose. Then it's the flash new suit, the Roland Cartier shoes, the new silk tie, and the shirt that best hides the rubbery paunch. Anne swoons playfully, and you tell her you're meeting clients. Today, you could do without bumper-to-bumper stress, so you drive to the DART station. Love has even dulled your competitive instincts and you allow three cars out of the objectionable short-cut slip-road near the entrance to Legoland. Their cheery waves of acknowledgement make you feel good about humanity. And at the train station the old bore of a newspaper vendor, whom you normally steer clear of, is delighted when you linger a moment to listen to his views on crime. "It's the parents I blame," he says in summation, and you smile, nod, glance at your watch and politely bid him goodbye. He ought to be installed as the Minister for Stating The Obvious, but today, there's none of the usual urge to grab hold of his newspaper stand and tip it over the railings, down on to the railway track.

The platform is littered with hastily-stubbed cigarettes and phonies yacking on their mobiles. A young guy wearing a light jacket, on the back of which is written, *Michael Collins, The Movie –Stunts Crew*, struts his way onto the platform like he was walking into a movie première arm-in-arm with Julia Roberts. He positions himself near the edge of the platform, continually adjusting his stance so that every new arrival gets the widescreen version of his claim to fame. He's too young and too immersed in his own self-importance to realise the real effect that this has on people. No doubt, like yourself, your fellow commuters visualise themselves tossing him in front of an oncoming train and saying, Right Stunt, show us how good a stuntman you are. And he's probably too much of a sap to guess that his short jacket has given the likes of your good self a perfectly reasonable excuse to stare at the tasty way his backside curves.

On mornings like this, you often see a face, a smooth neck, or perhaps even a shapely bum that catches your attention and lifts your spirits. A chance glimpse that is often dragged up and mulled over later. But this morning, you only have eyes for one person. It feels as though an anchor has been lifted and you have that uneasy, yet exhilarating, sensation of sailing out into uncharted waters. To other people, you are a snazzily-dressed executive with a briefcase waiting for the 8.04. Half-asleep, and more than likely dreading another day of drudgery. But what would they say if you tossed your briefcase up in the air, kicked your heels, and told them that you can't stop thinking about this wonderful guy, and that it's making the world a most wonderful place to be in.

The punctual 8.04 glides into the station and all the regular chalk-faces prepare to embark. The Stuntman presses the button to open the door, swaggers confidently on board, and your guess is that the crowded carriage disappoints him because of the limits it puts on his jacket fame. Like everyone else, you have perfected the art of avoiding eye contact, of staring into the middle distance like some sort of visionary. But this morning, you want to cross that barrier. You are tempted to break into a verse of "Morning Has Broken", or at least to smile at your fellow passengers, to encourage them to lose those frowns and acknowledge how splendid life can be.

The early morning sun shining on Dublin Bay reminds you of your father and, in particular, of his magical story regarding the origins of Howth Head. So many times he told you how, a long time ago, on a dark winter's night, a distant relative of his was involved in a game of poker in the Hellfire Club up in the Dublin Mountains. There were six men playing. Five of them knew one another well, but the sixth man was a stranger. And this stranger was losing heavily. A card was dropped, and when your father's distant relative leaned down to pick it up, he spotted the hoofs. It was the Devil himself who was sitting opposite him. A halt was called to the game, and in his anger Old Nick took a bite out of the Dublin Mountains, saying that he wasn't going back to England empty-handed. But out over the bay, the chunk of mountain became too heavy, and it slipped from the grasp of his fireproof teeth, plunged into the sea and, lo and behold, the people named it Howth Head. And you believed this story until you were eleven, when you made the mistake of telling it to some lads at school. The memory of how they ridiculed you causes you to smile, and the woman sitting opposite braces herself, clutching her handbag to her chest.

An involuntary shiver passes through you. If there is an after-life, the chances are that your mother and father will know what you're thinking. Would they try and pass some message from beyond the grave to Anne? It's bad enough that they never saw the baby, and that it's over a year since you have visited their graves, without subjecting them to this extra embarrassment in front of their afterlife colleagues. Waves of guilt are washing against your happiness. Maybe you should just tell Johnny Boy that there's been a mix-up. Give him £100 in compensation and wish him all the best. Nip it at the bud. Let the dead rest in peace. But your parents were the ones who encouraged you to study accountancy, and they must have known that the world of business demands family men. A better half to parade at all those social gatherings. So what did they expect?

* * * *

Teresa rubs the sleeve of your jacket between her finger and thumb and asks you what you've been accused of. But you don't have time to reply because in the background you see him stroll-ing up the corridor towards you. A surge of adrenaline pumps through you, your scalp jumps, the hair on the back of your neck bristles, and your heart beats so hard you're sure it's going to rip through the fabric of your high-quality shirt.

"Oh shit, I forgot the new lad was starting today," you say, before you duck into your office and, with every nerve-end in your body tingling, wait for that door to open.

Moments later, he's sitting opposite you, a pen in his mouth, his chair tilted back, intermittently pushing his tumbling hair back off his forehead, and in so doing, drawing even more attention to his eyes, so blue in the light streaming in through the window. His neat-sized nose and well-proportioned ears make you feel posi-tively elephantine. Now you notice his lips, his teeth, the high cheek bones, the almost Slavic features. You're experiencing the nervousness of a teenager on a first date; it's like there's a golf ball lodged in your throat. One minute you feel like you're going to start crying, the next minute you want to laugh. And while you're talking to him, the words seem to tumble about inside your head, only getting out by accident. You tell him all about Carney Textiles and the staff; stories which, from repetition, you can deliver on auto-pilot. Whenever he speaks, you absorb every word and phrase, knowing that you're going to scribble them into your diary in coded form that evening. You want to know everything there is to know about him but, for some strange reason, you're pretending that you're not terribly interested in what he's saying.

"Once you've survived one of our teabreaks, you'll know you can survive anything."

The moment you walk into the tearoom, you get that surge of pride heterosexual men get when they have a beautiful woman by their side. After performing the introductions, you fetch him a cup of tea and some biscuits, conscious that you are being watched. Doreen and Bernie make a point of showing off in front of him. They pick on Jason, the young lad from the post-room. Jason was in London the previous weekend watching his beloved Chelsea play, and Doreen claims that she saw him on *Match Of The Day*. "Brawling with a copper," she announces to the entire tearoom, and Jason's face looks as though it's caught fire. He's eighteen years old, and between his shaved head, his stud earrings, and his sullen expression, he bears a remarkable resemblance to practically every photofit on *Crimeline*. And if you didn't know him, you'd suspect he was the type of thug who spends his day loitering near traffic lights, waiting for the opportunity to ram a steel bar through your windscreen.

"And he brought the floozy along with him," Doreen says, tipping her ash.

"He did not." Bernie jerks back, feigning shock.

"Up to all sorts of shenanigans."

"His poor mother, that's all I can say."

"Sure she's the last to know anything."

"Well I hope he brought them condom yokeybobs with him."

"So do I. Otherwise we'll have to open a crèche down below in the basement."

Jason has reached a new peak of self-consciousness. Tears of embarrassment have welled up in his eyes and even the tips of his ears have turned bright pink. He tries to intervene but Doreen and Bernie are having none of it.

"Suppose he played tha' smoochy music to get her warmed up."

"And more than likely he was wearin' them silky black boxers we saw him buy in Marks and Sparks."

"They probably did the trick all right."

"But I'll tell you one thing, if he stays out in the sun any longer, he'll be mistaken for a Romanian refugee and he'll get himself deported, so he will."

Bernie nods. "Silky black boxers or no silky black boxers, the cops will be frog-marching him to the airport."

Jason is spared further embarrassment when the tearoom door opens and Sophie, Carney's secretary, sticks her head in, scours the faces, fixes on Johnny, and tells him that Mr Carney wants to see him. Johnny hesitates, and looks to you. You want to go along with him, but you are conscious that the secretaries are watching like hawks.

"Go on, he won't bite you," you say, casual as you like.

"Don't be so sure," Doreen says.

"He likes new people to call him Jimmy Joe Fat," Andy says, and he regrets this when Sophie casts a reproachful glance in his direction. Of course, through all of this, you are struggling not to stare at Johnny as he ambles his way out of the tearoom.

That's when the questions fly: What age is he? How much is he on? Is he an executive? Is he going to join the union? Where did he work before? Is he the reason why you're all dressed up? All these questions you stonewall with your usual calm control, but you very nearly choke with pride when Bernie announces that he's drop-dead gorgeous, and that she certainly wouldn't throw him out of bed for nibbling pistachio nuts.

Back in your office, you ask Teresa if there's been any word from Johnny. She looks at you, puzzled for a moment, and you privately chastise yourself for blurting his name out. Teresa is sharp. So you swiftly change the subject to work matters and you stand there, watching her fingers skip around the keyboard like those of a concert pianist, typing out your dictation, and not for the first time you wonder how she does it. Any repetitive task like that has you worrying about your sanity at least once every ten seconds.

Half an hour later, he returns, smiling, and asks if he can light up. You have never allowed anyone to smoke in your office before, there's a large *NO SMOKING* sign sitting on the desk, but still, you say it's fine if he smokes, and what's more, you give the impression that you actually approve of the habit.

"So what did Carney say?"

"God, he's fat."

"He said that?"

He smiles and you feel weak.

"The anorexic wanted to know my life story."

"That's our Jim."

"So I told him I was a crack-addict and a peddler in porn."

"So I presume he asked if he could do a deal?"

"Ah, he did, and he tried to get me drunk."

"Whiskey?"

"Two glasses of it," he says, resting his feet on the edge of the desk and letting his eyes go into what's supposed to be a drunken roll. "And now I'm anyone's."

The old ticker skips a beat.

"D'you smoke?"

"No."

"Only wussies don't smoke." He smirks, takes a pull and exhales the smoke in a series of rings. "It makes me feel so *cool*."

"Give us a drag." You take his cigarette and he laughs at the way you draw on it. You have never smoked before, but you just want your lips to touch the butt his lips have touched. Pathetic isn't the word for it, especially since both your parents died from smoking-related illnesses.

"Don't get in the habit," he warns, taking the cigarette back off you, and that's when Teresa opens the door and stands there, staring at his feet on the desk and the cigarette in his hand, and then at you. You shrug. She knows about your abhorrence of smoking, so of course she's puzzled.

"I made a special exception because it's his first day."

"It's a filthy habit," she says to Johnny, leaving pages of typed script on your desk.

"It's my only vice," he says to her, winking suggestively.

Every second Friday, a merry troop of executives head out for lunch together to a restaurant off Dame Street. You, Kevin Daniels, the Phantom, Sophie Hegarty, and occasionally Ronnie Burke, if it isn't possible to sneak off without him noticing. The company foots the bill so everyone tends to make it their business to be there. And when you arrive at the restaurant with Johnny in tow, Kevin Daniels looks anything but pleased. Having struggled his way up through the ranks, he naturally believes in rank. The Phantom, on the other hand, seems pleased with the new blood, and you just hope that he doesn't develop a crush on Johnny.

Without Ronnie Burke, the atmosphere is relaxed and pleasant. The conversation is about going for interviews and looking for jobs, and it's flowing along nicely until the Phantom brings it to an abrupt halt.

"You know, if I went for an interview now, they'd assume I was bent," he says.

Glances are exchanged. Under the table, Johnny presses his foot against yours. He's already downed two glasses of wine, and you're certainly going to encourage him to drink more.

"Gus, don't be so ridiculous," Sophie says.

"Well, I'm forty-five and as far as I know, I ain't married, so what else are they going to think?"

"They might think you've got a bit of sense," Kevin Daniels says with a short chuckle.

The Phantom shakes his head. "You know my theory, you meet one person in your life who was meant for you, and you either take that opportunity or you let it slip away."

"Ah Gus, you're such an old romantic, I'd nearly marry you myself," Sophie says.

A panic grips you. You've got to change the subject before someone mentions that you are married. It was crazy bringing

44

Johnny along. Anne is bound to be mentioned. There's high-delusion at play here, but you don't want him to find out that you're married. Not just yet. It's just as well you never wear your wedding ring. Wearing any jewellery gives you a claustrophobic, restrictive sort of sensation, which is no doubt an external manifestation of what's going on inside. In a way, your thinking now reminds you of those rare occasions when you went to school without your homework done, and when the teacher was selecting someone to answer a question, you used to convince yourself that you were invisible.

The moment of panic ends when Pierre glides up to the table and whisks a notebook from his pocket.

"And hoo vill have dessert?" he asks, and Johnny, who is mildly lubricated with expensive French wine, turns and laughs.

"Where did you get that accent?"

"*Excusez-moi?*" Pierre is flummoxed. The others are looking on incredulously. Everyone knows the accent is fake, but no one would ever even dream about questioning Pierre to his face.

"You're about as French as I am." Johnny's arm slips from the edge of the chair, and playing to the gallery, he points at the armrest and says, "Don't you move again," in a chastising voice.

"Pierre, I'll have the apple-pie and cream," you say.

"Verry good choice." "Tress biens," Johnny says, in a deliberately poor French accent.

"And for you, Monsieur?" Pierre addresses Johnny.

He studies Pierre. "Westmeath, I'd say?"

"Pardon?"

"Cork?"

"No, Limerick actually," Pierre admits.

A rush of air escapes from the Phantom's nostrils. Daniels sees that Sophie is smiling, so he forces what appears to be a smile onto his face.

"Limerick? D'you happen to know a fellow by the name of Carney, Jim Carney?" Johnny is showing off now, encouraged by the amused reaction.

"Indeed I do."

"Fit-looking chap."

"Indeed." Pierre isn't going to commit himself on this one. He knows who foots the bill here.

Kevin Daniels glances at his watch. "You better bring the coffee as well, Pierre."

You're actually pleased by this intervention, knowing that everything Johnny has said is more than likely going to slither its way back to Carney.

Sophie spots you topping your glass of wine up yet again. Her look of amazement is understandable. Before today, she's never seen you drink anything except mineral water on these executive lunches.

"Paul, you're turning into a regular wino."

"Ah, it's Friday." You are blushing. If she thinks about it, she will certainly link your drinking to the newcomer's presence.

The bill arrives with the coffee, and it irritates you the way Daniels grabs it and analyses it aloud. It's as though he's the one coughing up the readies. But one look at Johnny is enough to banish all irritation.

* * * *

At home that evening, Anne senses that you're behaving oddly, that you're preoccupied, so you tell her that you're stressed out from showing your new assistant the ropes. She says she'll have to meet him, that you'll have to invite him around for dinner some night. There's no answer to that. It feels like something's going to detonate inside. You want to phone him and ask him if he's hitting the town, if he'd like to meet for a drink, if you could drive over and watch TV with him, or if you could just sit there and watch him watch TV. The thought of a weekend without him makes you feel trapped. What are you thinking about? That'd be the first question you'd ask him.

"It's just, I've no time to get any of my own work done."

"Well, once he's trained in, you'll be able to get him to do the work for you. You'll be Mr Director by then."

Why did you have to tell her about the directorship? No doubt she's told her mother and her brothers by now. Probably half of Legoland as well.

"You didn't say that to anyone, I hope."

"No, I didn't."

She didn't. One thing about Anne, she never lies. Maybe that's what keeps you together. Truth and lies. Chalk and cheese. But it irritates you when she puts her arms around your neck and snuggles up to you. After the lovemaking of the past week, she feels confident and unhindered. You shrug her away by simply pointing to the TV.

On the RTÉ news, there's a shot of a group of people of varying ages holding a silent vigil outside Government Buildings. Their banners are calling for the government to change the laws to reflect the importance of family values. Many of the protesters look as though they've been snatched straight out of a 1950s all-night solemn novena. Even though they're bedecked with religious artefacts, including a faded papal flag, there's something very aggressive grim and even paranoid about their demeanour. They appear uneasy in the swashbuckling surroundings of modern day Dublin. It isn't difficult to imagine their views on gay people. But you do sometimes wonder what it is that really drives these people. It makes you think of one of the Phantom's favourite sayings, which goes: people have two reasons for doing everything, a good reason and the real reason.

Spurred on by these people, Anne tells a story about her day at school. Two of the kids' parents, one boy's mother and another boy's father, have decided to leave their respective spouses and shack up together. So the two boys, both of whom are called David, now have to share a bedroom, as brothers. She says that the two of them never hung out together, that, up until now, they have nothing in common except for their age and their first names. You laugh, delighting in the thought of the reaction this tale would extract from the merry band of protesters. The news moves on to a different item and you dash upstairs to take one last check on the baby.

She stares up at you as you place the bottle into her mouth.

Her soothing eyes hold you in their trance. Her tiny fingers grasp the plastic bottle. She emits a low purr of satisfaction when the air bubble clears. Sleepily, she once again brings your attention to the bright green nailvarnish Anne has painted on her fingernails. A smile is sufficient acknowledgement for her. You continue to sing a lullaby and rock the cot gently to and fro. With Teddy and Dolly on either side, and with her blanky snuggled up between the three of them, she's the picture of contentment. Gradually, her heavy eyelids close, she's on her way to the magical land of dreams.

A glance in the mirror does nothing for the confidence. The chin is definitely slackening. Some mornings, upon awakening, it feels as though your jowls are drooping down to your neck. You can't bring yourself to tilt your head forward and examine the crown. Recently, you've been getting an itchy sensation on your temples, as though a gang of little men are tugging at your hair roots, further exposing your own version of the Gobi Desert. A ray of light lands on your wrinkled brow. The grooves appear so deep and permanent now, you'd need a rope ladder to escape if you fell into them. And of course you make an unfavourable comparison to Johnny's smooth complexion. First thing tomorrow, you'll buy moisturising cream. The most expensive anti-ageing cream you can lay your hands on. You'll gladly fall victim to the stories of the marketing people. You'll believe them when they promise that you'll stay forever young. Every possibility has to be pursued.

The baby-sitter arrives and makes a big deal of spreading her schoolbooks out across the kitchen table. Her black drumskin-tight jeans look like they've been painted on, she's wearing no bra under that tight T-shirt and who daubs on that amount of make-up for a study session? But the question is, what's she going to be studying? There's a more than high probability that, as soon as your taxi's tail-lights make their exit from Legoland, the local lager louts will come tumbling in through the front door. No doubt they're taking up their lookout posts right now, as Anne makes one last check on the baby and you make polite smalltalk with her nibs. Maybe this is why the lager louts in the laneway always seem to stare at you as you drive past, as if to say,

Hey sunshine, we know all about your private life. Your wife's lingerie collection is bordering on the sexy, but your CD collection is bordering on the past tense imperfect.

*   *   *   *

You are sitting in a Chinese restaurant with your wife and your two closest friends, Bob and Karen, and it's obvious that your infectious good form pleases them. Just to think of Johnny leaves you feeling like you've pulled off a busy main road for an enjoyable picnic, recharged the batteries while lolling in warm dreamy sunshine, all the time watching those worried faces pass by. But something else also pleases you; the two guys sitting at a small corner table obviously aren't brothers or business associates. It's going to be fun watching them.

Bob is talking about a contract he's recently secured with some east European country. He's a computer genius. What he doesn't know about computers just isn't worth knowing. He votes Labour, writes frequent letters to the newspapers denouncing the greed ethos and what he sees as blatant social inequalities, but what he himself earns in a week could go a long way towards sorting out a medium-sized Third World famine. And Karen is no slouch on the financial front either. She's a solicitor who makes a big splash on the free legal aid front, specialising in taking on the cases of the underprivileged, so much so, that very often when a thug is arrested in the city they've been heard to ask for Karen by name. *I wanna talk to me solicitor, Karen O'Reilly.* Because Karen is a highly-perceptive person, she always makes you feel as though she's suspicious of you. Either she secretly fancies you or else she suspects your true sexual inclinations. The latter seems the more likely.

You like to believe that this low-level hostility may be due to the fact that you knew Bob before she did. You and Bob have memories, those shared experiences during that allegedly wild period of your lives. The college years, during which he was your companion on so many escapades. What you like about him is that he never preys, never asks those awkward questions that someone who knows you as well as he does might justifiably ask. Over the years, he surely must have noticed that your relationship with Anne is ever so slightly off-kilter. Maybe he does suspect something, but he has the politeness to pretend that he doesn't. Maybe he's waiting for you to say something, or maybe, like everyone else you know, he's just too damn busy to notice.

Between the four of you, you polish off a bottle of wine before the main courses arrive, but what makes the moment extra pleasurable is the fact that Bob smokes the same cigarettes as Johnny. The fan above the table is working full pelt but still you get that aroma, and that's enough to make you feel good. A dolled-up sexpot glides her way past the table, Bob turns his head to sneak a look, and you feel obliged to glance at her as well, earning yourself a playful slap on the wrist from Anne for your trouble.

"When you're on a diet, no harm looking at the menu," Bob says.

"And some of us could do with dieting," Karen retorts, glancing at her husband's stomach.

"I was speaking metaphysically," Bob adds.

Karen smiles. "I'd say you were all right."

The Chinese waitress arrives with the grub and Bob throws in an order for another bottle of the house wine. The night is beginning to warm up. Anne is already giddy and she leans forward, smiling, and points in the direction of the two lads at the corner table, who are holding hands under the table. The reaction is as you'd expect. Good for them, both Anne and Karen say. Beauty is in the eye of the beholder, Bob says. Aware of this scrutiny, the two lads unlink their hands and continue with their meal.

This ending to their display of open affection is timely because, moments later, three drunken lads stumble into the restaurant and proceed to announce to the entire clientele that they're on a break from a stag night. They've been drinking since three o'clock, they add, like they expect everyone to burst into spontaneous applause. In their early to mid-twenties, all three of them sport intimidating blade-one haircuts, their foreheads seem to be set in permanent ridges, and one of them has a tricolour tattooed on his forearm. They look the type who might spend their spare time loitering outside a post office on pension day. Maybe these are three boyos who have asked for their solicitor Karen O'Reilly in their day.

They're realising that they're in the wrong place when, with a certain inevitability, their attention focuses in on the two lads at the corner table. Nudges, unpleasant leers and the exchange of sly comments precede the opening salvo.

"D'yeh have a ligh'?" the one with the tattoo asks, a less than subtle hint of effeminacy about his tone.

One of the lads turns his head. "Sorry, but neither of us smoke."

This reply triggers a bout of childish sniggers from the drunks.

"Did I say something funny?"

"Nah, but yeh' are a bit funny." The one with the tricolour tattoo is warming up. The ugly leer contorting his face leaves the two lads in no doubt that they don't exactly fit into his vision of Ireland.

"A bit of a *you-know-what*," another one of the drunks says, letting his wrist fall limp.

"Well, you know what they say," the gay guy replies, smiling benignly, "it takes one to know one."

You sense a silent cheer from your fellow-diners.

"He's married." The one with the tattoo is pointing at his blade-one friend.

"So?" The gay guy loops his eyebrows.

"Married with kids."

"My sincerest commiserations, but surely you realise that being married is no longer a guarantee."

Anne, Bob and Karen snigger, but you're experiencing a sickly sensation in your stomach.

"What're you tryin' to say, bud?" The one with the tattoo is becoming aggressive. All semblance of humour disappears.

"It's John, actually."

Now, there's a name for you.

"Hah?"

John's boyfriend whispers something, but John boy shakes his head. He's on a roll.

"You seem to be mistaking me for someone called Bud."

This response brings sounds of mirth from around the restaurant.

"You callin' my pal a bleedin' faggot?" The one with the tattoo wobbles as he rises to his feet.

"Not necessarily, I'm merely stating a truism." John remains remarkably calm which causes you to wonder if he has an Uzi tucked away under his jacket. If you were him you'd be searching the table for potential weapons.

The tension eases somewhat when a young Chinese waiter appears at the kitchen door and stares at the three troublemakers.

"It's the karate kid," the heaviest of the drunks says, and he takes up what's supposed to be a karate stance.

"Hoo flung dung!" The one with the tattoo slits his eyes and speaks with an oriental accent.

This prompts the other two to also pull their eyes into slits and all three of them proceed to chant a singsong rhyme which is obviously their party piece for such restaurants.

"Ching chong Chinaman tried to milk a cow, ching chong Chinaman didn't know how. Ching chong Chinaman pulled the wrong tit, ching chong Chinaman covered in shit!"

Their bout of bawdy laughter fades abruptly when a second Chinese man, an enormous chef, emerges through the kitchen doors, wiping his hands in a towel. His stiff walk is like that of a wrestler, his every muscle seems to creak and twitch with each movement. He's so big, you imagine him being employed by the Chinese Space Programme to single-handedly catapult their rockets into orbit. His imposing presence seems to cast a shadow over the drunks' table.

"You have problem, guys?" Oddly, he speaks with an American accent.

"No problem, Boss," the one with the tattoo says.

"We not allow singing here."

"Righ' yeh' are, Boss."

"Game ball."

"Now I want you guys out of here, please."

The other customers breathe a collective sigh of relief when the drunks stand up to go. Fear has unearthed their manners. They have enough sense remaining to recognise a line that ought not to be crossed. They leave without a mutter of protest.

The hum of conversation slowly rises and before long the restaurant once again has the appearance of ordinariness to it. But everyone is watching the two lads at the corner table and pretending that they're not. The entire episode makes you feel justified in hiding away. Who would want to face such hassle on a simple visit to a restaurant? But if it were Johnny that was with you, you know you might just put up with it.

Then, with typical candour, it's Bob who stands up and, like an elected representative, goes over to the two lads and chats to them. This makes everyone feel better. Something in you wants Bob to ask them to join you.

"God, you'd feel sorry for them," Anne says.

To avoid replying, you pretend you're trying to listen to what Bob is saying to the two lads.

Karen says, "D'you know, I read about some recent sociologist survey where thirty per cent of the respondents said that gay people should be denied Irish citizenship."

"That's terrible," Anne says.

"The question is, what do they want to do with them? Ship them all off to Dalkey Island or somewhere?" Karen says.

"If they did, it'd probably become the trendiest place to go to," Anne says.

"You weren't watching the news tonight, were you?" Karen asks, and both Anne and yourself nod. "Did you see that family values crowd protesting outside Government Buildings?"

"Oh yeah," Anne says.

"Wonderful stuff," you say.

"Well, the leader of that group is separated from his wife, right, and a friend of mine handled the case. But d'you know what the wife cited as the reason for wanting the separation?" Karen pauses, like a teacher waiting for an answer from a class. Both Anne and yourself are baffled.

"He spent too much time protesting?" you say.

Karen shakes her head. "She said he was a homosexual."

This certainly wipes the grin off your face.

"Ah, go 'way," Anne says.

"And he's the very same fellow who blames homosexuals for everything from abortion to divorce."

"Aren't they?" you say, earning yourself a glare from Karen and a slap on the wrist from Anne.

"That's just typical of someone like that," Anne says.

"That which we say we'll never do is often what we want to do most," Karen says, and Anne stares at her in admiration.

Bob rejoins you and announces that the two lads are the soundest blokes you could meet. There follows the usual pieces about how talented and handsome and artistic gay guys are. "And they really know how to dress," Karen says, and Anne agrees, even though, to the best of your knowledge, she knows no gay people, aside from her husband. Some part of you wants to tell them all about this fellow who works with you, that he's ten times better-looking than either of the two lads. But it's time to go, and when Karen stands up, she swings her coat and very nearly takes the eye out of a woman at the next table. For a solicitor, she ought to know better. On the way out, of course, you all have to wave goodbye to the two lads, but all you can think of is Monday morning and seeing Johnny again.

Chapter Three

"I had a dream about you last night," he says, and this simple statement has the effect of blurring your vision momentarily.

Monday mornings aren't supposed to be like this. A funny taste lies at the back of your throat. The stomach flutters are out in force. Nobody has ever said anything so sweetly intimate to you before. Or so it seems anyway. The battleground of the office takes wing and flies away like a glorious albatross. This is the moment to open up, to give even a hint of how you feel about him, but something is holding you back. It's that sensible voice, telling you to be realistic, that it's only natural for two people who are around one another all day to invade one another's dreams at night. It's just that he's honest enough to tell you. Or maybe he has other reasons for telling you, just maybe.

"So, how often d'you have these nightmares?" With the sunlight streaming in through the window behind you, you think he won't be able to see that you're blushing.

"Made you blush."

"I'm not blushing."

He stands up, wets his finger, leans across the desk, touches his wet finger against your cheek and makes a hissing sound. Now you really are blushing.

"Whoooh, redner."

"So what was the dream about?"

"You'll be glad to hear that I've found an office for you. "Can't remember, but you were there, and I was there, and Mom and Pop were there, and so was Toto the dog." He stretches his arms out and yawns. You try to catch his yawn but it eludes you."

"Oh great, somewhere to sleep off my hectic weekend."

He tells you about his weekend and you absorb every word, and it's with sheer delight that you deduce that he doesn't appear to have a steady girlfriend. There are female names mentioned, but he seems to be making a point of also mentioning their boyfriends' names.

"Hey, what're you doing for lunch today?"

The question empties the air from your lungs.

"And don't say lunch is for wimps."

Not in a million years. And so it's arranged, you're going for lunch together.

"Guess who this is?"

You sit back and feign surprise. He has clambered up on to your desk and assumed a reclining posture. With his head supported by one hand, his other hand rests on his narrow waist, his shapely backside juts out, his shirt rides up to expose the elastic waistband of his boxers, and he pouts his lips at you. He's flirting, but what can you do? Flirt back? But what if he's not flirting? If he's just responding to your tacit encouragement for him to misbehave?

"A rabble-rouser reclining on a desk?"

"No, Madonna." He begins to sing. "Like a virgin, touched for the very first time, ooooh...D'you remember that song?"

You nod.

"Saw it on MTV oldies the other night."

You make a mental note to watch MTV occasionally.

And with that, the office door opens, and Teresa is standing there, surveying the scene in front of her, her brow knotted in utter bemusement.

"Have you two been drinking again?"

Johnny clasps his hands to his face in a display of mock fear. "Oh no, she's found out."

"Guess who he's doing an impression of."

Smiling now, Teresa looks at you and shrugs.

"You should know," Johnny says to her.

"I should?"

He turns to lie on his other side, and facing Teresa, he pouts and wiggles about as he sings. "Like a virgin, touched for the very first time, oooh, like a vir – rrr – gin."

Teresa is embarrassed now. She shakes her head and says, "You'd never believe you were twenty-three."

"I know, all my family look young for their age," he replies, and with that, he slides down off the desk, takes hold of Teresa's waist, and she giggles while he waltzes her backwards and forwards around the office.

"D'you come here often?" he whispers.

"He's mad," she blurts.

"I suppose a snog is out of the question?"

Teresa breaks free and adjusts her rumpled clothing. Red-faced and flushed, your normally collected secretary backs her way out the door. She has never met someone like him, and neither have you.

"Right, time we did some work," you say.

"Oh yes, I could think of nothing more appealing." He opens his lever-arch file, and then suddenly tosses it up in the air, catches it, and says,

"This is so incredibly boring."

"It's meant to be."

A sheet of paper with his notes lands in front of you, and you find yourself staring at his handwriting.

"Only on Fridays." "Are you shagging her nibs?" He cocks his thumb towards the door.

"I can just picture her with her high-heels dangling around your neck."

You are picturing him as your secretary.

"Hey, are you hitched?" A definite hint of a flush rises to his cheeks.

"Do I look that stupid?"

Now he's embarrassed that he asked this question. "When I was twenty-three, I had two kids," he says in a fair imitation of Carney, and then to round it off he feigns a wheeze, hauls an imaginary inhaler from his inside pocket and bangs his chest while he sprays the imaginary blasts into his mouth.

Under normal circumstances, your lunch hour is spent taking a stroll into town on your own. It's the way you prefer it. It's relaxing exercise, but more importantly, it circumvents the need to engage in petty conversations. At a brisk walking pace, it takes precisely eleven minutes to reach Grafton Street, where you immerse yourself in the flood of faces and browse your way through shops, buy a sandwich, take it back to the privacy of your office to eat it while reading snippets from the newspaper. It has often occurred to you that people must see you at the same time everyday. They probably set their watches by you. There he goes, you imagine them saying, the Walking Clock. But now, with Johnny walking by your side, you are oblivious to the busy swirl of the city life all around.

At lunch, the girl serving your table is pretty and once she's out of earshot, Johnny whispers, "Wouldn't mind giving her a slap of the wet lad."

You laugh, but inside you feel a stab of sharp pain, which you immediately assuage by convincing yourself that he's only saying this as a matter of course, the same way you used to yourself. But you would never say something like that if you were at lunch with a guy you fancied. However, this flicker of doubt is quickly quenched by your new-found capacity for self-delusion, which seems to hatch out of its shell that very day, take its first few tentative steps, adjust its eyes to the harsh daylight, flap its wings, and decide that it's ready for flight. There is no such person as Anne. He is never going to discover that you are married. If you close your eyes, no one can see you.

His office is down the corridor from yours and already there's a two-way path worn between them. No matter how many times you see him during the day, your stomach never fails to jump. For an entire month, the two of you go for lunch together. Layer upon layer of his life is laid down and delicately interwoven into the existing tapestry. Each day seems to throw up something irresistibly fresh and fascinating which you scribble into your diary in code that night, copying his handwriting. And what makes it all the more charming is the fact that he also seems to want to know a little about you. One day he asks Teresa if you're any good at football, and when Teresa tells you that you have an admirer there, you laugh it off, but her simple remark sends you into a dizzy spin. If you weren't living in an unreal world, it would worry you that he's asking other people about you. You would realise that it's only a matter of time before someone mentions Anne. But for this magical month, you are living in an unreal world and Anne and the baby are stuck somewhere out there on the peripheries of your consciousness.

However, the shadow of the weekend always looms. How will you survive two full days without seeing him? Outside office hours you inhabit different worlds, and now it's imperative that you somehow orchestrate it so that your social lives cross. Drink is the key to a man's heart. On the last Friday of the month you take the car into the city, and even the crazy rush-hour traffic fails to irritate you. It takes three quarters of an hour to get through Donnybrook and in that time you've composed a neat little letter for the problem page: *Dear Lucy, I have discovered the cure for stress. Fall in love with a handsome young man who works with you. Yours stressfreefully, Male Reader (married).* In another letter, you might explain why you took the car in on a Friday, the most hectic of traffic days. Lucy would understand that it's going to be essential to have wheels if you can summon up the courage to ask him to go for a drink after work. It's the most natural thing in the world, you tell yourself. If he were female it would be different. But he isn't female, so why worry.

Over lunch, you finally work up the courage to pop the question, and he crinkles up his nose and says that ordinarily he'd love to go for a drink with you, but that he's already promised to meet friends. His disappointment is palpable and this pleases you.

"Maybe some other time," you say.

He ponders this for a moment. It's exciting to watch him figure out a plan. Perhaps he'll suggest that you book into a hotel together for the weekend. Or maybe jet out to Paris or Rome or wherever's romantic right now.

"Hey, why don't you come and meet my friends?"

You hesitate. It's idiotic, but there is no logic in your life right now. Lovelorn is your middle name. His friends are probably all in their early twenties, at that know-it-all stage of their lives, who'll more than likely look upon you as something of a dinosaur.

"They're okay, you'll like them."

"Ah, maybe some other time."

And the moment he leaves the office that evening, you regret this decision. You stay on until seven o'clock to try and catch up on work you've let slip since his arrival. Up until a month ago you had no problem immersing yourself in tasks like this, but now your pen hovers idly above the page. It's impossible to concentrate. Endorphins are flying everywhere. The events of the month play themselves over and over in your head. His face, his smile, the things he said, they keep looming up at the front of your mind, elbowing all other thoughts aside. His distraction has caused other problems as well. Your normally ordered filing system has been thrown into chaos. Anything you filed in his presence seems to have been tossed in anywhere, like you were afraid you might miss something he said if you focused your complete concentration on what you were doing.

There's nothing you can do. Forces stronger than your will-power are at work. You phone Anne and tell her you're going for a drink with the crowd from work. She lists off the highlights of the night's TV programmes, and she seems pleased at the prospect of watching them in peace. For a moment, you feel sorry for her and have almost decided to change your plan, until his face tiptoes its way back into your thoughts and that's it, she's on the back-burner for the night. The show is on the road.

He has written 'THIS IS NOT A WHEELBARROW' in his easily-recognisable handwriting on the dusty side-panel of your car. It's like a love-note. A calling. Now you have no choice in the matter, of course you have to find him to tell him that you read his little message. The rush-hour traffic has cleared and you're rolling. The song about stumbling blue eyes comes on the car radio and you know that fate is on your side. There is no one else in the world you'd be bothered meeting for a drink now. It has to be him. Since the rocky years of adolescence you've deliberately kept your life on an even keel, measuring it out in little pleasures like a good TV programme, listening to music, a drink with friends, or playing football, tennis and golf. You had read somewhere that life without passion isn't really living, and in your customary defensive manner, you had pushed this notion right to the back of the already overcrowded suppression section of your brain. Only foolish people get involved in that sort of thing. It's for kids. You ought to have grown out of it by now. And up until recently, you actually believed that you had grown out of it.

The old ticker is pounding mercilessly, the legs are wobbly, the skin is tingling with goosebumps. A giddy, happy, uncertain feeling has you in its grip. Entering a pub has never been so thrilling. Nauseous with excitement and anxiety, you feel like a ship being tossed about on an unpredictable sea as you make your way through the tightly-packed bodies, the steady din of drunken voices, the dense fog of cigarette smoke. Snippets of conversation drift in one ear and out the other. Meaningless words spoken with the careful articulation of substance-abusers. You're looking in the mirror behind the bar, checking on how the hair looks, when you catch the eye of the Wax Hennessy, an acquaintance from college, who once spent a summer working in a candle-making factory in New York. If he was sober, the Wax would pretend he hadn't seen you, but he isn't sober. He shouts your name and it seems like the entire bar turns to gawk at you. If he keeps this up, you'll be featured on the *Nine O'Clock News*. And tonight in Dublin, the loudest shout ever recorded was heard in a busy pub. The person responsible was a stupid git called the Wax, who possesses one of those flat, expressionless, drip-dry faces, rounded off with a pair of those all-too-familiar beady, cash-register eyeballs.

You acknowledge his presence with the slightest upward movement of your head and the blandest of smiles. He's not alone. With him, there's a group of college contemporaries who you know to see. The receding hairlines, the greytops, the jowls and the portly bellies throw you off momentarily. These very same fellows were like whippets at college. They've fared worse than you and this gives you an unexpected lift. Peter Pan is installed as your middle name. The Wax shouts something else and you place your hand behind your ear and shrug. There must be fifty bodies packed between the two of you. He'd want to have a hotline to Moses to get through that lot. You heard what he said all right, but this isn't the time or the place to fill him in on how the "old job is going". You point towards the back of the crammed pub and contort your face into that of a fugitive's, the way people do when they want to give the impression that they are in a hurry. The previous Friday's business appointments page carried a photo of the Wax, along with details of his promotion. This is what he really wants to fill you in on.

Johnny isn't downstairs and on your way up the stairs a part of you hopes that he isn't up there either. Perhaps it would be better if you've missed him. Perhaps it would be better if he didn't know that you had come running after him. Anyway, if your college contemporaries were to see you with him it would raise eyebrows. People can spot passion a mile away. Even with their eyes shut, they can smell it. But all these misgivings are forgotten about the moment you see him. It's like a bright light has been switched on inside your head. He's sitting at a table with two other young guys. To speak, they lean forward, place their hand over their friend's ear, and shout. His tie is slung back over his shoulder, the top buttons of his shirt are open, his normally pale cheeks are flushed, a cigarette dangles between his fingers.

His eyes roll in their sockets until they come to rest on you. There's a moment's delay while he attempts to place your face, and you're sure you've made a terrible blunder. He doesn't even remember you, he only invited you out of politeness, he didn't mean it at all. You're from another planet as far as he's concerned now. It's one thing being friendly at work, but socialising is a different matter entirely. If he does finally manage to recognise you, he'll probably say, What the hell are you doing here? But you can always tell him that you're with friends downstairs. Yes, they just happened to be meeting in the same pub. Old Waxhead Hennessy and his cronies could step in and rescue you yet.

"Hey!" is all he says. And when he smiles your world slips out of its axis. Surely there's no nicer feeling than the one you adore being clearly delighted to see you. That bright light is getting brighter. He walks up to you, stands right in front of you, swaying ever so slightly, leaving you wondering whether he's going to shake your hand, embrace you, or even kiss you. Electric charges seem to spark between you. It's one of those intense moments that seem to last longer than they actually do, and which find their own indelible little storage space in the memory and linger there for decades. Forever maybe, who knows. And when he wets his finger, touches it against your face and makes the hissing sound, the light in your head shines so brightly you experience a light-headed dizziness.

"How's the rabble-rouser?"

"How come you're here?"

You mutter something about friends downstairs, but it's like the words you are speaking have a life of their own, laughing and giggling as they dance their carefree way out of your mouth and into his ear. One moment you feel like a gatecrasher at a kiddies' party, next moment you feel like the best pal of the kid having the birthday. And before you know it, he's introducing you to his two friends, whose names you don't even hear. They are actually younger than him, fresh out of college, barely shaving. This is kiddies' corner. Their music collections would hardly include The Smiths or Talking Heads. You've got to get control of yourself.

Johnny tells the two pals that you passed all your exams first time, that you're a financial controller and that you drive a brand new Beamer. Now they observe you with a mixture of admiration and puzzlement. They're wondering what the hell a hotshot like you is doing in their company. If accountants are the priests of the new faith, these lads are the seminarians, and you are well on your way to the rank of duplicitous bishop. But once you buy a round, you're something of a local hero. Drinkies children, you feel like saying. They're at the silly drunk stage and, pathetically, you join in their nonsensical babble. They're talking about how rich they're going to be when they qualify, the type of jobs they'll work in, the flash cars they're going to drive, the women they're going to pull, the houses they're going to live in, all the things they're going to buy. These are opinionated conversations you've heard so many times before, but because of him, you behave like it's all fresh and new. But you can't concentrate fully because you've convinced yourself that the older people down the pub are glancing at you like you are the strange man who has wandered into the children's playground.

So you finish your pint and criss-cross your hands above the empty glass when he suggests you have another. Disappointed, he asks why not, and you tell him that it's a smoky, stuffy joint and that if you're going to drink you want to drink in comfort. And as though to make your point, you wipe a smoke-induced tear from your eye.

"Let's roll," he says.

"But..." You direct a vague gesture towards his two pals who, red-faced from drink and red-eyed with lust, are competing with one another in equally pathetic attempts to chat up an unfortunate lounge-girl. If their parents could only see them now.

"They're only a pair of dorks. My real friends have gone home to get ready for Wexford tomorrow."

He stands up and tells the two dork friends that he's going on an expedition to the North Pole. They laugh like this is the funniest thing they've ever heard. A snot even flies out of one of their nostrils, and you spot Johnny's eyes rolling upwards. Feeling a little like a kidnapper, you follow him towards the stairs. The jitters have set in. Downstairs, the Wax Hennessy shouts what sounds like an offer of a drink, a minor miracle in itself. He's really willing to go to any length to fill you in on every last glorious detail of his promotion. But you're having none of it, you simply walk right on out the door the same way a man short of hearing would.

Outside, there are faces squashed up against the pub's plate-glass window. Young people's faces, clamouring for attention. They remind you of when you were at that age, when you took up those ridiculous postures, which you knew were ridiculous, but which you could never ridicule. Johnny tosses loose change into a begging child's cardboard box, and through this simple, unthinking action, you are imbuing him with mystical, saintly qualities. He is the new messiah. Aliens spying on the world will see his spirit shine brighter than those around him. Together you walk the gauntlet of the H people. "Homeless and Hungry", that's what their placards say, so what else can they expect you to call them. You don't like to admit it, but you've grown immune to their presence. However, outside Brown Thomas you see an undernourished and ragged-looking teenage boy, sitting behind a cardboard box, rocking continuously backward and forward in a demented manner. His hollow eyes stare out at the passing parade of Boomtown: Gucci and Armani, Celtic Tiger, the nightclub capital of Europe, the world's cultural capital, the city with money to burn. People are altering their routes to avoid him. Being with Johnny has triggered a dormant compassion and sharpened your sense of humanity. The demented-looking boy unsettles you and even the five pound note you put in his cardboard box doesn't ease this discomfort. But you can't deny that part of the reason for this moment of generosity is to impress Johnny Boy.

Twenty-five minutes later you are out in Sandyford, at the foothills of the Dublin Mountains, sitting together in his local, swilling copious quantities of beer and smoking noxious cigarettes by the score. Air flushes through your nostrils and seems to be following a clear unobstructed path directly to your brain, the oversupply of which has the effect of altering your perceptions. It's like you are a child again, seeing everything for the first time. Going for a drink has never felt like this before. The conversation ranges from work to exams to football, but somehow, it seems to be the most enlightened conversation you've ever engaged in. As well as adopting his gestures and inflections, you are behaving decidedly out of character; talking more than usual, reacting with uncustomary spontaneity and smiling and laughing like a bit of an imbecile. If people who knew you were sitting nearby, they probably wouldn't recognise you. But you don't care, there's an ease of conversation between you, like you've known one another for years. And being in his company fills you with a certain sense of almost proprietorial pride; you imagine the other drinkers are casting envious glances in your direction. That's a measure of how crazy you've become.

It transpires that he's heading down to Wexford for the

week-end. A friend's family owns a house there. And when he asks if you'd like to come along, you once again rejoice that no one at work appears to have mentioned Anne. But that plant of self-delusion has begun to sprout and flourish on the fertile grey matter inside your head. Reality is obscured. You are on your way to Wexford in the morning. The lounge lights flicker on and off, so he catches the attention of a lounge-girl and orders two more pints to celebrate. You feel light-headed now, unused to these quantities of alcohol. And what's more, you're going to drive home half-cut, something you could never have even imagined yourself doing before you met him. Your life is stumbling out of control. And after yet another unpleasant pull of a cigarette, your insides feel like a toxic waste dump. Both your parents are more than likely frowning down from their heavenly perch in dismay.

"What say we meet at ten tomorrow morning?"

"Ten o'clock it is."

"You drive and really impress my friends with the Beamer."

You want to tell him that you would circle the world in a hot-air balloon just to be with him.

It's unlikely that Anne will object, but in the remote event that she does, you know that you'll leave her. Any court in the land would understand. I wanted to go away for the weekend with this bloke, Your Honour, and she tried to prevent me. And was this "bloke" handsome? Indeed he was, Your Honour, and he still is. Well I fully understand your reasons and I'm a judge. Split the house down the middle and don't make too much of a racket during your manly activities.

A dangerous bend on the dark road shakes you out of this courtroom drama. Oncoming headlights flash the message to get the hell back on to your own side of the road. If you do knock someone down and kill them, you'll hide the body until after the weekend. Nothing must get in the way now. This is a back-road down from the mountains, free from roadblocks, you hope. It has all the signs of being the quiet old country road it probably once was. But now, behind the blurred hedges, there are ominous signs of new Legolands springing up. The give-aways are the

JCB tyre-tracks, and large billboards which feature the words "luxury", "detached" and "security."

Anne thinks it's a wonderful idea for you to go away with "the crowd from work" for the weekend. The break will do you the world of good, she says. And to avoid meeting her eye, you play with the baby, who has just finished a midnight snack and now seems intent on being tickled and played with until dawn. "I'll probably stay at Mum's on Saturday night," Anne says, and you agree that this would be a good thing to do. Her enthusiasm causes a flicker of suspicion. The thought of Anne having a clandestine affair occurs to you. Her and a bearded stranger. That would be the irony of ironies.

There's something mesmerising about the baby's eyes. They hold you in their spell. You can't stop playing with her. Just one more coochy-coo, followed by one more of her happy chortles. This game could conceivably continue until either one of you collapses from exhaustion. And she lapses into joyful hysterics when you duck down below her cot and suddenly pop your head up and say, Peep! Those ruddy cheeks, those laughing eyes, they are irresistible. Peep! You can't stop, she won't let you. Each peep is greeted by a burst of uproarious laughter. You crawl on the floor to the other side of her cot, and when you rise up onto your knees, you see her watching the far side of the cot, emitting little sounds of apprehension, her tiny fists clenched in anticipation. Peep, you say, and she swivels her head around in utter amazement. This unexpected peep shifts her frenzy of excitement up a gear, so much so, you fear that she might choke. So you return to tickling her, even though it's clear she wants the peep game to continue.

What will she think in years to come if she discovers anything about the weekend in Wexford? These things don't bear thinking about. Anyway, by then, gay fathers will probably be all the rage.

Out of the blue, Anne says, "Oh listen, you're not going to believe what I heard today," and you freeze momentarily. The guilt is getting to you. "The residents' association have got the county council to agree to put traffic lights at the entrance to the estate."

"Ah, great," you say, relieved. Jubilation. The authorities have relented. Money talks. Special treatment for special people.

Anne moves closer, sniffing the air in front of you. "Were you smoking?"

"I just had a pull or two."

"But..." This is unexpected. For you to smoke is similar to a vegetarian tucking into a blood-dripping steak. She's more than likely wondering if she really knows you as well as she thought she did.

"And you were drinking?"

"Only one or two."

"It was more than one or two Paul, I can tell by your eyes."

The eyes are the give-away.

"And you drove home!"

It's like a mother interrogating an errant son.

"Who was there?"

You list off the usual suspects.

"Was Teresa there?"

"For a while."

This sparks the martyred look. Does she think you'd be so pre-dictable that you'd shag your secretary? Johnny's image of the high-heels dangling around your neck causes you to smile, and this doesn't impress Anne. Back in the master bedroom, the blockbuster novel is hauled out and that's that, end of conversation. The drink has suddenly made you irritable, and you comfort yourself with the vengeful thought of someday plucking up the courage to rip out the last page of her blockbuster.

That night, you are anxious. It's too good to be true. Things like this don't happen to you. Maybe it's his idea of a joke. Maybe you'll call to his house like a thoroughbred sap and he'll have for-gotten all about the whole drunken plan. And even if he does turn up, what if he tells people at work and someone tells Carney? It would appear extremely odd. Two people who barely know one another heading off for a weekend together. The tearoom theatre would be ablaze with surmise and speculation. Break-a-leg Andy would be treading the boards with both wrists hanging limp. But then, you think, maybe Johnny will turn up and maybe just this one time things will work out for you. If this was the ecstatic feeling your friends experienced when they went on those first holidays with their girlfriends they did a good job at concealing it. Maybe it's just that they took these things for granted.

Eventually, as you had anticipated, the demented-looking teenage beggar from Grafton Street steps in through the front door of your thoughts. Every sad detail is there to see. Thinking about him makes you shudder. Where is he now? Is he too crazy-looking for the men who prowl the city streets in search of his type? What could you really do for him and all the others like him? But even thinking of him doesn't lessen your anxiety. Tossing and turning, no position seems comfortable. Anne is snoozing away beside you. Insomnia has a grip on you. It's well after three o'clock before you fall into a fitful sleep.

Chapter Four

Fittingly, for the morning that's in it, the early morning sun is shining down, sparkling on the criss-cross windows and the car chrome, drenching Legoland in its fresh light. The crows perched on the telephone wires explode into the air with a loud cawing and flapping of wings. The smaller birds sound like they're taking it in turns to imitate the ringing tones of mobile phones.

The metabolism goes into hyperdrive on the approach to his house. It's difficult to stop yourself making childish deals with a Higher Being. A new peak has been reached in your emotional life and you are susceptible. You will be a good loyal husband for the rest of your days if you can just have this one weekend away. You will climb the Sugar Loaf on Christmas Day in your bare feet, run naked around Stephen's Green on Paddy's Day, perform a daily moon for the citizens of Legoland. No Higher Being could resist such juicy deals.

It's a relief to see his house in all the splendour of daylight. It was no nocturnal mirage. Something still irks you though, like an unreachable itch that needs scratching. If he was gay, would he ask you to call to his family home? Surely he'd want to conceal his lover man, especially someone obviously that bit older. This reminds you to tousle your hair in the hope that it will land in such a way that the barren spots are concealed.

The intimidating teak door swings open and a teenager, who has to be his younger brother, is standing there. The family resemblance is uncanny.

"Hello, would Johnny be there please?"

"I'll see."

He slouches away without asking you to step in. Even his walk is similar to Johnny's. Of course, he's probably wondering what this old fellow is doing calling for his brother. The smell from inside the house hits your nostrils and it's his smell, that smell which will linger indelibly in your memory until your dying day.

Funny that, how every family has its own unique smell, you're thinking, when a door opens and a frisky red setter skids on the panelled floorboards, bounds in your direction and buries its nose in your crotch.

"Rusty! Rusty, leave the man alone." There's a definite hint of amusement in the younger brother's tone.

Despite your bodily contortions, Rusty continues to sniff at your private parts until the younger brother finally manages to grab him by the collar and haul him away.

Moments later, Johnny is standing there, and seeing him in casual clothes for the first time makes you want to embrace him.

"Thought you weren't coming," he says.

"Had a slight headache this morning for some reason."

"Better say hello to the old pair."

Reluctantly, you step into the swish oak-panelled kitchen. It's a shock to discover that his parents don't look an awful lot older than you do. The song lyrics, "Your Daddy's rich and your Mama's good-looking", spring to mind. They greet you cordially and it's obvious he's given them glowing reports of his new boss. They're delighted that their potentially wild son has fallen under such a steadying influence. It shows in their eyes. You are Mr Safe-and-Sound. That's what you like to believe anyway. They go on and on about Carney Textiles but you want them to talk about him. The parents' angle. The room is scattered with family snapshots. You sneak quick glances at him through the years. They give you a warm glow. But you fear that if you appear to be as interested in these photos as you really are, one of the parents will ask, Have you got the hots for our son or something?

The younger brother and younger sister lurk about in the background, staring at you with the mix of smirk and scowl peculiar to their age. There's no doubt they're giving you a thorough going-over and you're more than likely going to be the target of their sardonic adolescent mimicry. Your every word and gesture will be hauled out for the family game-show. But who cares? Not you. Once they get to know you, they'll like you. You'll take them out places and listen to them talk about their older brother. The sibling angle. This is the happy anxiety you ought to have experienced on your first visit to Anne's house. Watching her behaviour in the company of her family ought to have been something you revelled in, but all you can remember of that time was how you were constantly on the lookout for her good-looking brothers.

The phone rings for Johnny, and you experience a sharp stab of jealousy. How dare anyone else call him. It's to do with the trip to Wexford, he says. His friends are checking to see that he has a lift, and with that, he picks up the cordless phone and walks out into the back garden. So rather than stay with the family, you ask where the bathroom is. On the way up the stairs, you experience a pleasant sensation from holding onto the banister he has touched so many times. Also, there are further family photos to swoon over, but at the top of the stairs, the half-open door with the sign *Jonathan's Room* sends the insides of your head into a spin. The logical side of your brain is being wrestled to the ground by the illogical side. There is no option. It's mad, but you can't resist. Holding your breath, you steady the whirlwind, stand still and listen. Satisfied that there's no one about, you tiptoe towards his bedroom and cautiously stick your head around the door. The room is empty. With a sense of entering another time zone, you step inside and take a long, lingering inhalation of the same air that he had been breathing in and out throughout the night. The clothes which are scattered about are the latest in fashion and you make a mental note to go on a shopping spree and drag yourself up to date. A hairbrush catches your eye, and when you apply it to your head in long, lazy strokes the action seems to release so much static electricity you imagine the control panel of any alien spacecraft that may be hovering about in the vicinity lighting up like a Christmas tree.

An invisible magnet is drawing you towards the bed, and with the recklessness of love, you lie down upon it, wallowing in the pleasure of seeing the world the same way he sees it first thing every morning. The posters on the walls are neutral; New York City by night, and several famous films, but most importantly, none of female actresses or sex-kittens. There is hope. You close your eyes and almost believe you can feel him snuggling up along-side you. Then you imagine plucking a diary from under the pillow, flicking it open on page one, and reading his big admission: *I'm in love with my boss*. It's open season now so you kiss the pillow to suck up those flakes of shedded skin. A gorging cannibal, that's what you've turned into.

Approaching footsteps thumping their way up the stairs startle you. It sounds like a gang of machete-brandishing raiders are loose in the house. With catlike stealth, you cross the room and conceal yourself behind an open wardrobe door. Then, through the chink in the same wardrobe door, you see his younger brother and sister entering the bedroom, mischievous intent written all over their faces. The blood pounds against your temples with such force, you imagine yourself keeling over, victim to an inopportune bout of unconsciousness. They move out of vision. They appear to be at the other side of the bedroom, where you hear a drawer being slid open.

"Bingo," the brother says.

"How much?" the sister says.

"Three quid."

"Oh thanks very much Johnny, you're too kind to us."

This is followed by further rummaging sounds.

"Is Baldy still in the jacks?" the brother asks.

"Yeah. God, I hope the stink doesn't wither my plants," the sister says.

The brother launches into a range of different voices. "Hello, would Johnny be there please? Indeed he would, come on in, but please don't be trying to lead poor Rusty astray. Well Mr Lyons, slurp slurp, I joined Carney Whatever-it's-called in the sixteenth century and I've applied myself diligently to the task every since. Good man yourself, Mr Baldy."

It wouldn't require membership of Mensa to figure out who the brother is performing the unflattering imitations of. Your face feels like it's in need of an ice-pack. The top of your head feels itchy. It's one thing examining your hairline in a mirror, it's another thing hearing strangers confirm what you see there.

"And also, slurp slurp, I foresee a good future for Johnny, sorry Jonathan, at Carney Whatever-it's-called."

"Bingo squared!" the sister says.

"Ah, no way Christine, you can't take that." The brother's voice wavers with excitement.

"He's loaded now, he won't miss it."

That's when you hear Johnny shout from downstairs. "Hey, who's in my room?" "Oh shit," the brother mutters. "Quick, hide." The sister's tone is urgent. "Where?" "In the wardrobe." The sister's footsteps move in your direction. A drop of perspiration trickles across your ribcage. "Nah, too obvious," the brother says. The sister stops walking. "Yeah, but he's stupid, he'll never think of looking there." "Hmmm, that's true."

The pair of them are hovering about very close to the wardrobe door. Any moment now, they could pull the door open and see you standing there. What could you say to them? Ask them for directions? Claim you got lost? "Oh shit to the power of ten," the brother says in a panicky voice. "Spa-face alert."

There's the sound of a set of footsteps bounding up the stairs. "Scarper, it's every man for himself," the brother says, and it sounds as though they're running around the bedroom in circles. Through the chink in the wardrobe door, you see Johnny appear at the bedroom door, hemming them in. "What the hell are you two doing in here?" The sister speaks in a low voice. "You better not hit us, your friend will think it just a little bit on the weird side." "You're the very ones who'd be screeching the house down if I went near your bloody rooms." "We thought we heard a burglar," the sister says, and the brother sniggers. "Honest, we did. We chased him in here, he fell down onto your bed and he passed out immediately. From the smell," the brother adds, emitting a nervous guffaw which Johnny imitates in an exaggerated way. Then he turns his attention on the sister. "You know, if you were any uglier, we could charge people in to see you." "Ho, ho, ho, so original." "Now I know exactly how much money was in that drawer and if there's a penny missing, I'm going to – " Once Johnny moves away from the door, the sister and brother make a dash for it. They scarper out of the room with him hot on their tails. The three sets of footsteps pound down the stairs. Then you hear the sister roar. "Dad, Johnny's behaving like a juvenile again!" "Will you ever leave them alone!" the father shouts. "Honest to God, you'd never believe you're nearly twenty-four years old." The remainder of the exchanges are muffled. It sounds as though the mother is acting as peacemaker. Thirty seconds later, you slip out of the bedroom and head downstairs, and there at the end of the stairs is the younger brother.

"Did you find it?" he asks, polite as you like.

Can't talk, you feel like saying, my mouth is full of your brother's moulted skin.

"I did yeah, thanks," you say, conscious that you are altering your accent.

"Johnny's outside waiting for you."

"Oh right."

"See you again."

"Yeah, sure."

"You can give us a go in your car."

"No problem."

It's difficult to believe that this is the same lad you overheard upstairs. And there's the sister, smiling so sweetly at you, you can't help but think that she's guessed your intentions. This is one time you wish you wore a wedding ring, you're thinking, as you step outside into the bright daylight and spot Johnny being kissed on the cheek by his mother. And he doesn't flinch or withdraw. It's a beautiful moment.

Once you're out on the open road, drunk with the thrill of leaving the city, the younger brother and sister are soon forgotten, and you feel like a thoroughbred hotshot with the sunroof open, the wind whistling through your hair, the speedometer inching past 75MPH, blurred roadside signs warning that speed kills, and the one you love sitting alongside you. You wait for a break in the conversation before you self-consciously put on the tape which you have specially selected for the journey. Music can touch hearts. Music is when the human spirit soars up into the realms of the gods. This is like a test. The opening notes are pure heaven to you, but you're not really listening to them, you're waiting for his reaction.

He moans and says, "What's that crap?"

The omens aren't too promising.

"Beethoven. He was a bit of a star a few years back."

"Classical shite. Put on the radio, I wanna hear mind-numbing music."

You lean across and tune the radio into an oldies station on which Van Morrison is singing "Crazy Love". Mocking *sean-nós* singers, Johnny closes his eyes and sings along in a voice befitting a constipated ninety-year-old man. You very nearly blurt out that your wife likes Van the Man, but you hold your tongue. His denim-clad leg has caught your eye. Its alluring shape is too much to resist, so, to prolong the look, you pretend to fiddle with the radio-tuner. Moments pass with your eyes off the road, and when you look up again, all you see is a close-up of the back of an old-style cattle-truck. There they are, twenty yards in front of you, a row of expressionless cows, staring at you like you're the one on the way to the abattoir. While beside you, *sean-nós* Johnny is singing, "She give me love, love, love, love, crazy love."

It won't be possible to stop in time. You have to swerve. There isn't even time for a glance in the mirror. The cows are almost close enough to touch. A dizzy sense of panic grips you. Adrenaline pumps through your veins. Electrosensory reactions are on red alert. The internal motor goes into overload. The forehead is damp. Every nerve-end is shrieking. And then everything becomes dreamlike and switches to slow motion. Instinct takes control. The car, the cattle, the sweep of blurred peripheral shapes, the swerve into the other lane, the sound of a horn blowing, and Johnny's voice saying, If we die, I just want you to know that I love you.

There's a long silence. You drop your speed and settle your breathing. The big yellow ball is still sitting up there in the sky. The world appears to be still turning on its axis.

"Lucky I brought a change of trousers," you say, now doubting that you heard him say those words. But you did. People open their hearts and say these things in moments of crisis. At thirty thousand feet up, when the pilot comes on the PA and announces that the engines are shagged, that's when confirmed atheists become God zealots. That's when people have a tendency to say things they kept buried deep inside. It's probably better to pretend you hadn't heard it.

"Oh God, did you hear what I said?"

This is yet another one of his appealing features – his willingness to say what other people wouldn't dare.

"I thought we were going to die," he says.

There is no one you would rather die with.

"Will I do it again?"

"Keep your eyes on the bloody road."

Overhead, a jet aeroplane is hauling a trail of exhaust-smoke across the sky, and you imagine the pilot suddenly telling his anxious passengers to fasten their safety-belts and hold tight, before altering his path to swoop, dive, and zigzag until he had written *PAUL C. xxx JOHNNY L.* across the heavens.

Another moment of unwelcome reality awaits you at the twelve-bedroomed country residence. His friends, who are all in the twenty-one to twenty-three age bracket, have known one another for years. They grew up in the same neighbourhood and attended the same schools. It makes you want to turn the car around and hightail it back to Dublin. What do they make of you? What must they think? Is it that they are used to Johnny bringing older male companions along with him on these weekend jaunts? But surely they'd show signs. Or maybe they've just become used to it. But one thing's for sure, these are all upwardly-mobile people. Future high-flyers. Wealthy papas and mamas abound. No supermarket shelf-packers here. You've infiltrated a nest of rich kids.

Initially, they display almost exaggerated cordiality towards you, embarrassingly so, but very soon you're forgotten about, and they're off talking about past times, past events and people you know nothing about. But you don't mind, because most of these stories seem to concern Johnny's antics, or Jonathan, as some of them call him. It doesn't surprise you to discover that he's the heart and soul of the group. Anytime the stories move away from him, you want to say, Okay yeah, that's great but it's boring, let's stick to the Johnny stories please.

It's like piecing together a jigsaw. Their stories span the college holiday periods. You hear about the summer he spent as a street-sweeper in London, and the summer spent parking cars under the blue skies of Cape Cod, before he could even drive. They recall the reaction of American friends whenever they said that they were, "dying for a fag". The stories continue in the nearby pub and you continue to lap them up like the thirsty hound you are. And it's not only the stories you're lapping up. The drink is loosening your inhibitions, Johnny believes in letting his guests roam free, and you're finding out that they're a decent enjoyable bunch of people. But anytime you're in conversation with someone, you're all the time watching him. Like right now, someone, whose name you can't remember, is at your ear, yapping on about Arsenal, and you keep nodding like you're listening to him. It's so rude but you can't help yourself. The night would probably be great fun if you weren't so obsessed. By now, you've sorted out the romantic couplings. It's clear he has no partner, but there is this girl named Sara who he spends too much time chatting privately with for your liking. He seems to know her better than he knows the others. And the more you drink, the more green-eyed you become.

After the pub closes, everyone stumbles back along the dark country road. High spirits abound. And there you are in their midst, like you've known them all for years. Back in the house, a home-made disco lights system has been rigged up, a keg of beer has been acquired, and the music plays until the early hours. This would be such an enjoyable party were it not for the frustration of having to pretend that you wouldn't like to haul Johnny out onto the makeshift dancefloor and hold him close enough to feel his heartbeat. He dances with Sara, snogs her old-world style, gets off with her. You've moved beyond jealousy. It almost drives you insane to watch them. It'd be like dragging him out of quicksand to haul him away from her now. What a mess that'd make. And with everyone watching. Maybe it'd be better if you jumped in the car, drove back to Dublin, left his P45 on his desk and forgot all about him. But you can't. Just maybe he won't end up in Sara's bed and just maybe you'll share a room with him.

By three o'clock they're too tired to continue with the party, and the various couplings head off to the various bedrooms. Aisling, the hostess, asks if you wouldn't mind sharing a room with Jonathan, and you roll your eyes up like a big queen and remark that we all have to make sacrifices. The room you've been allocated contains only a double-bed. Naturally, this sends a thrill of excitement ping-ponging around your system, but it also irritates you ever so slightly that everyone seems to have jumped to conclusions. Do they all think you're a big poofter?

"Sorry about the double-bed," Aisling says.

"Don't worry, I think I might be sleeping elsewhere," Johnny says, and Aisling definitely spots the momentary flash of desolation sweep across your features.

He goes into the adjoining room to Sara, and there you are, left on your own, experiencing such an overwhelming dose of sadness, you want to cry. Their muffled voices are audible. Their laughter, the occasional shriek, and then those low murmurs. They're the worst. You want to tear down the wall and drag him back with you. Tell the prize bitch to go and find herself another man. Now you understand why people mainline. You lie there, staring out the window at the cold-blooded moon, listening. Now you've got that slap on the face you needed. The tree of delusion is starting to wilt and die. Now you can come down off that cloud and get back to real life. It'll still be possible to adore him from a distance, like some sort of glass menagerie, but that's as far as it will ever go and you will have to learn to accept this. And anyway, even if he hadn't gone into Sara's bedroom, and even if you had never met Anne, what were you supposed to do? Feel good about taking him to meet your family and friends? There would be no rituals, no celebrations, no joyous Christmas gatherings, no directorship, no permanency, no bricks and mortar, no piece of paper from the city hall. Just ridicule and scorn and abuse in restaurants. Who can really blame you for pretending?

Later, in that haze of half-sleep, the door creaks open and someone whispers your name. It's him. It's him. If you open your eyes, will you wake up and break the spell? If you start to breathe again, will he be whisked away out through the window?

"You asleep?"

"Yeah."

"Phew, at least I didn't wake you up."

You blink furiously to clear away the tears before you open your eyes. He's undressing. Does that mean he had his clothes on next door? Should you ask? He strips to his boxers and climbs into the bed beside you.

"Hope you don't snore," he says.

You make a snoring sound.

"Cold feet." He rubs his cold feet against your bare legs. This is too much. Something is going to short-circuit.

Who cares about stupid rituals, scraps of paper from official-dom, or even family approval. This is love and that's enough for you. That old tree inside is beginning to flower and bloom like a hothouse plant hooked up intravenously to high-grade fertiliser.

"God, I'm out of my box," he says and moments later he's sound asleep. Some motherly instinct takes over. You watch him sleeping, lying there with his head anchored in the harbour of his crooked arm. The hot-blooded moonlight is on his face. He looks like a different person. Innocent and vulnerable. Someone who needs protecting.

But very soon the motherly instincts desert you and you're on the prowl. With maximum stealth, your hand goes on the slither. Plenty of practise from putting the blankets back on the baby in the dead of night. That first touch of smooth skin, slim and muscu-lar. It's the stomach region. A bellybutton that turns inwards. Cute as a button. The gentle rise and fall. Slide down to the touch of cotton. Hold your breath. Steady that heartbeat. Slithery slip under the elastic waistband and down towards the promised land. He moves. He utters a guttural sleep sound. Retreat with haste and stealth. No careless movements in the heat of lust. Shut the eyes tight and listen. What are you doing? Molesting a sleeping man in a double-bed in Wexford. It's not something you'd want to dwell upon. Pretend you are dreaming if he says anything. Another move and then he settles. Minutes pass. You're dog-tired but there's no way you are sleeping yet. The slippery hand goes on the march again. Here we are in holiday town. Dum-dee-dum-dee-dum-dum. You've overshot the runway and landed on a leg. Firm and strong. Slender and long. Up along the chequered fabric. Stop. No movement. Just that steady breathing of sleep. Under the elastic waistband and hey-ho, let's go. Flaccid now, but for how long? Indeed, not long at all. It's all hands on deck time. Blow the whistle, sound the foghorn, we're off around the world. It's transformation time. From the Leaning Tower of Pisa to the Eiffel Tower and finally to a hot geyser shooting for the moon. Swift and glorious. You touch your tongue to your messy hand and think, Boy, you really are a regular fiend.

There's a thick layer of ice above you. You claw at it but your nails make no impact. "Air! Air!" you seem to shout. There must be some trick way out of this, so you bleat like a sheep, moo like a cow, bark like a dog, twist and turn like a trapped fish, until you awaken and discover that you are holding your breath and making a strange dolphin-like sound in the back of your throat.

Morning has broken. Bright light streams through the flimsy curtains, and there's a man inside your head banging a big gong. But the sound of the gentle, even breathing in the bed alongside you seems to encourage the man with the gong to take a break. The pain dissolves when you turn your head and see that his sleep-matted hair is so close you could stick your tongue out and touch it. And in your receptive state of awakening, it's a moment to cherish. The urge to wrap your arms around him is overpowering. All you'd have to do is close your eyes and mutter a female name. Maybe he will snuggle up against you, pretend that he too is adrift on that old sea of subconsciousness and call you Sara, so he can mutter sweet nothings into your ear. You are innocent when you dream, everyone knows that.

There are sounds of life in the house. Water gushes into a distant cistern, a door opens, footsteps pass on the corridor outside, the delicate footsteps of someone with a man banging a gong inside their head. From outside, there's the steady trawl of the waves giving the beach its morning wash. There's a cacophony of chirpy bird song too, and you imagine that the birds sound less stressed than their urban cousins do. Reluctantly, you let your feet roll out on to the floor and sit up. One corner of the room suddenly seems to tilt up, so you remain as you are for a moment. The man with the gong has been reinvigorated by his rest. His wild swings are landing well wide of their intended target and are instead splattering the soft tissue of your brain and crushing the bone and gristle of your skull. Why is he banging the gong in the first place? Probably because he doesn't approve of excess quantities of alcohol sloshing about in his domain. So why did you drink so much? Johnny. Why do you do anything these days? Johnny. And who was the person you spent an hour talking to about Arsenal? He was the shield to hide behind while you watched Johnny dance.

These are the type of questions that blur your vision as you aim yourself in the direction of the *en suite* bathroom, your every step restricted by your seemingly indeflatable hard-on. But a glance in the bathroom mirror brings you to your senses. Hurtling towards thirty and it's showing. That layer of scum congealed at the side of your mouth is not a pretty sight. Lucky he didn't see you before you showered. Nothing like a shower to make you feel that you look better than you do. Nothing like a wash of the hair to make you believe that there's more there than there was last time you looked.

Back in the bedroom, he's standing in front of the old-style mirror, examining his private parts, and your immediate suspicion is that he's searching for fingerprints. A shrill whistle-blast could be the signal for everyone to line up for a fingerprinting session. The forensic experts have been called in. The fiendish culprit must be found. However, your arrival prompts a little modesty. Now you see that his boxer shorts are decorated with a cartoon map of London, with Big Ben in poll position. Picking out the various landmarks gives you the perfect excuse to make a closer inspection. Covent Garden is on the right buttock and you almost touch it when you point it out. And this attention puts an end to his moment of modesty.

"Sara says I've got big balls," he says, lowering his shorts to give you the full frontal. "What d'you think?"

Well, even you, the master of control, can fall prey to a little dizzy spell at moments like this. There's no doubt, this is an image that's going to spend a long time nestled at the top of your memory charts. But you've got to be careful, hold yourself back and act casual, otherwise he could be running from the room, telling everyone that you're a pervert.

"Huge."

"Let's see yours."

If you were two ten-year-olds, this might not be unexpected, but when a man of twenty-three makes such a request to a man of twenty-eight, you know you're entering the realms of the unexpected. Anyone else would tell him to piss off, but you don't, you take that step into a foggy world by opening your towel and permitting him a five second glance, which he avails of with apparent relish. What is going on? A married man displaying the family jewels to his office assistant in a house in Wexford? The hurling county of amber and purple will never recover.

"Just remember, it's not for stirring your tea with," he says, and he drops his shorts, kicks them off, and you catch just the briefest glance of his bubble butt before the bathroom door closes behind him. And that's enough to send every blood cell in your body into a frenzy. Every last one of them drops what they are doing and rushes to take up their stations for penis-enlargement duty. Morning glory on a glorious morning. One thing's for sure, these blood cells are never such eager-beavers whenever Anne's rear is on view.

Five minutes later, he emerges from the bathroom, dripping wet, naked except for a towel wrapped around his waist. His matted hair glistens, and facing you, he asks if you would like to see him go on the horn. The old ticker palpitates perilously.

"Boinng!" he says, sticking the long, wooden handle of the toilet-brush out between the gap in his towel, and your burst of nervous laughter sounds like a foghorn.

Later that morning, after receiving permission to use the phone, you call Anne as you promised you would. There you are, chatting away, when he grabs the receiver out of your hand and says, "If he's making a pervert call, all you say to him is, great stuff, I usually have to pay for this."

You can just picture the flush rising to Anne's cheeks.

"Well, do you agree with me or do you agree with me?" he adds.

And now you can picture Anne, lost for words. She isn't one for quick responses and he seems to sense her embarrassment. You try to snatch the phone back but he moves too fast.

"Who is this anyway?" he asks, sniggering.

A long silence follows. His smirk fades.

"His what?...Oh, sorry."

The blood has drained from his face. "Never knew you were married," he whispers, handing the phone back to you. His sense of disappointment is palpable. But you are speech-less. Conflicting emotions have cut the link between your brain and your mouth. You want to tell him everything. You feel anger towards Anne for telling him that she's your wife. It's ridiculous, but that's what you feel.

"Who was that?" she asks.

"A messer called Johnny." It's nice just to say his name out loud.

"He sounds mad."

"You have to be mad to work for Carney Textiles." Now you're speaking for both of them as Johnny has stopped at the kitchen door with his hand cocked to his ear. It gets awkward when Anne tells you that Lia is teething again. He soon becomes bored with your monosyllabic replies and moves on.

For the remainder of the day, you spend your time trying to be close to him. But this is frustrating, because he's one of these itching-powder-in-his-pants types, a social butterfly, flitting from person to person in his own special way. Now that he knows you're married, he ain't interested. You participate in games of croquet and tennis, but you can't concentrate fully. And worse still, you get the impression that he's purposely trying to annoy you by flirting with the women, sitting beside them, draping his arm around them and asking them if they'd like to marry him. The women treat him like a mischievous rascal. But every time he does this, it gives you such a choking sensation of jealousy you can't breathe for a moment. It frightens you to think how you'd react if you thought he was being serious.

Late in the afternoon, an older sister of Aisling's drops by briefly with her husband. "Here come the wrinklies," you hear this older sister say, and you're sure you spot her glancing in your direction. There's a definite double-take. Both of them are around your age. No doubt, they'll ask later who the zimmer-frame candidate was.

Things happen fast with this group. One minute, there's a major game of charades in progress, next minute, everyone's jumping into cars and they're on their way to the nearby nightclub. In the mêlée, you lose track of him. You're standing there on the gravel driveway, wishing you could just call out his name. All around, car doors slam shut, shouts and screams ring out. The testosterone is high. The boys are going to have a car race. There are females to impress. Tyres skid on the gravel, horns are hooted, friendly insults are exchanged, and the stream of bright headlights weave and bob their way down the winding driveway and off out into the dark countryside. Aisling pulls up alongside you and tells you to hop in. He's not in the car so you assume he's gone on ahead, and more than likely left instructions with them to make sure to bring you along. Cheered by this thought, you regale the four people in the car with a few of the Phantom's top-notch jokes, and now that they witness you operate without Johnny's restricting presence, they see you differently. You actually have a personality. But really, it's the thought of them telling Johnny about the series of entertaining jokes you told that spurs you on. However, you haul in the topsails when you become aware that you're sharing the back seat with two of the weekend's single females. Is Aisling attempting to fix you up? You've been through all this years before, you know the signs, that familiar body language. But you can't deny that it's a relief to realise that they don't seem to have guessed your real intentions after all.

It's eight pounds a head to enter a sea of swaying bodies, a mirrored haze of coloured lights, and music that causes the eardrums to vibrate. The big consolation is that there's a full bar. No need to drink the usual overpriced muck which is so often passed off as wine. After you buy a round of drinks for the crowd in the car your eyes adjust to the dancehall lights, and there's only one person among the mass of bodies you are on the lookout for. Aisling's boyfriend Jerome, a jolly giant of a medical student, is entertaining the group with a hospital story. Everyone laughs when he describes the races the porters hold down in the mortuary. These races involve pushing dead people on trolleys along the labyrinth of corridors deep in the bowels of the hospital. The Stiff Race, they call it. Or Formula None. Wagers are made, a loud whistle blast starts the race, and he claims they even have a chequered flag for the finishing line. You give a fair impression that you're all ears, but all you're really thinking of is of how you might ask about Johnny's whereabouts without being too obvious. It wouldn't do to simply blurt out, "Where's Johnny?" or "Anyone seen Johnny?". A more circumspect approach is called for.

You are saved from further mental anguish when one of Jerome's pals walks up to you and asks where that bollix Johnny is. Without saying a word, you shrug, and adjust your stance so that the question is directed towards the others.

Aisling takes the bait. "He said he was going to stay in."

"Not feeling the Mae West," Jerome adds, rubbing his stomach.

It's difficult to maintain a calm disposition.

"Swine owes me a tenner," Jerome's pal says, moving away.

Almost instinctively, you feel like reaching for your wallet to pay off the debt.

Aisling and the others seem to be watching you, almost like they're waiting for you to make a run for it. This is the moment of truth. Are you really interested in their company at all? And about two songs later, their worst suspicions are confirmed if they happen to notice you slithering your way towards the exit instead of the toilets. One of the burly doormen asks if you want a pass-out, and you just shrug. He hands you one anyway, and you're conscious that all the doormen are looking at you as something of a curiosity when you set off at jogging pace towards the approaching headlights of the latest bevy of party animals. A jeep with a Dublin registration swings into the car park and disgorges its rowdy crew of lads practically at your feet. Their high-testosterone roars and pre-nightclub comments are ones you have heard a million times before: "Hold me back", "Lock up yer daughters", "Nothing in a skirt is safe". If they try and engage you in any friendly buddy-buddy chatter, you are quite likely to start a brawl. Drunk as they are, they seem to be able to recognise a potentially crazed person when they see one. They let you pass by unhindered.

The moon has emerged from behind the clouds to bathe the land with its ghostly light. Once outside the grounds of the night-club, you break into a faster jog along the coast road, from where you're treated to a grandstand view of the moonlight on the ocean. This peaceful scene really ought to have a soothing effect on you, but it doesn't. If anything, it makes you feel lonely and crazy. What the hell are you doing on your own running along some country road in the dead of night? It's a question you'd prefer not to think about, so you break into something approaching three-quarters pace. That madman moon is dragging you along, there's nothing you can do.

They're in the kitchen, Sara and himself, sitting together on a sofa, which you are tempted to grab hold of and tip over. Judging by their expressions, you must look wild-eyed and somewhat ruddy-faced after your exertions.

"How come you're back?" he asks.

For a crazy half-second, the alcohol in your system tempts you to tell the truth.

"Not feeling the Mae West," you say, rubbing your stomach.

"Me neither," he says, and you're sure you see him make a

face behind Sara's back.

"You should drink water," she says.

"Wouldn't you know she's a trainee nurse," he says.

She corrects him. "Trainee physiotherapist."

"Oh great, my leg has suddenly gone all stiff, would you mind giving it a rub-a-dub-dub please."

You take a half-step in his direction.

Sara proceeds to rub his leg, he leans back writhing in apparent pleasure, and you stand there, wishing you had remained in the nightclub.

So when he throws up in the kitchen sink and then lapses into a coma-like sleep on a downstairs sofa, you're not too peeved off. At least it means he won't be shacking up with the trainee physiotherapist. Upstairs in the *en suite* bathroom, you wash your teeth with his toothbrush and imagine that you're kissing him. Back in the bedroom, his canvas gearbag is too difficult to resist. A root through his clothes unearths his London boxers, complete with the hardened stain in the vicinity of Big Ben. You slip them on and stand in front of the mirror. Now you understand those men who write those furtive letters to *Dear Lucy* to tell her all about their secret fetish for trying on their girlfriends' knickers. The very same letters Anne and yourself regularly laugh at. Reluctantly, you slip them off and replace them in the canvas bag precisely as you found them. It's impossible to sleep, impossible to read, impossible to do anything except lie there in the darkness and think over every minute detail of the weekend. Hours later, the others arrive back, and judging by the way they tiptoe past your door, they've heard about your illness. During the night, you trek down the stairs on three separate occasions to check that he's still alive, and to wallow in the pleasure of watching him sleep.

The following day, you end up giving Sara a lift back to Dublin. She sits in the back, Johnny sits in the front, and in your crazy head, this is a triumph for you. Often, unknown to her, you catch her facial expression in the rear-view mirror. It's obvious that she's mad about him and that he's not too bothered with her. And once you realise this, your low-level hostility towards her ceases.

At her house, he carries her bag to the door for her, and when she bends down to extract her door keys from the side-pocket of the same bag, out of her vision, he pretends to boot her in the backside. He's showing off to you. But his expression alters dramatically when he spots her mother, watching everything from an upstairs bay window, her face registering a mixture of annoyance and bemusement. To make matters worse, he then pretends that he's in the middle of some sort of ballet routine, raising his foot up, so that when Sara turns to face him, he has more explaining to do.

"Oh, shit," he gasps, once he's back in the car. "Get the hell out of here, quick."

*   *   *   *

At home, you mumble details of the weekend to Anne, and when she spots you reading the horoscopes, she assumes it's hers you're reading, so you tell her that you're tired and you're going to lie down for a while. It's seven o'clock in the evening and already you feel the post-weekend-away gloom settling in. A large dose of Johnny DTs are coming on. The more you see of him, the more you want to see of him. If only you could phone him and suggest meeting for a pint. But even if you do meet him, you'll have to say goodbye again at the end of the night, so maybe it would be easier not to see him at all. You sneak into the baby's room to watch her sleeping. If she ever becomes a songwriter, her lyrics might include the words, *My Daddy's gay and my Mama's not bad-looking*. Back in your own bed, it's impossible to lie still so you take out the Johnny diary and it's something of a therapy to record the weekend in the by now familiar code. Everything he said is jotted down in your new handwriting, which is fast becoming almost identical to his.

Chapter Five

A strange thing happens at work on Monday morning. Kevin Daniels phones and asks you to join him in Johnny's office. Needless to say, you cover the ground between the two offices in something of a record time. On the way there, many possibilities filter through your thoughts, every last one of them spelling trouble. Surprisingly, Kevin Daniels appears to be alone in the untidy office.

"We've got a flipping serious dilemma on our hands."

"Hah?"

"Our friend has cocked up." There's no sign of Johnny. You scan the floor for his unconscious body, your thoughts now entertaining the possibility of Kevin Daniels living a secret existence as a martial arts guru.

"God is baying for blood."

This incenses you. "You told him?"

The colour drains from Daniels's face. He looks at you the way he might look at an errant child. "Of course I told him," he says, and with that he bends his puny frame and tugs at the handle of the bottom drawer of Johnny's desk. You soon see why he has difficulty in hauling the drawer open. It's crammed full of letters.

"See those statements. They were flipping well franked over a week ago."

What the hell are you doing snooping around someone else's office, you are tempted to say, but instead, for want of something better to do, you pick one of the letters up and examine the postage mark. Lo and behold he's right, it is over a week old. Something tells you that he's more irritated by the wasted postage money than he is by the non-posting of the letters. A desperate excuse presents itself. Daniels is a keen one for UFOs and all that rubbish. You could claim that aliens whisked the letters away from poor old Johnny, and these same aliens must be the ones who dumped them in the bottom drawer.

"We have fires to put out."

You want to commend him on his dramatic figure of speech, but you also want to deliver a sharp elbow to his groin region.

"It must've been an oversight."

"Well, we might believe that if it weren't for this." His stubby fingernail lands on the total debtors' figure for the month, an extraordinarily large figure, whose accumulation can only be due to the incompetence of one person.

Kevin Daniels is flicking through the large debtors printout like he was the Official Protector of Public Morals flicking through a copy of *The Layman's Guide To Smut*. Shaking his head, clicking his tongue in disapproval, but still drooling his way through it. You feel such a sudden surge of anger you suspect you could pick him up with one hand and toss him out through the window. Traffic chaos down below. It might even get a mention on the evening headlines: *Small man with irritating face falls to his death during slip-stream of morning rush-hour*.

"Paul, I don't for a minute presume to tell you what to do, but if I were you, I would keep a closer eye on our friend."

"I'll look after it, Kevin." There's a definite note of agitation in your voice, which he detects, and being the coward he is, he changes tack.

"Like, I know the two of you get on well and all that, but this sort of thing could have the lot of us in deep shit."

This causes both a cold shiver and a warm blush. Recognition is recognition, but it's also trouble. And what the hell does he mean by, "and all that"?

"No worries, Kevin." You make your exit before he has time to reply.

Eventually, you locate Johnny downstairs in the post-room. He's attempting to navigate his way around the room without touching the floor. Jason and Bernie are spectating, cheering him on like they were at a football match. A jump takes him to the top of a large filing cabinet, where he perches, sniggering, his tongue stuck between his teeth in concentration, and from there he leaps down on to the window-ledge where, with his hands spread like a tightrope walker, he strolls along the wooden ledge. There are people outside in the car park who are going to witness this strange scene. He isn't wearing a jacket, and it's an effort not to stare at his splendid physique.

"Johnny."

He holds his finger to his lips and makes a sssshing sound. Jason and Bernie look to you for your reaction.

"Johnny, something urgent has cropped up."

"Don't interrupt me now, we're talking *Guinness Book of Records* here."

From the window-ledge he leaps on to the large photocopier, balances himself, stands upright, and beats his chest Tarzan-style. He has control over you and he knows it.

"Daniels was in your office."

"What's he wanna do? Stick his tongue in my ear?"

Both Jason and Bernie snigger. A nervous sort of a snigger, mainly due, you suspect, to your apparent lack of control.

"He opened the bottom drawer of your desk."

This halts him in his tracks.

"Oh shit." He jumps down off the photocopier and says, "Oh shit, oh shit, oh shit," with his hands held to his face.

A phone call from an irate debtor moves the Johnnygate affair up another notch. This debtor, a man named Lawlor, has received a letter demanding immediate payment of a debt he claims he's already settled. Of course, the letter was signed in your name, but Johnny was the one responsible. He has made a serious cock-up, and you will dive in front of him to take the bullet.

"Could I have your name, please?" Lawlor demands.

You mutter your name.

"What sort of a dump are you running there?"

Your thoughts move into overdrive. There are a few answers you would like to give but you decide it's best to sound puzzled. "I beg your pardon?" There's a slight quiver in your voice.

"I paid that fucking invoice a week ago."

There's something quite threatening about a boss of a company using bad language.

"And I'm sick and fucking tired of receiving statements that say I haven't."

You pin the receiver to your ear. What if you just hang up and deny ever having taken this call? You picture the unpleasant Mr Lawlor, red-faced and obese, and wonder if, by irritating him sufficiently, you could cause him to keel over, victim to a timely cardiac arrest. You manage to eventually appease him somewhat by telling him a rigmarole story about a new computer package and a computer installation engineer of Asian origin who doesn't have a word of English.

"None at all?"

"No, just Pakistani."

"Oh?"

You wonder if there is such a thing as a Pakistani language.

But Lawlor is a crafty one. After giving you the impression that the matter is finished with, he then proceeds to phone Carney on his direct line and minutes later, you are summonsed to the Fat Man's office. Ominously, on the way up the stairs, you pass Kevin Daniels on his way down. A pleasant image of pointing an Uzi at the floor and seeing him dance to the spray of bullets enters your thoughts.

"Is God in his office?" you ask.

Kevin Daniels blushes. "Couldn't tell you," he says, and how you keep yourself from laughing out loud, you'll never know. The little rodent has the post-God-chat glow radiating from every pore in his lily-livered body.

Carney peers over the top of his half-frames, staring at you as though he's struggling to remember your name. His entire being exudes the afterglow of Lawlor's fury.

"Paul, I've just had the ear chewed off me by an irate customer."

You sit down opposite him, and somehow manage to contort your face into a look of shock.

"He's been billed for something he claims he's already paid for." Carney passes his handwritten telephone message across the desk. You furrow your brow like some sort of ace detective, all the while sensing that directorship slipping away.

"I'll look into it."

"Kevin Daniels tells me that there's been some sort of mix-up in your debt collection."

"Ah yeah, I can explain."

"I'm sure you can, but I don't want to hear it." Carney leans back in his chair. "After certain medical problems during the eighties, I let yourself and the rest of my well-paid lieutenants do the worrying for me."

For some reason, you register a compassionate look, as though you haven't heard about the Fat Man's two heart attacks at least two million times and counting.

"Just clear up the mess, Paul. I don't want to hear any more complaints."

"Right."

In the past, a bollicking from Carney would have had your stress gauge shooting up to the level marked "perilous". But now, you can imagine yourself simply telling him that you're having a little bother with the boyfriend, that he's gone and discovered that you are married.

"It gets worse. You sit down opposite Kevin Daniels, waiting for him to take his head out of his hands. You're in his glass icebox of an office, especially designed so he can keep a constant eye on his computer staff, who, you've heard, have been beavering away with great fervour ever since Eileen's departure. There's a poster of a red Ferrari on the wall behind him, alongside another poster of wild horses galloping along a seashore. If you were to judge him by his posters, you might get the impression that Daniels wants to go somewhere in a hurry.

"We have a really flipping serious dilemma on our hands."

Because his voice is distorted by his hands which are clasped over his mouth, a few seconds elapse before you realise that he has actually spoken. He hands you a bundle of about twenty cheques payable to Carney Textiles. The amounts involved are large. A quick glance through them and you realise, with a disquieting sense of unease, that these uncashed cheques date back over the period since Johnny's arrival.

"They were discovered in a large brown envelope." He pushes the envelope in your direction, and there on the front of it is Johnny's giveaway handwriting.

"Oh?"

"Behind a radiator in the post-room."

You lift your eyebrows. "They must've been mislaid, I'm sure he was looking everywhere for them."

He flashes a dubious look, which you pretend not to pick up on.

"There'll probably be a reward for whoever found them."

Now he's staring at you in puzzlement.

His telephone rings, offering you a brief respite. He turns away from you to whisper his baby-talk to his hypochondriac of a wife. The pair of them have developed their own private language for their numerous daily phone calls. Will Johnny get the bullet, you wonder. In your five years with the company, you can remember only one clear unequivocal dismissal, and that was Jason's predecessor, who was found by the tea-lady the morning after the Christmas party, conked out beside Carney's drinks cabinet. The rest of the dismissals have been ambiguous, like Eileen's.

Andy taps on the window of the icebox and points to the telephone on his desk. You point to yourself and he nods. No rest for the wicked. You make sure to shut the door to the icebox behind you. Andy is nodding at the phone and contorting his features to let you know that this is a troublesome call. It seems only right to pretend that everything is under control, so you smile at him before you lift the receiver. Confidence is everything.

"Paul Cullen speaking."

What follows is naked rage. Fury down a phoneline. A diatribe that has you expecting the telephone wiring to spark and crackle, a billow of smoke perhaps, and then a loud bang that will propel you back through the window of the icebox.

The Johnnygate affair has reached a new peak. The caller's name is Brady, and not only has he received a letter demanding payment for something he's already paid for, but his office also received a phone call, "in the past ten minutes", from someone in your office who refused to give his name, demanding immediate payment

"Well, if you give me your number, I'll look into it and get back to you immediately." You speak in a level tone, aware that Kevin Daniels has bid his wife cheerio and is now watching you from the icebox.

"No, you won't bloody well look into anything. I'll tell you what you'll do, Sunshine, you'll put me through to Jim Carney."

You place your hand over the receiver. The computer room staff are sneaking glances at you. They sense hassle. They see the beads of perspiration on your forehead. Kevin Daniels has his face pressed up against the glass partition in such a way that you are tempted to toss the phone at him. How did you ever get into this mess?

"Thank you, Mr Brady, I'll call you back as soon as I can verify those figures." Before you hang up, you hear Mr Brady make a burbling sort of noise which sounds as though someone is in the process of choking him. Maybe all hope is not lost. Maybe he has a vengeful secretary.

The door to the icebox clicks open, and Kevin Daniels is standing there, looking at you, expectantly.

"Have to dash," you say, leaving the computer room before he has time to draw breath.

When you get to his office, Johnny is in the middle of a phone call to a debtor. You signal to him to finish the call urgently. His eyes open wide when he recognises the brown envelope you place on his desk. Stress is written across his features, but the telephone voice retains its charm, to your ears anyway. How any debtor could resist immediate payment is beyond you.

Once he hangs up, you take the uncashed cheques from the envelope and spread them out across his desk.

"D'you know anything about these?"

He shapes his hands into a pair of binoculars, inspects the cheques, and then nods.

"They were found in the post-room."

"I couldn't find anything to credit them against."

You draw a sharp intake of breath. It appears that he's actually

96

admitting to hiding them behind the radiator.

"But Johnny, you should've asked me."

"You were too busy."

If this were anyone else, you would be angry.

"It doesn't matter how busy I seem, you know you can always ask me something."

He pushes his bottom lip out and lowers his eyes the way a naughty child would. "I'm useless at this job."

"Don't be stupid."

"I am stupid."

"No you're not, you're only learning how to do the job, you can't be expected to know everything."

"A chimpanzee could do my job."

A quick search back through the records confirms your worst suspicions. The old git Brady is correct. Johnny has credited the payment against the wrong account. There are two options facing you: admit to the error and let Johnny incur the wrath of his superiors; or alternatively, attempt to alter the computer records. The first option doesn't even merit a second consideration. Somewhere at the back of your brain, a faint warning light is flashing, telling you that the computer is a logical machine, that it won't accommodate the skewed logic of passion. After Johnny has explained exactly what he did, he once again pushes his lower lip out and wipes away an imaginary tear, and any lingering traces of professional judgement evaporate on the spot. He tells you that he's done a computer course and that he knows how to rectify the error. He's trying to impress you and you're there to be impressed.

There are moments in your life when you feel that you are making meaningful decisions, and this certainly isn't one of them. With a love-induced recklessness, you allow Johnny to press the Control key and the C key on his keyboard simultaneously. When you express doubts, he once again assures you that he knows what he's doing. You expect to see desks levitate and walls reduced to rubble. This is the manoeuvre to get into machine language, a manoeuvre every employee has regularly been warned against executing. But, just like a cosmologist delving deep into the stars, this is where you have to go to alter the past. This is where your loved one has to go to save his pretty ass. What follows has you wishing that you could turn back time. The screen freezes momentarily, then it slips into gibberish. Squiggles and symbols flash past your eyes. He switches the machine off, but the gibberish is still there when he switches it back on again. His frantic repeated pressing of the Control and C keys has no effect now. Things have spiralled out of control.

He says, "Flee the scene of the crime, that's my motto."

And without a second thought, you are out of that room and into the maelstrom of office activity. Judging by the gasps of surprise, others are viewing the same gibberish on their screens.

"Methinks our Japanese friends are trying to tell us something," Doreen says, unable to conceal her delight that the daily routine has been broken.

"Peoples, are we receiving strange messages on our screens?" Bernie says, also imitating Kevin Daniels.

Jason taps your shoulder. "Here, what d'you get if you cross a nun with an apple?"

You smile, shaking your head.

"A computer that won't go down on you."

Jason is blushing wildly, and because you like him, you erupt into laughter.

An order is issued from the computer room. Every terminal is to be switched off immediately. The computer is down. Work has halted. The executive staff pretend to be put out by this stoppage, while the non-executive staff funnel their way directly to the tearoom, where the spirits are high. Carney has been spotted in the icebox. The tearoom fills up to watch Andy perform the scene in the icebox. The climax of his performance features nineteen-stone Carney sitting on top of ten-stone Kevin Daniels, squeezing every last trace of air from his lungs. "Oh please Mr Carney, we promise we'll be a good boy if you'll just get up off us." There's uncontrollable laughter everywhere. Andy has to be in line for a tearoom Oscar.

* * * *

Just before midnight, you dial Kevin Daniels's home number, and once you hear his not-so-chirpy answer, you hand the phone to Bob.

"Hey man, we're the party people and we're on our way over to your gaff to party all night long."

You peg your finger and thumb to your nostrils.

"The party people," Bob says.

There's a pause.

"What d'you mean you never heard of us?" Bob shakes the phone. "He hung up."

"Surprise, surprise." This little deed makes you feel better. A sweet little kick of revenge. Bob must really be wondering about your maturity.

The office block looks almost benign in the moonlight. As you had anticipated, the light in the Phantom's office is still on. But one thing is certain, if the Phantom sees a light on in another office, that office is the last place he will go into. Wearing woolly hats and upturned collars, you're on your way towards the building when a crouched shadow mooches past the illuminated window. The Phantom is packing up to go. He's knocking off early. The shadow moves away from the window and the light goes out. So, feeling a little like special agents involved in a stakeout, you sit back into Bob's car and wait. Minutes later, the Phantom's black car, which is known affectionately by the crowd in the tearoom as The Hearse, emerges from the underground car park, turns cautiously on to the empty street, and heads off at a ridiculously slow pace towards the southside of the city.

"It's all systems go," you say.

The two of you stride towards the small groundfloor window which you have left open. You move fast, afraid that if you stop to think, the logical side of your brain will grab the illogical side in a headlock and force it into submission.

Up the back stairs you go, your rubber-soled shoes soundless on the tiled steps. Adrenaline pumping, you step out on to the second floor corridor, half-expecting Jim Carney to appear suddenly and ask, with raised eyebrows, if your friend is involved in industrial espionage.

"Step on the gas, wipe that tear away," Bob sings, pushing you forward. "One sweet dream came through today." Bob is the luckiest person you know, so you feel that with him on your team, things can't go wrong. He's the type to walk into a supermarket, get tapped on the shoulder, and have some respectably-attired PR man say, Excuse me, sir, you are our one millionth customer, and to mark the occasion, you have won yourself an all-expenses-paid trip to the Caribbean.

The door of the computer room is locked, so you open the cleaners' cupboard and take the spare key down from its hiding place behind the dusters and rags. The computer room is awash with little nerdy notes scribbled on dainty squares of sticky yellow paper. The system makes a whirring sound as it cranks into action. Bob positions himself in front of a terminal, makes a comment about the dinosaur system, and stares at the on-screen mumbo-jumbo with the eagerness of a mad scientist on the verge of discovering the secret to world annihilation. While he works, Bob slips into a coma, uttering the occasional expletive, oblivious to your presence. He doesn't even seem to hear the door of the icebox click open.

Feeling the satisfaction of a socially-deprived car vandal, you take a black marker to Daniels's poster of the red Ferrari. The long scratch mark you draw along the side looks almost authentic. Sniggering, you insert a pair of spectacles, a replica for the Kevin Daniels square-framed specs, on to the lead horse on the poster of galloping horses. They give the horse an intellectual look, and appear, in some way, to slow it down.

Whenever Kevin Daniels took the key to his desk down from its secret hiding place behind the coat-stand, you always, for no apparent reason, pretended not to notice. Could it be that some future memory was telling you that a night like this could materialise? Daniels has rummaged through Johnny's desk, so it's only fair that you should reciprocate. You slide the top drawer open, half-expecting to have your fingers snapped off by a mousetrap. Inside, the only eye-catching item is a black diary. Would you stoop low enough to take a snoop at someone's diary? No one is ever going to find out, so what does it matter? It's not as if you're going to broadcast it around town. Anyway, if there is anything private in it, Daniels would hardly have left it lying in his desk for any burglar to peek at. And you almost succeed in convincing yourself to believe this.

Daniels is insane. His diary is crammed full of crazy nonsensical sentences written in his idiotic scrawl. Initially, you smile at the thought of him, straitjacketed and foaming at the mouth, being dragged from his office by a group of men in white coats. All it would take would be a phone call to the relevant authorities. But then you experience something approaching pity when you discover a soppy poem written about his wife. What a sap. It is strange to discover a quirk of vulnerability in someone you suspected of having no human emotions. But before you replace the diary, one of the crazy sentences stirs a memory of one of the office binges. It reads, "The donkey swallowed the cat." It was the punchline of one of the Phantom's particularly black jokes. Then it slowly dawns on you that, apart from the soppy poem, the diary is a collection of joke punchlines. In some way, Daniels's quest for popularity is touching.

The next drawer contains internal memorandum files and the one marked "Strictly Private" instantly catches your attention. The first memorandum reads:

PRIVATE AND CONFIDENTIAL

TO: Jim Carney, Managing Director.
FROM: Kevin Daniels, Computer Services.

Johnny Lyons, a clerk in the accounts
department, arrived into work at 9.20 am
this morning.

You wrack your brains but you have no recollection of Daniels ever mentioning this memorandum. Is it all part of a massive book of evidence being collated to use against Johnny? Is it all going to be served up in one fell swoop to oust him? It's quite likely that if Kevin Daniels were to walk into the icebox right at this moment, you would murder him. A swift violent encounter with a large stapler. But you read on and discover that Johnny is only one of many employees who have fallen victim to the bird's-eye view of the front entrance available from Daniels's office window. There's no doubt that this vigilance could backfire on him. Carney must wonder about Daniels's productivity between the hours of 9.00 am and 10.00 am.

Bob doesn't even appear to notice you walk past him and leave the computer room. The first stop is Johnny's office. As soon as you step inside, you smell lingering traces of his familiar after-shave. On the desk, there's a page with his doodlings, and a list of urgent tasks to perform. The room looks different without him. The ghost of his presence hangs heavy in the air. It's a lonely feeling, like you're stepping on his grave. In a drawer, hidden beneath his Walkman, you find a letter he's writing to a friend in London. It's all about you, celebrating your friendship. How you introduced him to classical music, how you're a really decent boss, and how he can actually see himself persevering with his exams after all. Your face is aglow. But most importantly, it's dated after the Wexford weekend. There is still hope. His openness is so appealing, but how can you warn him not to be leaving private letters like this lying around, that there are unscrupulous people around who will read them? By the second page, a pang of guilt wings its way in from somewhere and you replace everything as you found it, shut the drawer and leave the office.

Upstairs you go to God's office. Surprisingly, the door is unlocked. At last you have the opportunity to satisfy your juvenile curiosity and find out once and for all if the rumours about the specially manufactured extra-large toilet in the *en suite* bathroom are true. They appear to be. The bowl could double up as a jacuzzi. Maybe they did have to lift it in by crane. Back in the office, you unlock the French doors and step out on to the balcony. Down below, the street is deserted. In the darkness, you accidentally tip your toe against a potted plant. It wobbles on the ledge for what seems like an eternity before it disappears from sight and lands with a hollow thud, scattering the pavement below with fragments of ceramic and clumps of the specially-fertilised earth. You don't wait around to witness the reaction of the locals. Love has driven you to do crazy things, but this has got to be the craziest. Breaking and entering is a jailable offence.

Taking two steps at a time, you dash down the stairs, and on the second floor, you run into Bob, who's out roaming the corridors in search of you. His task is complete. The man is a genius. As you drive away, you console yourself with the thought that like so many other office misadventures, the incident will be blamed on the ghostly crew of night-cleaners who spirit their way into the office under cover of darkness.

Chapter Six

"Their heads were shaved, you know like them toothbrush heads you see everywhere." Tom is breathless with excitement.

"Wooooh." Doreen points at Jason's new blade-one cut.

"He's for the high-jump," Bernie says.

"I was at me kick-boxing," Jason says.

Doreen slants her eyes, raises one foot, and holds her hands up in what's supposed to be a kick-boxing posture.

Andy asks, "But Tom, how d'you know their heads were shaved?"

"Ned saw them, didn't he?"

"But he said they were wearing balaclavas."

"Took them off for a moment, didn't they." Tom is chancing his arm but no one gives a damn.

There's been a buzz of excitement around the office since early morning. It's now tea-break time, and the previous night's break-in is the only topic of conversation. Tom is revelling in centre-stage. He's been talking to Ned, the night-watchman. There was a gang of them, he tells everyone, "Four or five of them, carrying guns and wearing balaclavas."

Heads shake, tongues make clicking sounds of concern. Everyone's delighted with the drama, even though everyone knows that Ned the night-watchman is practically deaf, and even if he does happen to hear the slightest sound, he locks himself into a storeroom, switches the light off and buries himself beneath a pile of cardboard boxes. Someone else announces that they heard that Carney's office was ransacked. Tom nods sagely. "It has all the hallmarks of a Dublin criminal gang," he says. "You know that crowd that steal computers."

Again, everyone nods and tut-tuts even though they all know that the antiquated computer system couldn't be given away. Doreen is the one to break the spell and introduce a dose of reality to the proceedings. "Why would anyone want to steal that heap of junk," she says.

"A community school in Tallaght can't be wrong," Bernie says.

"They could use it for automobile spare parts," Andy says, no doubt feeling a little left out with Tom hogging centre-stage.

"The detectives are taking fingerprints," someone else says, and you experience a moment of panic until you assure yourself that there's nothing to worry about, that your fingerprints are everywhere anyway.

A secretary from design bursts into the tearoom with a look on her face which promises news and demands silence.

"You're not going to believe the latest," she says, smirking.

Everyone looks to her expectantly. This morning is one where the ordinary everyday humdrum has been blown out of the water. The living is wild.

"The experts are baffled," she says, and she reveals that whatever the burglars did, they tampered with the computer and that, by some fluke chance, it's up and running again.

The loud spontaneous burst of laughter rocks the tearoom. People are jerking and flicking like they are in the throes of mild epileptic seizures. Years of dental work is on display.

"Come on peoples, all hands on deck, it's all systems go." Striving for attention, Andy is rubbing his hands together, performing an imitation of Kevin Daniels.

Back in your office, you switch the VDU on, half-expecting it to cause trees to bend and the sky to fall in. But it doesn't. Bob truly is a genius. Immediately you access the Brady file and, lo and behold, the payment is there, backdated to the time of its receipt. It's like time-travel, or one of those abstract relativity concepts which straightline minds like yours have difficulty grasping. But now you have the problem of explaining how Brady's payment didn't appear on the printout. A software problem, you will say. Kevin Daniels hasn't much of a clue when it comes to software. He knows it's a mess, he gets well paid, so you suspect he has enough sense to know when to keep his gob shut.

The whole caper is beginning to take it's toll. Your energy is flagging. A feeling of inertia has spread right to your bones, and the only way to spark life back into your weary limbs is to think of Johnny. This has the effect of electric shock therapy. An involuntary shiver ripples through you, you sit upright, haul in those wandering thoughts, and concentrate on the work at hand. But not for long. He's like an undertow. Just when you've steadied yourself, got control of things, along comes another tug to whisk everything out from under you. No matter what your mind is concentrating on, every thought pattern eventually circles back to him. Despite your best intentions, you go to his office, where you find him listening to REM on his Walkman. He tells you to take a listen, and you do, but all you can think of is the letter in the drawer.

"Would you say I'm the worst employee ever to work here?" he asks.

"Long way to go before you achieve that honour."

"I'm going to set up a new organisation: Clerks Raging Against Promotion." He smiles. "Of course it'll be abbreviated, using the first letter in each word. D'you get it?"

"I do."

"You know, when my uncle was at UCD, the students there started a magazine called *Catholic University News and Times*. They put the first letter of each word in huge lettering, except for the 'and'."

"No need to draw pictures."

"That was when Ireland was a holy Joe country."

After confiding in him about Bob's rescue mission, he suggests a celebratory drink after work and you don't spend too long contemplating the decision.

The problem is what to tell Anne. You could simply say that you're going out for a drink with your new assistant, but you know you won't. Greg or Harry, two friends from college whom she rarely sees, are other possibilities. You can't say Bob. She sees him too often. But then, Bob knows Greg and Harry, so it might be necessary to say to her not to mention to Bob that you were out with Greg or Harry. You could claim you were protecting Bob's feelings, that he might be jealous at being left out. But then she'd wonder why you don't just ring Bob and invite him along. Because Greg and Harry don't like him, you'd say. It's all getting to be such a complex web of deceit. A feast of lies. A crazy situation altogether.

"Poor thing," Anne says, after you use the trusty old excuse of entertaining clients.

"It's a pain in the you-know-what." You can barely contain your exhilaration.

You drive way out into the suburbs, passing within a risky half-mile of glitzy Legoland, to a pub in Loughlinstown. It's doubtful that you'll meet anyone you know out here. Also, this is close to his home territory, and that's enough to warm your cockles. It's as though the roads and the trees and the buildings have been imbued with his magic. The pub isn't busy, so there isn't a major problem in locating an isolated table. It's ludicrous, but you can't help sensing that everyone can read your intentions.

Once you're settled with a drink, you fill him in on the finer details of the previous night's adventure. You sense a hint of jealousy regarding this "Bob person", so you let on you barely know Bob, and this enables him to enjoy your re-enactment of the tea-room reactions. The letter about you to his friend in London has definitely altered your thinking. He's opening up areas of your heart you never knew existed, excavating feelings and emotions you thought were buried forever. He's released a spontaneous side of you, you're letting go for the first time without weighing up and considering every word and syllable you utter. The blood cells are in riotous form, racing through the veins, making you feel pumped up, omnipotent, ready to go. You are connecting and both of you know it.

By ten o'clock, you've both downed five pints of lager, and for the first time, he expresses concern about you driving in this condition. He glances at the TV page in the newspaper and sighs. "Right, I've already missed *Big Wheels*, *Tractor-Pulling*, and alas, the *Bat-Racing from Tunisia*," he says with a smirk. "Another rare feast of televisual entertainment lost to alcohol. No point in going home yet." He suggests a walk to sober you and you don't take much convincing. "Hey, ever been to the top of the old railway bridge?" he asks.

You shake your head. He beckons to you to follow him, and you leave the pub and stroll with him, up the quiet road.

The old disused railway bridge resembles a giant knuckle-duster punching the sky. A fine structure, raised about a hundred feet above the road on its long concrete legs which support its series of arches. He points to a dusty pathway up the steep bank. It's madness, but love and the full moon make you do these crazy things. Two men, dressed in suits, clambering their way through the summer foliage of brambles and weeds. It's a sight to behold. He's leading the way, you are close behind, feeling like a young-ster. The moonlight is almost as bright as daylight, and when you reach the top you have to adjust your trousers to get your hard-on to sit comfortably.

Away from the glare of the city lights, the stars seem closer, the moon almost touchable. With mere centimetres separating you in the night stealth, he proceeds to point out the landmarks. You inch closer to catch the fragrance of his aftershave. Car head-lights approach and with a juvenile exuberance, you both drop blobs of spit as it passes below.

"So what time's the missus expecting you home?"

The question hangs in the air between you. It was asked in a tone you've never heard before. A serious, yet vulnerable, tone. His eyes appear too big for their sockets. There is only one answer to give right now.

"What Missus?"

"The ball and chain."

"There is none."

"But..."

"Do I look stupid enough to get hitched?"

You sense his transition. The changing of the guards.

"But I was talking to her."

"That was my sister you were talking to." You laugh. "Wait'll I tell her that she fooled you."

He points at you in a mock-threatening manner, before slicing his finger the width of his throat.

"Well what time is the chick expecting you?"

Talk about testing the water by plunging in.

"Who would have me?"

Moments pass, during which the world seems to turn a somersault.

"Lie to me, would you?"

He feigns annoyance and grabs hold of you, attempting to wrap his arms around your neck. It develops into one of those playful wrestling matches in which there are no losers, where touch is all, and when his hand happens to brush against your crotch, everything turns surreal.

"Is that a telescope in your pocket or are you just glad to see me?"

You simply look at him, hold him in your stare. The moonlight is splashed upon his face. This is true beauty, the likes of which you have never seen before. Your eyes go out of focus, your head is dizzy. Your entire life seems to hang upon this moment. Your past flashes by like an old black-and-white newsreel. Something is telling you to pull back from the brink, not to open up. Something else is urging you to let yourself take that free-fall.

"Is it because of me?" He asks in a whisper. He has moved closer to you, and the back of his hand is ever so gently tracing the outline of your erection. Now there is no doubt.

"Indeed it might be."

You expect time to do a swift about-turn and discover that none of this is really happening, that it's just another plunge into the giant old swirling sea of delusion which can appear in so many shapes and guises, and into which you can submerge yourself so deep, you begin to believe in it.

His hands circle your waist. Your life seems to skip out of a groove. The old ticker definitely skips a beat. He fits into your arms in a way no one has ever fitted before.

"I sort of knew the first time we met," he says.

"So did I."

Did you really say that?

"But I never thought it would come to this."

"But...what about Sara?"

He utters a low, gurgling laugh. "What about her?"

"Cover?"

He nods. "Have to give my friends the right impression, don't I, and besides, I was just trying to make you jealous."

The weekend in Wexford dissolves in your head and all the various parts are reassembled in a new pattern.

"When that sister of yours said she was your wife, I nearly puked, and because of that I got really pissed and then I did puke."

You touch his hair, trace the outline of his face, run your fingertip across his lips. It's like meeting him for the first time. You're so happy and excited, you're afraid you'll forget to breathe. This is a once in a lifetime, of that you have no doubt.

And when you kiss you expect the moon and the stars to spin out of their orbits and collide in a massive fireball. You are touching the raw nerve of intense passion you knew as an adolescent, a raw nerve you thought had long since withered and died. It's total abandon time, letting go time, so much so you want to cry with joy. At such an untimely moment like this, you feel like letting the waterfall of pent-up emotion cascade down your cheeks in tears.

He sinks to his knees, undoes your belt, opens your buttons, and pulls your trousers and shorts right down around your ankles. He takes you in his mouth. The sensation is warm and sensitive but it doesn't seem the right thing to do just now. You don't want someone you love like this to think they have to do anything degrading. But one look at him banishes these reservations. It's time to really let go, to merge as one, to lose yourself in blissful pleasure which is somehow enhanced by the sensation of cool evening air on your bare legs, and by the fear of being caught.

You become aware that you are moaning and gasping as Johnny, without a hint of a tooth, increases the tempo of his expert motion. Everything becomes hazy, pleasure seeps from every pore, you're sure you can hear music. It feels as though you're levitating, looking down from a hundred feet. There's the city lights blinking down below, the dark outline of the winding coastline, the crab-claw harbour, the steady stream of car headlights; up further, you can see the mountains circling the city, you're among the stars in the heavens, and when you look down you see Johnny's house, and in the back garden, there's the swirl and style of a wedding party, and when you focus you see Anne and realise that it's your own wedding you're looking down on, and that all the guests are pointing up at you and they seem to be saying, Oh look, there's Paul in the future. Is that Anne with him? No, it's not. It's a man. What are they doing?

This thought has the same breath-wrenching effect as when an aeroplane suddenly dips during turbulence. But Johnny seems to have read your mind. He adjusts his rhythmic motion and proceeds to massage your thighs like he's trying to rub away the wedding image. And he succeeds. Every thought and image empties from your mind to be replaced by a beautiful light. It's like you're outside yourself, that you've relinquished control of your innermost being to some greater power, and you believe that you're being afforded a momentary glimpse into heaven. Stroking his hair, you arch your body back to signal the impending crescendo. And with perfect timing, he withdraws and brings you to climax manually. The floodgates open, a tidal wave explodes, the arching spurt is a glistening thread in the moonlight. Overwhelming torrents of pleasure capture your every nerve-end. You want to roar out and hear your voice echo and reverberate across the countryside. You want to tell the world how happy you are.

"Don't worry, it's biodegradable." His voice, which seems to emerge from a mist, startles you momentarily.

"Thank you."

"I love you," he whispers, and these three simple words scrape away the tough, congealed layer around your heart. You can't say anything. Words like cherish and love and truth fizzle out before you manage to utter them. His words have rendered you helpless, like a delicate infant, pure and innocent, so vulnerable to the actions of others. You hear music in your head, a voice of purest pitch. But he understands. It's enough that you simply embrace him and hold him close. This is real love, a love you can't possibly live without. The Phantom is right after all; one special person in a lifetime, that's the quota. You always thought it was his excuse for being on his own, but now you realise that maybe the man is wiser than everyone thinks.

On the drive home, every detail of the evening is replayed over and over in your head. You had reciprocated, copying his every move, while somewhere in the dark recesses of your mind lurked the thought that he had obviously done this before. But what the hell, that didn't matter. It was something so many people would find so repulsive, but not you. This was so different to those early dating fumbles with Anne. Back then, you felt a constant pressure, a discomfort, an overwhelming sense of uncertainty. It was like trying to hold a gaseous substance in a birdcage. You knew it was all wrong, but you persisted. Maybe it would all change. Maybe you would wake up one morning and it would all be different.

Back then, you were the master of excuses. Study, work, football, and even "Snogging outdoors is for juveniles". But if Johnny had spun the same yarns up on the railway bridge, you wouldn't have given it a second thought. He could have flapped his arms and taken flight right there in front of your very eyes, floated about for a while, and you would have simply said, With you Johnny dear, nothing surprises me. This causes a little pang of conscience. It's hard to imagine, but the chances are that Anne was as much in love with you then as you are with him now. Why else would she have put up with you? How else could she have been so blind to you? It's an awkward thought to entertain on such a night.

At home in bed, she snuggles up to you, rubbing her warm feet against your cold feet. Old perky's going to have to spring into action again by the looks of things. She senses your good form, and you're so tempted to tell her just how happy you are. Just how much in love you are, and how that love has made her so much more appealing to you. How that love has made the whole world so much more appealing to you. Surely she'd be pleased to hear that. But you don't, you button your lips and act like an adoring husband.

*　*　*　*

"Where were you last night, you look like you were in a fight," he says in your office the next morning and all your overnight worries evaporate. He glides his way around the desk, his eyes never leaving yours, until he reaches your side. There's that love scent of his aftershave mingled with tobacco. He slips his hands into yours, silently challenging you to a first-blink contest. He's facing the window, the first little ripples of laughter appear on the colour part of his eyes and quickly spread across his face.

"Have you ever seen *A Bridge Too Far?*" he asks, letting his hands slide up from your stomach to your chest.

"Was that filmed up on a disused railway bridge?" You copy his every movement, discovering, as you do so, that he has severe tickles.

"Yes, I believe it was filmed last night."

"In the moonlight?"

He jerks like a rabbit in a trap. Another tickle spot has been located. "Indeed, and I hear the Censor had a mild heart attack while viewing the same motion picture." He unzips your fly and wriggles his hand in through the tight gap.

"And why was that?" You shiver involuntarily when he cups a cold hand around your balls.

"Unadulterated filth, that's why."

"Where's the League of Decency when you really need them?"

"I don't know what the country's coming to," he says, and he prevents you from replying by placing his mouth to yours. His eyes are closed, his lips are moist, his tongue is moving about like a gymnast. It's 9.15 on a Tuesday morning, there's a management meeting due to start at 9.30, but at least you won't have to worry about lipstick smudges.

There's only the tiniest click of warning. That familiar click the doorhandle makes, a noise the handyman has promised to sort out. And it's just as well he hasn't, because it affords you those crucial few milliseconds to disentangle before Teresa's face appears around the door. Her smile vanishes. There's that give-away moment of hesitation, that look of puzzlement. If she didn't see anything, she's certainly going to be able to smell the passion. Women have a nose for such things. She's wondering what the hell Johnny is doing behind your desk, so you act fast, and point to figures on a printout and say, "Check out this one first and then get back to me."

"Right." He looks up, pretending to have just become aware of Teresa's presence. "How's Teresa? Sobered up yet?"

She smiles and pulls a face. But you're sure you see her eyes flicker down towards the give-away bulge in Johnny's trousers. Who says men have all the biological advantages?

You go to the management meeting with a skip in your step and a belief that you can achieve anything. Even Kevin Daniels is treated like he's one of your best buddies. During the day, the sweet fog of love clears somewhat when you begin to ponder the practicalities of this relationship. It's not going to be the lie-free zone you might have wished for. So it's something of a minor relief that Johnny has to go to lectures after work, and when he asks for your phone number, you tell him that the phone is out of order. So he gives you his number, a number you have already committed to memory from your snoop through his CV, and he makes you promise to call him later.

"Absence makes the heart grow fonder," he says, and this simple everyday cliché suddenly makes absolute sense to you.

The traffic comes to a standstill about fifty yards from the entrance to Legoland. Exhaust fumes shimmer in the heat, engines snarl, fingers are drummed on rooftops, the occasional horn is hooted, fists are thumped against steering wheels, contemptuous lips are curled and angry words are mouthed. Sometimes it seems that people in traffic jams feel they have to behave the way people in traffic jams on TV behave. The sun comes out momentarily and the scene is reflected in sweeping images racing across car windows. It really is a bummer to be caught so close to home. But today, you don't give a toss. There's no amount of gloom that won't lift by just thinking of him.

Then you spot Tight Jeans, Lia's baby-sitter, looking on while a youth scribbles graffiti on a bus shelter. They both stand back to admire the artwork, and they're laughing. Then Tight Jeans spots you, and her smile disappears to be replaced by a blush. You wave at her and she waves back, muttering something to the youth. He turns around to look and he too blushes. What do they see? A middle-aged man stranded in traffic. Little do they know, but you're now going through that first-love sensation you ought to have gone through when you were their age. They walk on down the road and you see that he has written, 'IF YOU CAN'T READ THIS YOU NEED GLASSES' on the bus shelter. Good old Tight Jeans and her boyfriend have gone up in your estimation. They have style.

On the car radio a woman is talking about her deceased son. She remembers how, when he was fifteen, her son came home from school one day and told her that there was a boy in his class who the other boys jeered because they thought that he was gay. And when she asked her son if this boy was him, he called her a bitch, stormed out of the room, locked himself in his bedroom and turned his music up so loud the walls of the house shook. Years later, when he was dying, he admitted that yes, of course he was that boy, and that he had cried on his pillow for two hours that day. It almost pleases you when the programme goes into a musical break. These sort of stories are too close to the bone for comfort. Emotions like that have been pushed so far into the obscure backrooms of your memory, you almost believe that they never occurred.

Up ahead, the cause of the delay becomes apparent. An elderly man is attempting to turn his car into the driveway of one of the old detached houses, which would have been surrounded by fields ten years before. But he has misjudged his angles and he rams his brand new car into the stone gate-pillar, upon which the house name *Sans Souci* is written in all its ironic glory. On his third attempt, he hits the pillar once again, but this time, there's no stopping him. He revs the engine up and, like a cartoon character, tries to force the car through the stone pillar.

This is too much for the onlookers. Contempt switches to bewilderment, even compassion. Why is this old man prepared to destroy both his gate and his car simply to avoid causing an obstruction? What has it all come to? The hazard-lights of the car directly in front of you go on and a well-meaning man hops out and goes to the elderly man's assistance. This is a relief, a conscience-easer. Someone else is doing something, you can pass on by and blank it from your memory. But then, something strange happens. After just a moment's thought of Johnny, you switch on your own hazard-lights and go to the man's assistance.

Between the other driver and yourself, you manage to coax the flustered old man from his car. Sweat is streaming down his forehead, his hands are quivering; he looks like he could do with popping a pill or two. The thought of mouth-to-mouth resuscitation is not a pleasant one. To appease him, you give the impression that ramming a car into a pillar is a common everyday occurrence, but he doesn't seem to hear a word you are saying, nor does he seem to notice the gang of youngsters who are staring up at him like he's some sort of exotic species. The other driver takes the wheel of the elderly man's car, and the front tyre makes a whirring sound against the crushed chrome as he manoeuvres it through the narrow gateway and up into the gravel driveway. The traffic on the road begins to flow again, the crowd of onlookers disperse, and you assure your fellow do-gooder that you'll make sure the old man gets to his front door in one piece.

But once inside the house, it's like the old man has secretly jabbed a needle into his arm. He springs to life, introduces himself as Rob and proceeds to talk non-stop about the faults of modern cars, until a second elderly man comes down the stairs, who is introduced as Neil. When Neil hears what happened, he laughs and calls Rob an old fool. And with that, both of them engage in a brief, but sprightly, shadowboxing contest. Then they turn their attention to you, and they give you the distinct impression that your answers to their questions are the most fascinating snippets of information they've heard in decades. Everything is flowing along nicely until you tell them that you live in Legoland. That's when you're sure you detect the slightest of grimaces. Legoland is definitely not high up on their list of favourite travel destinations.

They point to a framed aerial photograph of the area before the bulldozers moved in. Fields, hedges, trees and even the odd cow. They take delight in listing off the array of cement-saving items they witnessed the builders tossing into the foundations of the Legoland houses. Trees, planks of wood, shopping-trolleys, barrels, dustbins, and maybe the odd gangster or two. Is it any wonder the kitchen floor slopes. You tell them about the slope and they laugh so hard, you fear you might be carting the pair of them off to the Accidents and Emergencies department.

"So, are the two of you brothers?"

"God no," Neil gasps, as if this was the worst possible thing you could say about him.

"I'm not that ugly, am I?" Rob asks, his face contorted in feigned horror.

They tell you that they're both bachelors and that they've been living together since their college days. It gradually dawns on you that they are actually a couple. The walls are full of photographs of them holidaying in exotic locations around the world. The smiles are smiles of people with high disposable incomes. It's nice to see them as they were when they were young. Happy and carefree, warm in one another's company, the way only lovers can be. And here they are, still together. Anyone could see the chemistry between them, the easy relaxed way they have together. They compliment one another, finish off one another's sentences, smile enthusiastically, and when they jeer one another, there's a fondness in that jeering. So many people you know would be repulsed by this fondness. Right now, it seems difficult to imagine why.

You bid them farewell after reminding them that your car is parked outside with its hazard-lights flashing. They stand at the door, waving goodbye, until you are out of sight. They've made you promise that you'll call again, but really, all you can think about is telling Johnny about them. Fancy that, you imagine him saying, is the entire city turning gay?

At home, you almost blurt out the story to Anne, but you hold yourself back, deciding that there's no point in drawing unnecessary attention to the subject. After all, later that evening, you're the very one who's going to be sneaking upstairs to the extension phone in the study to call your lover man. The simple act of reciting his telephone number in your head gives you a lift. But when you do actually dial that magical sequence of numbers, you hand is shaking so badly, you have to re-dial three times. And when you do eventually get hold of him, he tells you, in a whisper, that the rest of his family are heading down the country for the entire day next Saturday.

"So, if you're around, you might drop out for a game of scrabble or something."

A tingle stirs in your groin.

"A game of something sounds interesting."

"A game of something it is then."

After you hang up, you have to lie down for ten minutes to let your system normalise again. Then you go downstairs and give Anne such a bonecrusher of a hug, you very nearly snap her spinal chord in half. Not surprisingly, this uncustomary display of passion startles her.

Chapter Seven

Halfway up the ornate staircase, without looking around to check that you are there, he says, "Honeypots, see if you can carry me," and he lets himself fall backwards into your waiting arms. Funnily, this is precisely the sort of little game Anne used to play back in those early days, the sort of game that used to irritate you almost to the point of physical illness. But from him, the words seem right, and even if he weighed a tonne, you suspect you might still manage to summon the strength to carry him. But someone as hyperactive as him couldn't put on weight even if he tried. He wraps his arms around your neck and stares intently ahead of him, behaving as though he's being rescued from a raging fire.

"Excuse me Mister, but would you by any chance have a room to rent here?" he asks.

"Indeed I just might have."

"Wonderful." He points towards the door bearing the name-plate that reads, *Jonathan's Room*. "Now I may not be able to pay for this room in cash, however, I might be able to pay in another way."

"And what had you got in mind?" you ask, hoping that he has double-checked that the house is in fact empty.

"Perhaps we should go inside this room here and discuss the matter further."

He kicks the bedroom door open and you're struck by an overwhelming dose of his odour. There surely is no nicer feeling on earth than knowing that you are about to hop into bed with someone you would gladly lay down your life for; especially when it's someone who, you suspect, might do the same for you.

"Drop me on that trampoline, please."

You dump him onto the bed where he writhes and contorts like a swimmer who has run into a drift of jellyfish. Then he flips over onto his stomach, rests his chin in his hands, so that his eyes are catching the light from the window.

"I could vacuum your house from top to bottom."

"Hmmm." You play the role of the prospective landlord, rubbing your temple, deep in thought.

"I could dig your garden from head to toe. I could polish your shirts and iron your shoes." He stares into your eyes. "Or I could do other things for you."

You lie down beside him. "Other things?"

"I could brush your teeth." He rubs his finger across your front teeth.

First you kiss, let your hands go on a thrilling roam, until he frees himself from your arms and, with a shy flutter of his long eyelashes, he tells you that he wants you to undress him slowly. And who are you to object? Although you do wonder for the briefest of moments what his parents would say if they were to walk into the room and see their son stretched out on his bed like a stranded starfish with his boss kneeling over him, in the process of removing his shoes and socks. It's no easy job to get the clothes off someone in a recumbent position, but you persist, and when you tug his jeans down you discover that, especially for the occasion, he's wearing a rather fetching pair of slinky blue briefs. A thought occurs to you. Whenever Anne splashes out on slinkies, all you can think is that it's such a waste of money. But with him, it's worth it. And looking into his eyes, you let one hand tantalise his inner thigh with the lightest of wispy strokes, while your other hand slides down his chest, across his stomach, and comes to rest over the satin fabric, cupping that bulge.

For the first time in your life, it isn't love by numbers. It doesn't matter what you do, or what he does, or whether you have to do this because he does that. You're operating on a new level now, you don't have to think, everything just takes its own natural course. All that matters is that the two of you are here, lying in one another's arms. To stay like this until the end of time would be paradise. You're touching levels of pleasure you never thought possible. Things take on a new perspective. Things like the flash car, the house in Legoland, the hotshot job, the fat cheque at the end of the month; they don't matter now. In a moment of revelation you see them for what they are, merely elusive stimulations. With him there's no need to justify yourself. For the first time in your life you've lost yourself in an otherworldly way; you feel a sense of heightened being, an almost spiritual glow. There's no stress, no worry, no pretending, just plain old love.

He tells you that his first sexual experience was at boarding school, when he was fourteen, with the priest who was in charge of the cross-country team. Shaking his head in feigned solemnity, he insists that he led the poor cleric astray by wearing scandalously short running-shorts. "With slits up the side," he adds, bowing his head in mock shame. "I tweaked a hamstring muscle during training one day and he told me he had some cream to rub into it." He sniggers at the memory. "So we went to his private changing-room, he closed the door, started his rub-a-dub-dub, one thing led to another, and next thing I knew, the randy old so-and-so had both his hands up where they ought not to have been."

"And did you take any pleasure in it, my son?"

"Absolutely none at all, Father."

You pretend to give him absolution.

"But I made a nice mess of his clean soutane. I'm sure he had trouble explaining those stains to his superior."

Then one day, he tells you, during a religion class, the same priest announced that homosexual activity was a mortal sin, and such was the spontaneous burst of laughter that erupted from the class, he realised that he wasn't the only one to receive the "injury treatment". A truckload of complaints materialised and the priest was shipped off to another school at the far end of the country. The mind boggles. Then he asks you what your first experience was and you say him, and he laughs and says,

"I bet you say that to all the boys."

You snuggle up under the bedclothes, your arms wrapped tight around one another, staring into each other's eyes. The passions are rising. The time for talk is over. It's down to the real business. The bedclothes are discarded. His special occasion underwear are tossed aside. It's all-in rough and tumble on a bed which exudes his odour, in a room which seems to glow from his aura. Displaying unexpected strength, he manages to pin your shoulders down with his knees, and mesmerising you with an impish grin, he inches slowly backwards until he's sitting on your stiffy, whereupon he moves about in a circular motion, all the time staring at you, talking to you with his eyes. Moments later, with a supple adjustment of his rubber limbs, he's flipped around so that he's kneeling above you, devouring your dick with a relaxed and methodical motion. It's sixty-nine time. *Deep Throat* comes to town. You adjust his legs so you can get an angle on his beautiful love truncheon which is throbbing in anticipation. And once again, it's like you're outside yourself, losing control, relinquishing your grasp, pushing your way out into the waters of delightful unpredictability, succumbing to a sea of blissful abandon. You come together, delaying, speeding up, before shooting your dual loads of hot love simultaneously. With his back arched and with his hands extended above his head, he lets his head fall back and purrs with total pleasure.

In the midst of a post-coital snooze, you are awoken by a moist tongue meticulously licking every square millimetre of your ear. With a smile, he beckons to you to follow him out of the room. You see red marks on his buttocks, left by your nails. It pains you to think that you caused him even the slightest discomfort. The strains of Brahms play on a radio-cassette player he has plugged in in the corridor. In the bathroom, a large blue-tiled bath tub is filled to the brim with steaming, bubbly water.

"The three Bs," he says, stepping into the tub. "Bubble-bath, Bacardi and good old Brahmsey."

You're tempted to ask him if he learned about the three Bs at boarding school, but you don't, because you don't particularly want to hear anymore about his escapades with the randy old cross-country cleric.

"And where, may I ask, did you get that tape?" You point to the box of the compilation tapes you prepared for him.

"From a chap I work with."

"Work?"

"Well, perhaps work is too strong a word to describe what we do, but anyway, this poor chap likes classical shite."

You take the glass of Bacardi off the silver tray he has stuck in front of your nose. He downs his in one gulp and you do the same.

"Never drink and swim at the same time," you say.

"You'll just have to save me, won't you," he says, drawing a heart in the fog on the mirror. He fills both your initials at opposite ends of the heart, and then rubs it all out again, claiming that his *mater* and *pater* would want an explanation.

He's overdone it with the bubble-bath. All you see are rolling hills of foam. The last time you were in a foamy bubble-bath was when you were very young, when your parents used to use it as an enticement. You immerse yourself in the foam, facing him. But not for long. He slides his way up to you, straddles you, his legs apart, and tells you that he's lubricated himself and he wants you to make love to him. You can do nothing but smile at the intensity with which he says these words. He peels a condom from its wrapper and pulls it on for you. Slowly, you inch your hard member inside him. His face is contorted in a grimace of what looks like excruciating pain, beads of sweat have formed on his forehead, but still he tells you to continue. Above you, condensation has formed on the ceiling. The tight outer rim is passed and it feels like it's never felt before. You are leaving this world and plunging into a new one. In time with your rhythmic motion, water and foam lap against the edge of the bath and slop out onto the floor. His nails are digging into your back. He's gone through the pain barrier and he's bucking and riding like a rodeo king. It's in to the hilt now, each new thrust slaps your stomach against his balls. The thrill reminds you of an exhilarating helter-skelter ride. Thoughts are racing through your mind: Has he done this before with anyone? And what happens if someone arrives home unexpectedly? But these worries are forgotten when you approach climax. Now you lose yourself completely, gasping, saying anything that comes to mind. He's kissing you and gasping and moving back and forward, up and down. Sweat is stinging your eyes. Every nerve-end tingles. The orchestra is reaching a climax. And so are you. Fast and furious. The second coming. And like a man possessed, you emit a sigh of sheer delight.

After a long kiss, you lie back and you feel like you could compose music, that you could be the new Brahms if you put your mind to it.

"Should be a little easier next time," he says, and you lean forward to kiss his eyelids.

* * * *

At home, Anne looks at you strangely and a shiver of guilt runs right the length of your backbone.

"Harry phoned for you." The words seem to splash from her mouth, out onto the floor like slops of water.

There's a liar's delay. Just that fraction of a second while you're reassembling the forces of deceit. The baby isn't around to use as a distraction, so instead, calm as you like, you bend down, unzip the side-pocket of your golf bag and take out your rain gear. You were supposed to be playing golf with Harry for the afternoon. Lucky it wasn't raining because your rain-gear is bone dry. How would Anne react if you simply said, Look, I met this amazing guy, you'd fancy him too, and he invited me to intertwine my thighs with his for the afternoon. How could I resist? Her first instincts would probably be to laugh.

But what were the chances of Harry phoning today of all days? He hasn't phoned in months. The secret is not to get in a fluster.

"Oh, what did he want?"

"They were short one for indoor football."

"Shit, I'd have preferred that to the golf." You say this with such conviction you surprise even yourself.

"But...weren't you playing golf with Harry?"

You lift your head, wrinkle your brow, and look at her in puzzlement. "Harry? No, Johnny." It feels so good just to say that name out loud.

"Who?"

"Johnny, my new assistant."

"Oh." She believes you. Just about. Close shave. The names Harry and Johnny are probably tumbling about in her head. A sound-alike name-check is running, a cloud of doubt is forming, and that's when the doorbell rings. The moment dissolves. But you can't deny that there's a certain excitement in living so close to the edge, more than likely it's similar to the rush of adrenaline a pickpocket experiences at the moment of the dip. But it's definitely an exhilaration that the approaching middle-age part of you would prefer to do without.

It's good old Drumskin-tight Jeans, the baby-sitter, to the rescue. She parades her way into the kitchen, plonks her suitcase full of study books down on the table, admires Anne's hair and her new boots and her new jacket. How to slurp your way to a payrise. You stand there, smiling like an imbecile, and for some reason, this chatter between them reminds you of those days when Anne was pregnant. You had joined the proud ranks of the fathers and the fathers-to-be. Anne did the talking but you were with the real men. You hung out with them, joked your manly jokes, all the while tacitly excluding those who didn't yet qualify for the mile-high-testosterone club. Acceptance? Is that what it was all about? Imagine telling the same macho lads that your love-machine saw better action in a young man's house that afternoon than it did at any other time in your life.

In the taxi, Bob asks where everyone would like to go and you can't resist it. You really have no interest in going anywhere now unless there's a chance of meeting him. Yeah, it's time for a change, Karen agrees. So long as they serve beer, Bob says, and while you are giving the taxi-man directions, you can sense the heat from Anne's laser eyes. If you were her you'd probably do a lot more than stare. Of course she suspects that things are happening, things she doesn't understand. Her hubby, Mr Calm-and- Control, is behaving decidedly out of character. Almost snapping her backbone one minute, ignoring her the next. So to ease the tension, you casually remark that you once went to the pub with clients and that you were very impressed. It works. And even Anne admires the old disused railway bridge at Loughlinstown which you point to, regurgitating snippets of historical facts Johnny had managed to relate before you plugged your lips to his. Lucky it's dark because your face feels like its luminous, so much so, you expect the taxi-man to glance in his rear-view mirror and warn you not to stay out in the sun so long, or, more then likely, to ask if you ever thought of getting your blood-pressure checked. Karen points to a mansion and says that it once belonged to a drug baron. Everyone glances at the mansion and you file this little snippet of information away for discussion with Johnny.

He's nowhere to be seen. The others are taken aback. The pub is ordinary, so ordinary in fact, you can sense them thinking, Is this what he dragged us halfway across the city for? They're casting sly glances around in search of the hidden special features. Elephants dancing on giant footballs, lions jumping through hoops, giraffes blowing up balloons, or at least a bit of live music, and not the awful supermarket *muzack* that's pumping through the PA system.

Bob orders the first round. As long as you've known him, Bob has always bought the first round. It's such an appealing trait. You'd have to knock him out, or set his shirttails on fire to get an order in ahead of him. And as though the buying of this round by her hubby somehow permits her the privilege to moan, Karen proceeds to tell you that the eldest of their three boys is being bullied at school. You stare at her intently, as though the trials and tribulations of a snotty-nosed seven-year-old are the most fascinating details you've heard in quite some time, but your attention is firmly fixed on every new arrival coming in through the door behind her.

Bob then tells you about a new security device he's invested in. It's a tape-recording which simulates the sounds of a pack of half-starved Alsatians.

"Great for when you go away on holidays," he says.

"And all you have to feed it is a little electricity," Karen says.

"You'll have to tell us where you got it," Anne says.

And believe it or not, Anne is talking about the Harry and Johnny name mix-up when good old Johnny Blue Eyes parades his way in through the front door. A herald of trumpets sound inside your head, a drum beats to his every step. The interior of the pub seems to change colour. Suddenly you feel pumped up, omnipotent, euphoric, like a half-starved Alsatian, ready to devour him. He's wearing clothes you've never seen him wear before, and they make him look all the more devourable. He's got two male friends in tow, neither of whom you've laid eyes on before. One of these friends says something to him and when he smiles you feel like a lovestruck adolescent. Helplessly numb.

He doesn't spot you until he's almost level with your table. He hesitates for that split second which, in other circumstances, might have meant death. The music in your head fades out abruptly. The world seems to stop revolving. Time stands still. Your eyes meet. A tiny inaudible gasp escapes from between your lips. You hold your breath, shake your head ever so slightly, and flick your hand to motion him away. If you introduce him, Anne will know you came here to meet him, and he might find out that Anne is your wife. But why did you come here? To see him? To get that boost? Or just plain old crazy love? He reads your signals, takes a good look at Anne and the others, before he continues on his way to the far side of the lounge. Why is he so complicit? He's done nothing wrong. It must be that the subterfuge is catching. It's getting to be like a drug.

The music recommences inside your head. Your skin tingles, goosepimples rise on your arms, you're drinking faster than you normally would. At the far side of the lounge, he has positioned himself so that he's looking straight across at you, and like you, he also appears to be drinking faster than he normally would. The subterfuge is taking its toll. As the night wears on, more and more of his friends arrive until they've taken over the entire section. None of them were in Wexford with him, which makes you wonder just how many friends he actually has. Your middle name is Sir Glance-a-lot. But their behaviour amuses you. It's like their seats have been sprinkled with itching powder. They move around like grasshoppers, changing places with regularity, engrossing themselves in an intense conversation one minute, having a laugh the next. People your age don't move about because they have nowhere to move to. Maybe growing old is all about isolating yourself. At one stage, he sees you looking at him and he places his pint glass on his crotch and proceeds to rub it slowly up and down.

You haul your attention back to your own table and you notice that first flush on Anne's cheeks. The wine spritzer has begun to take effect. A subliminal signal ricochets around your brain notifying your hidden self that it's okay, she ain't going to notice anything now. She's a pleasant drunk, who loses her sharpness after two, gets giddy and slurs her speech after three, and simply smiles and giggles after four.

"God, you're like the proverbial fish tonight," Karen says when Bob gestures to the lounge-girl. What a simple pleasure it is to have a good friend ask what'll you have to drink when he knows full well what the answer's going to be. Even Bob and Karen are drinking more than usual tonight. It must be the excitement of the change of venue.

He doesn't need to, but Johnny takes a circuitous route to the loo, twice passing close to your table on his journey. Maybe it's your imagination, but you're sure you spot Anne cast an admiring glance at his bum. Now there's something the two of you never knew you had in common. You stand up to go, relaxed in the knowledge that there is no chance that Bob, who's probably bursting to go, will come with you. It's only women who do that, mainly, you suspect, because they don't have to stand together at the same urinal.

He's alone in the gents, relieving himself. And like a 1920s gangster, you push the two cubicle doors open to check that they are empty.

He turns and smiles drunkenly. "Honeypots, what a surprise to find you here."

"Zee walls have ears," you whisper.

"Who's the fancy lady?"

"Jealous?"

"Green-eyed."

You throw your eyes up to avoid his gaze. "Another futile attempt to fix me up."

"So why didn't you want to introduce *moi*?"

"Because I didn't want you keeling over with boredom."

"If she's wealthy, marry her." He shivers involuntarily before he zips up. "Hire me as your gardener and we can both be kept men." He opens his eyes wide.

"And I suppose we'll shack up together in the gardener's shed."

"Which will be about this size." He nods to one of the cubicles, his eyes roll seductively, in a way that wrenches away all control from you.

The cubicle is small and cramped. There's a full twelve-inch gap between the door and the floor and the dividing partition between the two cubicles ends well short of the ceiling. This is a high-risk venture, an utterly crazy thing to do, but in the haze of alcohol, you do it. Aptly, some juvenile scrawler has written 'SEX' on the cubicle door. If it was a public convenience the walls would feature a more physical sort of graffiti. You have read those raunchy scribbles, and also those pitiful attempts to make dates. Cries in the wilderness. Sometimes you wonder what would happen if two scribblers did meet up, and clicked, and went to a dinner party together. So how did you two meet up? their host would ask. Through a note on a bog wall actually. How romantic.

He wraps his arms tight around you and seems to be attempting to shove his tongue down your throat. Drink is the aphrodisiac. Love is the drug. You keep your eyes open and your ears on red alert. Inevitably, hands go on a tour down below. Buttons open, skin is caressed, blood pumps through the veins. He pulls your trousers and shorts down to your knees and once again takes you in his mouth. The liberating alcohol almost fools you into believing that this is the first time you've met. Worries are suspended. Sweet music plays in your head. You look down and caress his hair. Waves of pleasure ripple through you. One of Ronnie Burke's sexist jokes springs to mind. It goes, What's the difference between a penis and a bonus? The wife will always blow the bonus. You'll have to advise Ronnie Boy to find himself a willing man next time he's in line for a bonus.

And then, as he raises himself up to kiss you, Johnny sways drunkenly, stumbles over the toilet-bowl, crashes against the partition, and slides to the floor where he places his hand to his mouth to stifle his sniggers. It's then you realise that there are other people in the toilet. You place a finger to your lips. Fear replaces bliss. Anxiety replaces excitement. Johnny raises himself noiselessly to a standing position. Your ears are on such red alert, you barely notice him licking your eyelids. How long have you been in here? Could they possibly have heard the sound effects outside? Are they pointing to the locked cubicle door, and telling every new arrival that there's a pair of bum-boys up to all sorts of shenanigans in there? Roll up, roll up, for the unforgettable toilet show. All it takes is for one inquisitive person to peek under the door, or a tabloid journalist with a curved lens. Your feet feel naked and exposed.

A door closes outside. Everything goes quiet. Either they're all standing out there like statues, attempting to lure you into coming out, whereupon they will stare at you like you had twenty heads and maybe hurl an insult or two; or else they've gone to fetch the manager, who, in turn, has probably gone to fetch the vice squad. It's difficult to think straight. It's not everyday you get trapped in a toilet cubicle with the man you love. The lowlands of your brain are obscured by a haze of alcohol. There are noises outside. The main door into the toilet opens and closes a couple of times. There's the splash of piss and the sound of someone farting. A tap gushes water. The hand-dryer goes on. It seems that loo life has returned to normal.

Johnny has fallen asleep on your shoulder. The alcohol haze has reached the highlands of his brain. You shake him until his eyes open. He smiles, and he is in the process of moving his mouth towards yours when Bob's face appears over the top of the partition wall. It's a moment of sheer panic. Every muscle in your body turns rigid. You feel like a hunted animal. What are you doing in this confined space? Why aren't you out there, roaming the wide open spaces? Slowly, you focus your thoughts, and the horror of the situation dawns. It's hard to tell who's the more shocked, Bob or yourself. To judge by his expression, you'd swear he'd just seen the bowels of hell. His face pales, and a vacant sort of gaze comes over his features, like he doesn't really want to understand what it is he's looking at. His eyebrows flicker in silent greeting. You hold his stare, somehow hoping that by doing this he won't look at Johnny. He says nothing, because there really is very little he can say. He remains in his bird's-eye perch for a matter of seconds, that's all; but it may as well have been a couple of days.

There's a knot in your stomach, a queasiness at the very pit of your existence. Johnny, who has remained blissfully oblivious to Bob's presence, is vaguely aware that you are blocking his attempted kiss. It's a problem to communicate anything to him, let alone a dilemma of this magnitude. Gradually, his face registers alarm, he sits down on the toilet seat, turns his head to look at the place where Bob's face had been, as though he's going to find the solution up there. Somewhat disconcertingly, you realise that your trousers and shorts are down around your knees. Did Bob's line of vision enable him to see down there? And if he did, could Johnny possibly pass for a female from that vantage point? It's very doubtful. A look at Johnny, in need of assistance, causes a surge of protectiveness, and momentarily you consider blowing your cover. But that old sensible logical side tells you that it's the drink that has you by the goolies. In the morning he will be sober, and you'll still be in need of respectability.

A knock on the door braces you. This is followed by another knock and a voice that says, "Johnny?"

Johnny's eyes open wide, his cheeks swell with air, and he points to himself and nods. Then he points to you, points to your mouth, urging you to speak.

"No, it's not Johnny," you say, calm as you like.

"Oh, sorry."

"That's okay."

You don't breathe until you hear the outside door close. The search parties are out in force. And it's not surprising, because when you check your watch, you see that you've been missing for over twenty minutes. There's constipation and there's constipation. Why the hell didn't Bob knock on the door instead of being an over-the-partition pervert? Maybe he did and you didn't hear him.

You open the cubicle door. There's no one about. You wave good-bye to Johnny and as you emerge from the loo the space in front of you seems to open up into an airport arrivals area and you're the one whose flight has just touched down. People have jostled for position to stare at you as you emerge, bleary-eyed and jet-lagged. One moment you're a famous rock star, the next moment you're searching for the held-up sign which says, "Toilet fiend, Paul Cullen. This way."

Now for the worrying part. Your stomach is like a butter-manufacturing factory operating at full pelt. If you were Bob, what would you do? You certainly wouldn't tell the women, not yet anyway. In some weird way, it pleases you that he saw you. He is, after all, your closest friend and maybe, in some subliminal way, you wanted to tell him and break free from the shackles of secrecy and repression. But what a way to let him know. One thing's sure, he'll think twice about taking a shower with you after the next game of tennis.

On your approach to the table, Bob reminds you of a small child the way he's looking at you while pretending that he isn't. There's no doubting that his world has been flipped head over heels.

"What kept you?" Anne asks with the careful articulation of an infrequent drinker.

"Met someone I know."

"Who?" Anne's elbow slips off the table and she looks at it as though it belongs to someone else.

"Fellow from school." Bob is now observing you thought-fully. "We smoked a joint together."

"You what?" Anne is incredulous.

"Grass, man. We blew some fumes for old times."

Bob is actually smiling. Maybe he does believe you. Maybe he's doubting what he saw. Maybe it wasn't even him at all, just someone that looked the spit of him. A clone even. Modern science knows no bounds.

"*You* were smoking grass?" Anne's brow is knotted and she's pointing at you like you'd just told her that you were from planet

Pluto. "First it was cigarettes and now it's...it's drugs!"

When she puts it in such stark terms, it makes you wish you had invented a different tale. Bob and Karen are eyeing you the way people do when they've been discussing your problems behind your back and suddenly the opportunity presents itself for them to launch into their pre-prepared lectures.

But you're having none of their lectures. As a distraction, you point towards a group of Johnny's capering friends. "That lot could do with a drug or two," you say, when one of the friends is pushed off the end of the long seat and tumbles onto the floor.

Karen exposes her tombstone teeth in a compliant smile. Bob's face is expressionless. By the time the four of you are squashed into a taxi, you've convinced yourself that Bob saw nothing untoward.

Chapter Eight

Kevin Daniels will never admit it, but he knows that the company's computer ought to be quietly placed onto a scrap-heap in the dead of night. The only other proud owner of this particular model in the country is a comprehensive school somewhere out in the depths of the city's sprawling western suburbs. Old kickback Ronnie struck the deal. In the tearoom theatre, Andy has often recreated a scene where he plays Ronnie Burke opening the front door of his Foxrock home. He turns the key in the lock, but he can't push the door open because it's blocked by the pile of kickbacks or "gifts" as Ronnie euphemistically calls them. Sometimes, Andy plays it so that Ronnie gets the door open, steps inside and is promptly buried under an avalanche of "gifts".

Despite the computer's shortcomings, Kevin Daniels still has no particular trouble in tracing the latest mishap to Johnny's terminal. You're on the phone to a fabric supplier in South Africa when he slithers into your office. Such is the look of utter shock on his features, you expect that he's going to tell you that a revenue hit squad is forcing their way in through the roof. It's tempting to prolong the phone call to irritate him, but South Africa isn't exactly next door.

He asks you to accompany him to Johnny's office, and you make sure you're the one who opens the door to give Johnny ample time to create the impression that he's hard at work. And it's just as well you do, because it gives him the crucial few seconds required to remove his headphones and conceal them in a drawer. While Daniels demonstrates what has been done on the terminal, he behaves as if Johnny is not in the room. He only looks at you when he's talking. This low-level hostility makes you suspicious. Is it caused by envy? Envy of the friendship between Johnny and yourself? Maybe Daniels has the hots for you and he sees Johnny as unwelcome competition. This thought causes you to smile, and this smile necessitates Kevin Daniels to draw a sharp intake of breath. With expert timing, Johnny snaps a loose-leaf invoice folder shut, and its resemblance to the sound of rifleshot startles Daniels momentarily, very nearly causing him to duck.

It turns out that Johnny has written a cheque for £9,999,999 on the computer's dodgy cheque-writing facility. The giant-sized figure has caused the system to overload and crash. And what's more, this large cheque was made payable to Bernie. It's a real problem keeping a serious look on your face. Kevin Daniels acknowledges Johnny's presence for the first time when he turns to him and asks, "Why did you write the cheque?"

Johnny shrugs.

"You make out a cheque for almost ten million pounds payable to one of your fellow-employees and you can't give me a reason?"

Johnny glances at you, but what can you say? All you want to do is kiss him.

Daniels shakes his head. Illogic is alien to him. "I just don't get it, have you nothing to say for yourself?"

Again, Johnny shrugs. "I thought I'd be able to cancel it."

"Cancel it?"

"Yeah."

"But why would you want to cancel it?"

"Because it was only done as a joke."

"A joke?" Daniels looks set to hyperventilate.

"I'll sort it out, Kevin," you say, and with that the phone rings. It's Carney's secretary. Carney wants to see you in his office immediately.

"Better not keep Big Jimbo waiting," Johnny says, and Daniels eyes him as something of a curiosity.

Carney certainly isn't happy. His fury induces a facial ruddiness, spittle sprays his desk. Who is this Johnny Lyons? What sort of qualifications does the fucking eejit have? How are we supposed to steer a steady ship with gobshites like him on board? What about the two drunken captains, you feel like saying, but you don't. Because there isn't much he doesn't hear about, your guess is that Carney more likely knows that you and Johnny have struck up a friendship, that you've been doing lunch together, heading off for weekends together, having the occasional snog. But he isn't one for treading on eggshells when it comes to his business. All of what he says is promptly consigned to a dark cellar in your brain. Another emergency will trundle along later in the morning to distract him. Something will supersede this. A strike. A fire on the factory floor. A sexual harassment suit against the entire senior management. He may even keel over himself, clutching those drill-marks on his chest.

For all the attention you're paying, he could be telling you that he's cultivating his prize plants in his ears; that is, until you hear the words, "He has to go". These words certainly wrench you up out of your semi-slumber.

"Look, Paul, I know you're pally with him."

Of course, a big rosy flush rises to your cheeks.

"And that's why I overlooked the problem with the debtors…If it wasn't for the fact that you two were pals, he'd have been out of here before his feet had time to touch the ground. So I gave him a second chance." Carney shows his palms in a gesture that says it all. It's over. There's no point arguing. There's no point falling to your knees and offering to take a pay-cut to cover Johnny's salary.

Johnny is waiting in your office, and when you break the news he seems indifferent, preoccupied, and the way his attention drifts you might as well be describing any old meeting with Carney.

"I'm really sorry."

"Don't worry about it."

"Let it lie a few days and he'll probably change his mind."

He shrugs. "Ah, I don't give a toss either way."

You look at him.

"I was going to leave anyway."

"You were?" You feel deflated. He's obviously been thinking about this for a while. So why didn't he say anything?

"Yeah, I'm not cut out for this sort of crap." There's a hint of a smile, but that's it. It dies a death. Evaporates. Goes wherever dead smiles go.

A silence follows, and for some reason he can't bring himself to look at you. This is so unlike him. All the fun appears to have vanished. It's as though he's bursting to say something, but can't decide on the exact wording to use. The only reason you can think of is that he's blaming you for not saving his job.

"Have you any idea what you'll like, emmm, do now?"

"Probably move abroad."

This is painful to hear. There really is nothing else you can say except, "If you do, I'll go with you."

"What about your wife and kid?" Now he turns to look at you and you see that his eyes are moist. "I was talking to her just now." He points to the phone on your desk.

It feels as though you are on board a speeding snow-sleigh which has hit a patch of dry earth. The steam-train of love comes to an abrupt halt. Every scheme and plan is thrown up into the air. What can you say?

"You told me you weren't married."

"I can explain."

"I just wish you hadn't lied to me."

"Johnny, I..." You've never seen him like this before. You want to hold him in your arms, but it doesn't seem possible. It's almost as if his body is emitting invisible signals warning you to keep your distance, and of course, this only serves to further endear him to you. In his eyes you are a cad, but not in your own. If he was older he'd understand the tide you were swimming against. Times may have changed, but not so in the conservative world of business.

And it's just as well you didn't hold him in your arms, because Teresa walks into the room, hesitates for a moment when she sees him standing there, as if she expects to catch the two of you rollicking about naked on the floor. She senses the palpable gloom. She's either guessed what's happened, or else she's heard it from the Fat Man's secretary. The news is probably raging through the building right now.

"Phone message," she says, before beating a hasty retreat out of the office.

The message reads: Urgent – phone Anne.

"It's a little girl, isn't it?"

"Hah?"

"Your kid."

"Yeah." You wonder what sort of conversation they had. Could this even be the reason for the urgent message from Anne? Thoughts like this cause palpitations.

He exits the room, and you stand there staring at the door for a full five minutes before you reluctantly lift the phone and call Anne. To your surprise, she's beside herself with exuberance and excitement.

"You're not going to believe the little bit of news I heard this morning!" She almost shrieks, and you wonder if this is an expression of some form of mild lunacy brought on by her chat with her husband's male lover.

"What?"

"Guess."

What would she say if you told her that you've been through a bit of a romantic trauma, and that it's difficult enough working up the enthusiasm to speak to her without having to go through the extra hassle of having to guess what it is that's making her behave like an imbecile? What if you just told her right now that you wished you had never met her?

"I'm pregnant."

Talk about pregnant pauses. You almost ask her if she knows who the father is. And then you think that, indirectly at least, Johnny is. After all, he is the one responsible for your recent spate of lovemaking.

"Paul? Did you hear me?"

"Yeah, I'm just catching my breath."

She laughs. "I couldn't believe it."

"That's fantastic news." You're not even sure if your voice is infused with the correct note of joy. How can you take all of this information on board? Your mind is going to short-circuit and you'll end up a madman, sitting cross-legged on the floor, babbling on about government conspiracies and the like.

In a daze, you walk into the tearoom where the cheque for ten million is all the rage. In his absence, Johnny is the toast of the tearoom.

"I've a good mind to put him across my knee and roast that lovely bum of his," Doreen says, simulating a spanking action.

"Let the millionaire speak." Andy is pointing at Bernie, who has the cleaning lady's fur scarf wrapped around her neck as a symbol of her new-found wealth.

"We are going on a cruise." Bernie speaks in a posh accent, fluttering her eyelids.

"Well don't forget yer pals," Doreen says.

Bernie blinks at her. "Sorry, do I know you?"

Jason taps your arm. "Is he gonna get the bullet?" he asks, and you shrug. "He's gone home, yeh know."

You think fast and let on that you know this. They're watching you, especially Andy. You gulp back the remainder of your tea, glance at your watch, and say, "No rest for the wicked," before you leave the tearoom.

The direct line is ringing in your office. You race along the corridor, certain that it's him. It's not, it's Bob, and for a moment you assume he's ringing to congratulate you. He's not, he's just checking that you're still on for the game of tennis after work. He's probably hoping you will say no, but you don't. A brisk game of tennis is just what you need. Clear the head. It's obvious that the toilet incident is still sloshing around in his head and that he doesn't really believe your "spliff with an old schoolpal" story. He knows you never smoked anything. There's a detached air about him, almost like he's speaking to a stranger, and in many respects, if he saw what you think he saw, he must feel that he is. You wonder if he'll claim that he forgot to bring a towel, or maybe he'll wear a tracksuit so he can take a shower at home after the game? And how will he react if you happen to nip into a toilet cubicle? Or if you were to haul Johnny along to do umpire?

What's most noticeable about the game is the lack of Bob's questionable line-calls. His heart isn't really in it and you gain a surprisingly easy victory. You don't need to be a neuropsychologist to figure out what his brain cells are preoccupied with. In the changing-rooms you strip off quickly, step under a steaming hot shower and close your eyes. And there's Johnny's face staring at you. Next thing you see is the bedroom door with the sign - *Jonathan's Room*. Then you're carrying him up the stairs, so you open your eyes and alter your thought patterns before the eager-beaver blood cells get their call-up for erection duties.

Bob is in a shower opposite, scrubbing his hair. How would he react if you let the eager-beaver blood cells have their way? Would he freak out? Unlikely. Many people would consider Bob okay-looking, but to you, his body is repulsive. The words scrawny and puny spring to mind. How you'd love to tap him on the shoulder and say, Hey Bob, I like you man, but you can rest assured that even if the pair of us were marooned on a desert island together for the remainder of our days, I could think of nothing worse than to do what you undoubtedly imagine I'd want to do. He'd probably tell you that he would be more freaked out from not having a key-board at his fingertips.

"Any more problems with the computer?"

"Hah?" That certainly caught you unawares.

"The boneshaker computer."

You laugh and tell him the story of the latest breakdown, omitting the fact that it was the guy he saw you snogging in the toilet cubicle who was responsible.

Back in the changing-room, you're drying off when two college students stroll in and proceed to strip off. There's no doubt that Bob is sneaking glances at you to see if you are sneaking glances at the two lads. It's not your imagination, you know him well enough to know that he is. And it's a real nuisance because one of the two lads is a stunner. Sweet-faced, firm-assed, with a dick down to his knees, and you have to make it your business not to feast your eyes on something you normally would have no prob-lems admiring. What makes it worse is that you've often looked forward to this day. This particular guy has caught your eye out on the courts before, but you have never yet had the good fortune of landing in the changing-room at the same time as him. Up until this day, of all days. This frustration of holding back transforms itself into a feeling of intense anger against old hawk-eye Bob. This is one of the few advantages of being gay and he's trying to ruin it. Stupid nosy so-and-so, you think, how you'd love to pluck those sneaky all-knowing eyes out of their sockets and hang them up on the towel rack. As the stunner leaves the changing-room, you snatch the quickest of looks, and then quickly swirl your head around to catch Bob staring at you like you had just told him that you had contracted a terminal illness. The fire in your eyes certainly appears to unsettle him. And then you think about Anne's pregnancy and you feel good. Bob is delighted when you tell him. New life has this effect on all right-thinking people.

At home, Anne is sitting in front of the TV with her feet up, and the happy, resigned mother-earth look on her face. She's started to knit already. The new baby's going to plop out onto a mountain of wool. Feeling a moment of intense fondness for her, you place your hand on her stomach, pin your ear to it, and listen for that tiny heartbeat. But all you can really think of is Johnny's stomach, and how much more appealing it is to you. And all you want to talk about is Johnny's imminent sacking. The new baby will be the topic of conversation for months to come. It's insane, but now you almost feel a bitterness towards her for deliberately planning her pregnancy to eclipse any conversations about Johnny. These sort of meandering thoughts worry you. They have to be stamped out, trampled underfoot, immediately eliminated, otherwise they'll be fitting you out for that straitjacket. It cheers you up when you decide that if it's a boy you're going to suggest the name Jonathan.

"You know, Paul, I think it might be a good idea if I took leave-of-absence."

"Yeah," is all you can say.

"Like, we can easily afford to get by on your salary. It's just, I'd like to be with the children." She pats her stomach.

"It's entirely your decision." For some reason, you're suddenly hit by this image of Anne and the two children sitting on O'Connell Bridge, a cardboard box on the pavement in front of them. It's a sobering thought.

The following morning gets off to an inauspicious start when the Wax Hennessy ends up in the same DART carriage as you. As always happens on these early morning encounters, both of you pretend not to notice one another. It's an unwritten charter for all commuters. There are so many distractions when you need them: the overhead map of DART stations, poems by Anonymous, the back page of a newspaper, the view of Howth, the people waiting at stations, the blurred patterns of a grey wall. Anything but the Wax.

At Sydney Parade, there's a delay when an insistent woman sets her mind on barging her way on board the already over-crowded carriage.

"Please stand back from the doors, there's another train coming right behind," the driver announces over the PA system. But this woman's having none of it. Like a prop-forward moving towards a ruck, she drops her shoulder and makes yet another unsuccessful charge against the wall of bodies, and once again, the automatic doors touch her padded shoulders and slide open. All around, stressed commuters sigh. Clasping on to anything she can, the woman attaches herself, limpet-like, to the solid wall of passengers, her expression similar to that of a woman experiencing advanced labour pains.

"You're not in Tokyo now," a man mutters, and his fellow commuters instinctively turn to stare at him.

The impasse finally ends when a tall man, in a green coat, reaches out what appears to be a helping hand, but with a deft flick of his wrist he pushes the unfortunate woman and sends her sprawling back on to the platform, where she loses her footing, backs into an elderly gentleman, and the two of them end up in a tangle on the ground like a pair of ungainly lovers. A surly youngster standing next to you removes his hissing headphones, guffaws, and then turns bright pink when he sees that everyone else in the carriage is pretending not to have noticed the incident. Everyone is watching the tall man in the green coat while pretending that they're not. 'Giving someone the flick' takes on a whole new meaning.

The train glides away from the station with the woman whacking the windows with her umbrella and screaming that she has witnesses. It's a sharp lesson on the rigours and stresses of modern living.

"We may experience a little turbulence," the driver says over the PA system, and your fellow commuters now feel justified in permitting themselves the faintest of smiles. Instinctively, you think about the simple joy you will get from relating this incident to Johnny, but just as quickly, the grim events of yesterday wriggle their way back into your thoughts.

The incident has encouraged the Wax to catch your eye and send a slimy smile in your direction. You lift your head and act like you've just become aware of his presence. Both of you glance at the tall man in the green coat, exchange the type of look people exchange when they find themselves in the company of a madman, and then it's back to reading the poems by Anonymous and watching the blurred patterns of grey wall. Anne's pregnancy enters your thoughts and you experience a warm glow inside.

Johnny doesn't show up for work until the afternoon. Dressed in jeans and a casual shirt, he arrives in to collect his personal belongings. You only learn about his presence when Teresa phones you. She tells you that he has already handed in his resignation, that Bernie and Doreen are taking up a collection for him, and that everyone is going to the pub at 5.30 for the presentation. It all leaves you cold. It's all unravelling too quickly.

He's alone in his office. The same canvas bag he had with him in Wexford is perched on the desk, filled with his personal belongings and what looks like a year's supply of stolen stationery.

"Oh, hi," he says, like he's greeting anyone from Doreen or Bernie to one of the geeks from design.

"You've had enough?"

"Yeah."

"So you're having your going-away piss-up tonight?"

"So I believe."

You just can't bring yourself to say what you really want to say. Instead, you make small-talk about the buoyant jobs market and some upcoming football match, all the time acting like there was never anything between you. You do this because you know him well enough to know that this is how he wants you to behave. You put it down to the shock and disappointment he's experiencing. In a day or two everything will be back to normal between you. When you remember the incident on the DART that morning you experience a surge of joy. At last you have something decent to relate. Something humorous is what the moment calls for. He listens, matter-of-factly, his eyes appearing to glaze over. He utters a feeble laugh and says that it was hardly funny for the woman who was pushed from the train. A silence follows, during which you decide that you will have to say something else. The problem is what.

The opportunity is lost when the Phantom arrives into the office. "You're leaving us?" he says, his face contorted into a look of shock, which appears to be genuine. And what's more distressing is the fact that Johnny chats to the Phantom as if he's the closest friend he's got in the place. He's deliberately using the Phantom as a shield against you, he has even turned his shoulder ever so slightly to exclude you, so, in revenge, you say that you've got things to do, and you leave him alone to continue his riveting conversation with the Phantom. Of course, the moment you're outside, you wish you had stayed inside.

In the pub after work the clock hits 6.30 and people realise that Johnny isn't going to show, so they begin to drift away. However, before they leave the pub, they come up to you and ask you to give him their regards. This makes you wonder what people think is going on. Has Teresa yapped? You're even more defensive when Ronnie Burke, who you guess to be about a quarter-cut, comes up to you and says, "I'd say you're really going to miss him." There's no doubting the mischievous glint in his eye. You want to make some nasty retort about his kickbacks but you hold your fire, and instead simply shrug your shoulders and say, "Yeah, I'll miss Jimmy all right."

But the comment is lost on Ronnie. He's more pissed than

you thought. His brain can only just about concentrate on what he himself is saying. And then, without any prompting, he says, "What's this?", and he proceeds to stick his tongue out, curling it into a tight curve so that it resembles a lizard's darting tongue. You shake your head. "A lesbian on the horn," he says, and during the guffaw that follows, he sprays your jacket with gin, tonic, saliva and morsels of food.

There's no doubt that you would remain on in the pub until closing-time if you thought there was just an infinitesimal chance that he might walk in through the door. But once Bernie reveals that she gave him his going-away present at lunchtime, you say your goodbyes and head straight home. Anne asks about the evening, but you're too listless to reply, so you tell her you have some work to do and you go upstairs to the study and sit there looking out the window, unable to focus on anything. Before you met him, weeks and months used to glide past without you taking any particular notice, but how every moment seems highly charged, precious, there to be grasped and lived.

Chapter Nine

Two weeks pass and there's no contact. You phone his house what seems like half a million times and leave half a million messages, but he doesn't return any of your calls. His younger brother and sister appear to live beside the phone. Two rings and one of them plucks it from its cradle. Most times they just say, Sorry, he's not in. Occasionally though, they holler his name out, and you hear it echo around that house you think about so often and your pulse begins to quicken, but they come back to the phone and say, Sorry, he's out at the moment, would you like to leave a message? It's embarrassing that the same two people keep answering. You can almost hear them think, Oh God, it's Baldy again, how'll I get rid of him this time. So you try to alter your voice, but this back-fires when they ask if you'd like to leave a message and you have to give the same name that must be filling their phone-message pads by the score. You don't pursue them for further information on his whereabouts because you're sure that they either suspect your motives, or he's warned them not to give anything away.

So, for those two weeks, you do little else except think about what he could be doing. You never stray too far from your phone, and this leaves you constantly on edge, constantly waiting, con-stantly stressed. Now you see the benefits of a mobile. Whenever it gets really bad you take a stroll down to his old office, sit on his chair, dip into the drawers of his desk, take out old scribble pads and stare at any little snippet of his handwriting. They're full of nonsensical drawings and words, but you're sure it's just a matter of staring at them long enough to decipher some secret coded message.

A replacement is found for him, a twenty-four-year-old newly-qualified accountant named Janet. She was one of the original inter-viewees, the one the Phantom thought ought to get the job, and naturally, the fact that choosing her is going to cause further irritation for Kevin Daniels is undoubtedly instrumental in your decision. She's a pleasant type, exceptionally bright and meticulous, but it somehow jars with you to see her sitting at Johnny's desk. Like the Vikings, you feel that his entire office should be set alight and pushed out to sea in a longboat.

There are memories of him everywhere, and each one inflicts a sharp stab of bleak pain. You feel like someone who has stayed behind in a holiday resort after the summer has ended, and all your friends have departed; the weather has turned cold and your desolation is amplified by all the lingering memories of those carnival times. Everywhere you go in the building you can recall things he said, things he did, the way he smiled, the easy way he stood with his arm resting on his hip.

By the Friday of the second week, you're almost frantic from the craving. You feel like you're going to die if you don't see him. If you thought it'd work, you know you'd take out a full page ad in a newspaper to arrange a date. Now you understand what people mean when they talk about the throes of addiction. If you see him just one more time, you tell yourself, that will be it. One more fix will satisfy you, you tell yourself, even though you know you're fooling yourself.

And that's when the tiniest chink of light appears from an unexpected source. Bernie arrives into the tearoom and announces that she bumped into the "mad lad" on Dame Street. She's aiming her comments in your direction, and you're soaking up every word she says, while at the same time, you're pretending that you're listening to some other conversation. Andy has his sharp eyes upon you. One slip and he'll do his merciless impersonation. He once had the Phantom building a wooden artefact of Marcus in his bedroom.

"He said to say hello to you," Bernie says when she catches your attention.

"Who's that?"

"You've forgotten poor old Johnny already."

"Oh, Johnny," you say, struggling to maintain that look of indifference, while inside, everything has gone into a mad spin. "Has he found another job yet?"

Bernie laughs. "Yeah, in the circus."

The others laugh and the conversation steers away out of your

147

control. The moment slips from your grasp. Andy is doing the part of Johnny as a lion-tamer and Jim Carney and Ronnie Burke are the lions. To interrupt Andy in creative mode would be an error of gigantic proportions. Your left ear would be in danger of bursting into flames anytime you were absent from the tearoom theatre. So instead, once you discover that Bernie is going for a drink after work, you know what you have to do.

It's clear that your presence causes all the regular Friday night drinkers to perform a double-take. They're trying to remember what the occasion is, whose going-away booze-up is on tonight, since that's the only time they see you here. Ronnie Burke buys a large round of drinks and then, with his face set in that mould of sincere and serious conversationalist, designed, of course, to entice colleagues to remain on in the pub with him, he proceeds to tell a story about an incident which involved an acquaintance of his. This acquaintance was on his way into a pub in Dun Laoghaire when a young man asked him if he'd like to buy *An Phoblacht*, the republican newspaper. According to Ronnie, his acquaintance let fly verbally, calling the young man a murderer's accomplice and a fascist among other things. Three hours later, when his acquaintance left the pub, he was set upon by a group of thugs and beaten up.

Ronnie holds his palms out and shakes his head in concern, but he almost glows with the satisfaction of having related what he considers to be a top-notch anecdote. "Of course, there's no way anyone could link the two events, but..." Ronnie lifts his eyebrows, expels a rush of air through his nostrils, and contorts his face into a look which says, Who-are-they-trying-to-fool?. The group of listeners display their concern with little nods and tut-tutting sounds. Ronnie's true interests become obvious when he takes a split-second glance at his empty glass. But that's long enough for someone to ask him what he's drinking. To crown it all, Ronnie delays a moment, as though he's thinking of heading home to the family or something, and then he laughs, remembers aloud that it's Friday, and the way he says, "Ah sure, one more won't go amiss", he makes it sound like he's doing the drink-buyer a big favour. But

Ronnie isn't stupid, he must know that everyone realises what his real motives are.

So, to distract people's attention, he calls Andy over and says, "Andy, I hear you do a good mimic of me."

Andy is flummoxed. "I do?"

"Look at him, butter wouldn't melt."

To say that Andy is mortified would be an understatement.

"Go on, Andy, do it now," someone else urges.

"Yeah, go on Andy." Others join in the chorus of encouragement.

"Ronnie, there's nothing about you I could mimic." Andy the chancer is in diplomat mode.

"Ah, go on."

"I can't, Ronnie." Andy finally manages to squirm his way from Ronnie Burke's grip and he moves away at speed back to his group, no doubt to perform an imitation of Ronnie Burke asking him to do an imitation of himself.

As luck would have it, the timing mechanism on your bladder happens to coincide with that on Ronnie Burke's bladder. He's alone in the gents, standing at the long urinal, with one hand resting against the wall and with the other hand holding his dick out for all to see. It's obvious that he's proud of his member, so you make sure you don't give him the pleasure of sneaking a glance. Not that you'd want to anyway.

"This is one hell of a costly slash," he says, pissing away merrily, and despite your best intentions you find yourself uttering a sycophantic guffaw of laughter.

It would be so appealing just to nip into a cubicle, but you can hardly do that now. Decisions like that have to be made spontaneously. So you take up position a respectable distance away from Ronnie and prepare to relieve yourself. The pressure on your bladder is immense, but nothing comes out. Seconds pass. Still nothing. A psychological clamp has tightened around the exit from your bladder. The secret is not to think about it, but it's another matter carrying this off. After fifteen seconds or so Ronnie becomes aware of your plight, and he seems to take pleasure in increasing the pressure of his discharge.

"We're holding the future in our hands," he says, and again you laugh, and by sheer brute force you manage to discharge a squirt, the measliness of which you're certain didn't escape the attention of old beady-eye Ronnie.

The arrival of Joe Corcoran from the design department saves you from an extreme case of stage fright. He enters the toilet, hesitates a moment, then slips away into the sanctuary of a cubicle. Ronnie Burke catches your eye and smirks. You return the smirk. Those few moments of distraction had the effect of opening the invisible clamp, and something akin to the Niagara Falls is gushing out proudly from within you. The moment is made all the more pleasurable by the involuntary shiver that racks your insides. Now you're one of the boys, you can smirk about the wussie in the cubicle.

Moments later, Ronnie is at the hand-dryer and you are at a washbasin when, in the mirror, you spot the expression on Joe Corcoran's face upon his emergence from the cubicle. It's a look of uncertainty, of someone who senses that they have strayed into the wrong neighbourhood, a place they don't belong.

"Joe my man, those latest designs of yours are top-notch, absolutely top-notch."

Joe Corcoran turns crimson. "Thank you, Ronnie," he says, in a voice which puts you in mind of a husky woman speaking while she holds a hair-clip between her teeth.

"I have to hand it to you gay lads, you really have the edge when it comes to detail," Ronnie Burke says.

"Would you say so?" As is his wont, Joe Corcoran contorts his face into an exaggerated grimace which is supposed to convey wide-eyed wonder, but which you suspect is really a manifestation of years and years of insecurity. No one is going to convince you that someone as effeminate as Joe had an easy time at the boys' school he attended.

"You've got the Midas touch, you lads have."

"Thank you, Ronnie."

And with that Joe Corcoran exits the toilet, and Ronnie Burke waits until the outside door closes before he does an imitation of

Joe Corcoran's dainty voice. "I really ought to be going to the ladies' toilet," he says, sucking his cheeks in to pout, and letting both his wrists hang limp. Not satisfied with this, he tiptoes his way to the cubicle Joe had occupied, pushes the door open and says, "Surprise, surprise, he was alone in there." Ronnie then proceeds to tell you that most queers can only function sexually in toilets, that they associate the smell of urine with turn-on. You're tempted to ask him how he knows this, but you don't. Instead you remark that Joe Corcoran doesn't have a wife waiting to interrogate him when he gets home. This changes the shade of Ronnie's complexion. His wife has recently threatened to leave him. How it took her so long to issue these threats you'll never know.

It makes you feel like you've done your little bit for the cause of Joe Corcoran, or Design Joe as he is affectionately known. In his mid-thirties, he makes no bones about his sexual orientation. If the truth be known though, he really has no choice in the matter. "As gay as Christmas" is how you've heard various people describe him in his absence. Sometimes you wonder what it would be like to be as effeminate as Joe, if you had all the mannerisms that screamed out the message. Schooldays would have been a major hassle, but after that, your life probably would have been a lot less complicated. If your persuasion was so patently obvious, there'd be no point in hiding from the truth and driving yourself insane.

Before you leave the bathroom, Ronnie Burke says, "Hey, remember Eileen?", and you nod. Ronnie points to the first cubicle. "One night, I fucked her in there till her ears popped," he says and guffaws loudly. Your initial reaction has him immediately on the defensive. He realises that he's said something he probably ought not to have. "Total nympho, she practically raped me," he adds, with no guffaw. Now you react with neutral ambivalence, leaving him with the option of believing that you believe him. But the puzzle behind Eileen's mysterious departure has been solved. Her silence had been bought. It's a sobering reminder of what lies behind the façade. But once again you've succeeded in unsettling Ronnie Boy. How could you explain to him that, as far as you can see, one of the major positive features about being married is that you no longer have to join him and his motley crew on their tedious Friday night "skirt chasing" exploits? Those long, boozy nights which are peppered with a steady misogynistic stream of derogatory and juvenile references to female bodily parts, particularly their private parts. They call the women horrors and ugly dogs while never appearing to see what stares back at them in the mirror. Any objective observer would definitely conclude that they didn't really like these women. This is the irony, that they spend so much of their time trying to be with women who they don't really like. And it is also ironic that some of the lads actually admire you for your apparent loyalty to Anne, while others, mostly the married ones like Ronnie Boy, are more than likely relieved that you no longer tag along, casting what they perceive as your judgmental eyes upon them.

Back in the bar, you eventually manage to isolate Bernie and since you've lowered five pints by this stage, you're far more relaxed in asking her about the details of her encounter with Johnny. She jokes about her cheque for £9,999,999 and you consider turning her upside down, holding her by the ankles and shaking the information out of her. But you have to retain control, pretend that you find her plans on how she's going to spend the imaginary money just riveting. When she eventually tells you that she thought she heard Johnny say that he was going drinking in town tonight, you want to whisk her up off the ground and hug her. Instead you buy her another drink. How you'd love to be able to ask her what he was wearing, what exactly he said about you and, more importantly, how he looked when he mentioned your name. But your resolve has weakened. The clock is edging its way towards ten, and you need a fix so bad you'd run barefoot over hot coals to get to see him. When you make the mistake of announcing your departure, Ronnie Burke lunges forward and rugby-tackles you in front of a group of bemused strangers. And, without a second thought, you use Anne's pregnancy as the excuse to get him to untangle himself from your midriff. How low will you stoop? But there's no doubting it, just to think about the new baby boosts the spirits.

The show is on the road. A sprint down the length of Grafton Street with your hands jammed into your coat pockets to keep the change from jangling. This is not the time to have the beggar population of Dublin chasing after you with their cardboard boxes and their paper cups. A fleeting glimpse of your reflection in a shop window confirms the suspicion that you don't look anything like the kindly image of yourself which you conjure up at times like this. Halfway up the street you pass the spot where you saw the demented-looking beggar boy, but he's not around tonight. "Maybe he's dead," you say aloud to yourself, and it doesn't cause you a scintilla of bother. Nothing else matters now. "Or maybe he's a millionaire," you mutter, appreciating the attraction of happy Hollywood endings. If someone were to walk up to you, tap your shoulder and say, "Hey, the world's going to end in half an hour", you'd tell them that you can't stop right now, that you've got more important matters to attend to.

The moment the pub comes into view your heart begins to thump. This is a foolish thing to do but you can't stop yourself. You imagine the entire pub ridiculing you behind your back: Oh God, would you look who it is. Does he ever give up? But still you can't stop yourself. It's the not knowing that's driving you insane.

Just inside the door, you encounter one of his young dork friends sitting alone on the stairs nursing an insipid-looking pint. He's pleased to see you, he thinks he's found someone to drink with. "He's not here, he left hours ago, he says with a discernible slur in his voice, and you simply nod like this means little to you. But it worries you. Is it so obvious to everyone that you only came to this pub to see him? And then, in another way, it pleases you that people acknowledge that there is something between you.

"Bit packed," you say, grimacing as though you'd tasted something sour.

"It's all right upstairs," he says.

"Think I'll give it a miss." You leave him alone with his flat pint and his disappointed expression.

It's 10.10pm when you pull out onto the main road, almost

convincing yourself that the drink-driving roadblocks won't be mounted for at least another half-hour. This is a mad thing you are doing, but you have to see him, no matter what. It's a relatively clear drive out to the suburbs, and the car park attendant at his local waves to you and assures you that he'll take special care of your motor. You smile, mutter something incomprehensible and hurry into the pub. Every head seems to look around when you step inside, and then turn away again in disappointment or relief. Everyone seems to be waiting for someone. And you're waiting to hear him shout your name, or even to sneak up behind you, cover your eyes and say, Guess who?

One of his friends from the Wexford weekend, whose name you can't remember, catches your eye and nods. He's with his girlfriend, who was also down in Wexford, and her name also eludes you.

"Hiya, Paul."

"How's the Wexford mob?" You feel a little like Ronnie Burke the way you stumble your way towards their table, exuding that cordial look of sincerity. Like Ronnie, it's important that you don't blurt out what you really want until the right moment. They offer to buy you a drink and you refuse it. That's the difference between yourself and Ronnie Boy. He's focused on his drink, you're focused on your man.

"Hey, is Johnny about?" The words blurt out in a most uncasual manner.

"No, not tonight," the fellow says, his smile vanishing because he now realises that you really have no interest in talking with them aside from asking about Johnny. The only way that you'd stay in their company now is if they suddenly began to tell the most wonderful anecdotes about Johnny. This might ease the craving somewhat, but it's doubtful that it would satisfy you completely.

"Okay thanks, have to dash."

You leave them in a nonplussed state. You are a man with a mission, racing against time.

It's 10.40pm when you pull up outside his house. It's hardly a proper hour to call for someone but, along with your jacket, your

154

decorum has been slung onto the backseat. You just walk up that driveway and press that doorbell. His younger sister answers and, oddly enough, she doesn't appear in the least bit surprised to see you.

"Hi Christine, is Johnny in?"

She's chuffed that you remember her name.

"He's gone to the Burlington with some friend of his who's home from England," she says in her vague way and you want to hug her.

"Thanks." You look at your watch. "Better get the skids on."

"Rachel's her name."

"Oh right, Rachel." You give the impression you know who this Rachel is.

"See yah." She waits until you reach your car before she shuts the door. Maybe she's got a crush on you. That would be something. You could get a divorce, marry her, and then you'd be his brother-in-law. That'd certainly keep him attached to your apron strings, and keep you from chasing around the city like some sort of demented lunatic.

It's panic on the streets of Dublin. The journey back into town is a reckless one. Red lights are crashed, startled pedestrians have to move fast, major pileups are avoided by the narrowest of margins. The 520i is a blur. It ends with you parking in a flowerbed in an unlit section of the hotel's crammed car park. It's 10.55pm when you fix your tie, pat your hair into place, spray your breath, and stroll nonchalantly into the crowded public bar, where close to half the population of Dublin seem to have amassed. It's like an obstacle course, people cast reproachful glances at you, resenting your efforts to search the bar. I have to find him, you feel like roaring at the obstinate ones who won't budge out of your way. A good knee in the nuts is what they're asking for. The dense fog of smoke makes your eyes water. He's going to think you were crying, and if you don't find him soon, you could well be. A surge of panic rises within you. You feel like a child who has wandered out of his depth in the swimming pool. To calm the nerves you buy a pint and swallow a long gulp to make it look like you've been here awhile.

And then you see him, and you imagine you hear the tension leave your system with the hissing sound of hydraulic brakes. Everything is all right, there he is, a little drunk, sitting with a friend, enjoying a laugh and a joke, and no doubt missing you. But the friend is not female. He has spun a yarn. But why? And who is this friend?

He's utterly flummoxed when he sees you steering a path towards their table. The smile vanishes to be replaced by what looks like the uneasy gaze of someone who suspects that they are being stalked. Your spirits sink but you can't let it show. You have a decision to make: do you say that you're here with friends and that you just happened upon him by chance? If you do, you're relying on four people not mentioning your mad exploits – his sister, his geek friend in the pub and the couple who were in Wexford. It's too risky. The parameters of whatever story you invent would have to be stretched between the city centre, his local pub, and his house, all within thirty minutes of one another. Maybe you could claim the gift of bi-location. It might impress him, but your guess is that it's best to say nothing unless he asks.

"It's all right, I've just heard that the world isn't going to end at midnight." You direct the comment at him, touching what you hope to be the correct note of fun. None of your inner turmoil must show. Uninvited, you pull up a stool and sit down opposite them.

He stares at you. The person sitting alongside him stares at you. The entire bar seems to be staring at you. Eventually, he performs the introductions.

"Derek, this is Paul. Paul, Derek."

You exchange a weak, reluctant handshake with Derek, whom you take an instant green-eyed dislike to.

"He's the one who gave me the bullet."

You register dutiful playful protest.

"Oh, you're the married man?" Derek blurts.

You look at Johnny and he shrugs. But what he doesn't know is that you're experiencing a little rush of joy. If he's been talking about you, it's not all doom and gloom. But this little rush stutters to an abrupt halt when you notice that their feet are touching, an observation which very nearly causes you to spit out your drink. You know you ought not to, but you can't help yourself instinctively casting a disapproving glance at Johnny.

"It's all right, I won't say a word," Derek says, winking with mock slyness, and now your dislike turns to burning hatred. Instinctively, you zone in on his weakest feature, his oversized nose. Beaker Nose, you name him, conveniently ignoring the fact that if an independent jury were to compare the two of you in the looks department, young Beaker Nose would sweep the boards. There's such a strong urge welling up inside you, an urge to tell him to buzz off, to go and jump off a high building and see if he can fly, and he seems to sense this too, because moments later he stands up and heads off to buy cigarettes.

"Want me to go with you?" Johnny whispers, playfully tugging at his sleeve, and you want to go outside and howl up at the moon.

And so the two of you are left alone, and he's clearly more uneasy than ever. Despite your best intentions not to mention Beaker Nose, you immediately ask who he is and he tells you that he met him in town.

"Where?"

"In town," he whispers, his eyes flickering back and forth, his way of conveying a wariness of eavesdroppers.

"Where in town?" you persist, even though you know full well where they met. And when he tells you that he went to a gay bar, you feel utterly betrayed. It's desolation row. This was something you had planned to do together. And he went in there without you and, worse still, he met someone.

He moves closer to you and speaks in a whisper. "Look Paul, it's over between us."

The din all around you seems to suddenly go quiet. Your body goes numb. His eyes are staring at you, his lips are moist with drink.

"I'm sorry I lied, I just – "

He cuts in, "It has nothing to do with you lying. Believe me, I understand why you did. But...it's just...Listen, you have a young child, and a wife you're obviously fond of, you'd be mad to throw all of that away. Absolutely bonkers."

The words are tearing you asunder. It's obviously his nice way of telling you it's over, but you don't want to hear it that way. Love is touching hearts, you want to say to him, you touched mine, and surely I touched yours.

"I mean, you're obviously bisexual or whatever. Anyway, whatever you are, you're not as gay as I am, and if you want to know the truth, I'd love to be straight. Life would be so much easier. Like, I'd love to have kids and that, and not have to put up with all the pretence. But I'm not, so I've got to get on with things. But with you, it's different, you have a choice..."

"I don't," you mutter.

"Ah, you're only saying that."

"I love you."

Judging by the way he flinches and glances to his right, you're speaking too loud. The eavesdroppers are closing in like a shoal of blood-frenzied piranhas.

"Let's talk about it some other time," he says, with a note of finality. He's seen Derek fighting his way back through the crowd. You glance to your left and see a woman looking at you. She immediately turns away, her face burning with an eavesdropper's guilt.

Desperation takes a stranglehold. There is only one path open to you now, and that's Beaker Nose. You turn your attention on him, lure him into a one-to-one conversation with your back half-turned to Johnny, purposely excluding him. You leave no gaps in the conversation, and anytime Johnny tries to force his way in, you frown at him the way you might at a child for speaking out of turn. It transpires that Derek has been living in London for the past two years, and that he has recently returned to Dublin. Your head goes dizzy when he reveals that he has an apartment. All you can think of is that the two of them have a place to go to. A knocking shop. It's too much to take, so you blank it out of your mind and listen to him go on about the interviews he's been to in his search for a job in advertising.

"Maybe you could find him a job," Johnny says, and you don't even turn to look at him. Surely he realises that if you find this clown a job it will be somewhere in the further reaches of Outer Mongolia. Instead, you press on, talking about the jobs market, saying things you've said a thousand times before, which is just as well, because you are certainly short on concentration here. Half your brain is taken up with trying to visualise this apartment of his, while the other half is taken up with schemes and tactics. And when Johnny goes off to the loo, you tell Derek he's mad coming back to Ireland, that London is the place to be. It's a pathetic attempt, but you are desperate.

At closing time, they decide that they're going to the hotel's nightclub. Johnny asks you to come along, but you've never heard such a half-hearted offer. It's ten pounds in and they're counting their pennies. A long queue has already formed outside. "It'd be worth your while holding a toy pistol to the nightsafe-man's head," Derek says, and you are tempted to encourage him to try this. What if you pulled out your wallet and offered him the contents, On the condition that he never sees Johnny again. And what the hell are they going to do in a heterosexuals' nightclub anyway? Dance together? Hold hands under the table? You can't help comparing your relationship with theirs. They're the same age, so Johnny can't act the kid the way he did with you. And he likes acting the kid, having attention lavished upon him, having tributes showered upon him, being adored. He's definitely more subdued. So maybe all is not lost. But then they crack a private joke about being one of the zombies walking through Ranelagh, carrying a plastic bag containing a carton of milk and a loaf of bread. They roar with laughter at something you are not part of and it's painfully difficult to pretend that it means nothing to you.

You feel numb, constricted, claustrophobic, disorientated, like you're running down a long, dark tunnel. There's no way you can stay here any longer. Johnny comes out to the car park with you and advises you to take a taxi.

"I hope I crash," you say, with all the heartfelt intensity of a lovelorn teenager.

He says nothing. He just looks at you like he doesn't really understand you. And this is not surprising since he's only ever seen your happy jolly side. All you are doing is probably ensuring that you'll never get back together again, but you can't stop yourself. You want to plead with him to take a lift home with you, just like the old days. You could drive to the disused railway bridge to look at the stars. If he wanted to, you could drive to the airport and fly to the sun that night. There's a gold credit card in your pocket.

"How come you're here anyway?"

It's time for some honesty.

"To see you."

He laughs. "You're mad."

"I know."

His laughter fades. "Oh shit, I wish you didn't feel this way."

Maybe now's the time to fall down on your knees and beg him to come home with you. Tell him that you can't endure life without him.

But then, the sight of that git Derek emerging through the revolving door like he's Brad Pitt or someone, causes you to experience such a sharp stab of intense hatred, you realise you better leave before you really lose control. You rev the big engine with maximum noise, the skidding tyres send little flowers flying everywhere, and you roar out of the car park like someone with a deathwish. Let him worry about you ending up entangled in a mesh of chrome and plastic. Hopefully, it will spoil his night.

How you actually get home, you'll never know. The drive is a haze of anguished what-ifs and blurred headlights. Tight Jeans, the baby-sitter, is sitting at the kitchen table, performing a fair impression of someone in the midst of deep concentration on her school textbooks. But there's a definite whiff of passion about, and you get the distinct impression that some hot-blooded young buck has recently bolted out through the back door and is now probably scaling the walls of Legoland, ripping his favourite jeans on barbed wire, setting off timer-lights, causing dogs to go into frenzies and prompting neighbourhood shotguns to be loaded up.

Anne is out at her creative writers' group meeting. She

doesn't know it, but her hubby could give her something really creative to write about. You pay the baby-sitter, and because you don't speak to her, you suspect that she leaves the house with the notion that you'd like to get the knickers off her. No doubt she's read about that sort of thing in Anne's stash of magazines. You wonder how she'd react if you tell her that nothing could be further from your thoughts.

"Lia is fast asleep," she says, and you simply nod and shut the door.

It's like you are sleepwalking. Your vision is blurred, your mouth is parched. A slow clock ticks inside your head, too slow. The soft ticks remind you of the rise and fall of telephone wires you used to watch as a kid, while travelling in the car. The group wedding photo in the bedroom seems to expand and grow to gigantic proportions. All those people whose names elude you. Their faces expand and their mouths spout illegible bubbles of dialogue. The picture springs to life, and those long-forgotten guests are ridiculing you, mocking you. They no longer need the bubbles of dialogue, they can talk and shout now. There are voices everywhere, disembodied voices. Some howling, some speaking in whispers, others speaking gibberish. The past and present are mingling. An orchestra is playing somewhere in your head, a violin holds a long note. Control is slipping. You pin your hands to the sides of your head and press hard in a vain attempt to hold it all together.

You lie down and the world stops spinning. A deep chasm seems to open up inside your head, filled with the blackest of black shadows. Demons have been released. You fall deeper and deeper into the chasm. You are shaking uncontrollably, salty tears are trickling down the side of your face, into your ears, down onto your neck. You have never felt so low. The years of holding back are in those tears. There's no one you can talk to. Six billion people on this earth and not one you can tell. Your life has been built on quicksand. The entire fabricated structure is sinking now. All those false certainties are slipping into the gurgling mud. He's all you care about, nothing else matters. You've glimpsed paradise, and now you feel utterly alone. Cold, numb, paralysed, alone. There's a deep nothingness inside you. It's like your sanity is being pulled in several directions at the one time. Your control is certainly slipping now and there's nothing you can do about it. What's going to happen? Are you going insane? Perhaps it would be better than this blackness, this awful emptiness.

You hear the click of a switch, and an indeterminate length of time seems to drag past before you're aware that the light is on.

"Paul?"

Anne's voice is lost in a dense fog. It's proving difficult to focus, but she's there beside you. For how long, you can't tell.

"Paul. What's wrong?"

She's kneeling by your side, she's flustered, she's asking so many questions. Is it work? Is it medical? Are you drunk? Speak to me. You try to speak but there's a constriction the size of a football lodged in your throat.

The words of an old song keep repeating themselves like a mantra in your head. "Better stop sobbing now, better stop sobbing now." Anne is shouting now. She's slapping your face and shaking you. "Have you taken pills?" she keeps asking, but all you want to hear is the voice singing the stop sobbing song. The insides of your head are a winding catacomb of tunnels meandering off in different directions. You're standing at a cross-roads. The choice appears to be yours. One of these tunnels leads to madness and if you wander off down that tunnel, you are in a spot of bother. The front door to your sanity is flapping. Gentle voices are urging you to go that way, that there's nothing to worry about. Other voices are laughing mercilessly. It sounds like they're coming through an echo-chamber. A growling, fire-breathing demon would be better than this. It gets so frightening you attempt to say comforting prayers from your childhood, but you can't remember the words. A magnet seems to be tugging you deeper into the abyss.

It's quiet now. You prise your eyes open. The room is empty. A car passes outside and the headlights send shadows chasing across the ceiling. Maybe you are in control again, maybe the worst has passed. But when you close your eyes, his voice comes into your head and he's talking to Beaker Nose. They're in a dingy bedsit, lying naked together on a bed, doing all the things you and him once did together. Mocking laughter mingles with the sound of footsteps running through the tunnel of madness. Then it all goes quiet. The footsteps are still running but they make no sound now. It's the eerie calm before the storm. The roar rumbles to life somewhere in the depths of that tunnel of madness. It's like a ball of fire ripping its way along a trail of paraffin, burning through your head, down to your lungs and up again, trundling through your throat, clearing all in its path, freeing all constrictions, before it bursts forth from your mouth, exploding out into the dark night. It's like a train emerging from a tunnel. It goes on and on. A howl that shakes the world to its very core.

Far away, you hear the baby screaming, you hear footsteps running. Closer, you hear people's voices and someone is saying your name. A cold jab of a needle and that's it. Out for the count. Lights out. Voices cheering. Euphoria. Bright, bright lights.

Chapter Ten

A week in space follows, a medication-induced drowsiness. Freed from the straitjacket of reality, your dreams nudge their way into the strangest territories. Like way back into your childhood, to the very first friends you had in primary school, where you relive moments of absolute vivid happiness. At other times, crazy delirious thoughts swirl around in your head the same way they do during a high fever. But you know that the black clouds are still lurking there somewhere in the nether regions of your mind like a menacing gang of corner boys, hanging around, just waiting for the opportunity to return. What's he got to be depressed about? you can almost hear people thinking. But you can't get out of bed, you can't budge. It's almost as if you're afraid that the slightest movement will allow the corner boys to make their charge for the front seats.

One time you seem to wake up, and you're lying in the bed you slept in during your youth. There's someone in the bed beside you, concealed beneath the blankets. Next thing you know, your mother's standing there, a breakfast tray in her hand. You little scamp, she says, who's that you've got hidden under the blankets? Is this your friend Johnny? And with that Johnny's head pops out, that impish grin lining his features. Paul's forever talking about you, your mother says to him, and his eyes twinkle on a merry dance. D'you like Johnny? you ask your mother, but she just smiles that elusive smile of hers and says, Oh now, that'd be telling. And who walks into the room but Anne and the baby. You squint to make out the shadows near the door. It looks like the crowd from work. And like a football match official, Bob is telling them all to keep back behind an invisible line. Then that mad thumping beat of a nightclub starts up, the bedroom changes into a dancefloor and there's old Beaker Nose dancing with Johnny, so you close your eyes and everything goes black. Depression black.

Gradually, you become aware of your surroundings. It seems as though every get-well-soon card ever printed is propped up around your bed. The hospital smells of boiled vegetables and cleansing materials. The nurses regularly ask you your name, your address, the name of the hospital, who the president of Ireland is, and, of course, what day, month and year it is.

There are patients here who really are insane. They wander around with crazy, wide-eyed, preoccupied expressions, chatting away to themselves, seeing no one else. It surprises you how quickly you become institutionalised. Meals and cups of tea take on major significance. There's a hospital radio station, and you join the saner of your fellow inmates in a competition to see who can request the least suitable song. These include such songs as, "If You Leave Me Now", "The First Cut Is The Deepest", "Help Me Make It Through The Night", "Suicide Is Painless", "Killing Me Softly", and "anything by Madness". It's the only way to survive. One of these inmates tells you that he filled in "atheist" in the space marked "Patient's religion" on his hospital admissions form and, that same day, two nuns arrived at his bedside, pointed to the word atheist on his admission form, and asked him what this nonsense was all about.

Visitors begin to arrive: Anne first, then a trickle of close friends, and then a flood. Every time the door opens you wait for his face to appear, but it never does. The ward soon resembles a pedestrian thoroughfare. People seem to have nothing better to do than hang around hospital beds. They make you feel like the failure you don't want to be. It's enough to lapse anyone back into depression. People from work visit, including Kevin Daniels who tells you that God sends his regards. If any of the doctors had overheard him say that, they would have clamped a straitjacket on him before he had time to draw his next breath. Daniels relates a story he heard Spike Milligan tell on television. One time, Spike had to get electric shock treatment for his depression. They carried out the treatment in Spike's home and Spike felt great after. However, a month later, when he received his electricity bill, the amount he owed caused him to be more depressed than he was before. As soon as he's finished, Daniels realises it's a story he shouldn't really have told. But you pat him on the shoulder and he feels okay again.

Many of those people from the group wedding photo also come to visit. These are your college contemporaries, and among the males you're quite certain that you detect the silent surge of satisfaction they secretly experience from a competitor's perceived weakness or failure. Not that they wish you any harm, but it's always nice to know that there's someone worse off than yourself. No one understands this better than your good self. But, in others respects, you scare the hell out of them. This place scares the hell out of them. You sense it behind their heavy-handed words of encouragement. They all know that they could be next.

There are times when you feel so low you are sure you can take no more. Once they let you out of this place, you decide, you will end it all. Jump into the sea off the end of Dun Laoghaire pier one night and they'll fish your body out three weeks later. And, ironically, making these plans for the saddest journey lifts your spirits. It's like a light at the end of a dark tunnel. An escape. Deep down, you know you'd never have the nerve, but it's comforting to think about it.

After a week, the hospital staff decide that you've lazed about long enough taking up scarce resources. So a female psychiatrist called Dr Kelly is assigned to your case and you are actually brought to her office in a wheelchair. The young nurse pushing you speaks to you in that loud voice people reserve for the elderly, for children and for the insane. She gives you a funny look when you say, "It's just like travelling in a wheelbarrow." She answers, "It certainly is, Mr Cullen, it's just like travelling in a wheelbarrow," in her booming voice, which you imagine can't be too good for the patients in nearby wards, especially not for the ones who hear voices in their heads. Talk about getting a different perspective on the world. It's like riding in the sidecars they had on old-fashioned motorbikes. If you were so inclined, you could easily burrow your head down into your shoulder and sneak a look up a dress or two.

Dr Kelly takes a few minutes to browse through your file and you feel like you're back at school. It's a pleasant feeling to entrust yourself to someone else's care. You're the helpless child, she's the nice mammy who will make everything better. She's around five years your senior and she sits with her back to the window, but somehow you doubt that it's to admire your eyes. This thought causes your memory to flash up the image of the first day Johnny sat in your office. Those blue eyes. This, in turn, jolts you somewhere inside and triggers the panicky fear that the corner boy shadows are on the march again. You hear Dr Kelly say that you're suffering from a severe case of depression. So, after the initial formalities and careful tiptoeing, she assures you that anything you say will go no further than this room, and you decide that you can trust this Dr Kelly. You tell her that you're in love with someone other than your wife and that's what's caused all the problems.

Whatever sympathy she had for you evaporates there and then, like a morning mist on a scorching hot day. It's solidarity against the big, bad oppressor. No doubt she's thinking, This clown's off getting his jollies behind his wife's back and now that he's been dumped he's feeling sorry for himself. How sad. What a pity. He expects sympathy. A good knee in the goolies will sort him out.

"And where did you meet her?" she asks, jotting down notes on a pad, more than likely to avoid having to look at you.

"It isn't a her."

"Oh?"

This shifts everything. There's nothing like a dramatic revelation to alter people's perceptions and attitudes. Her stern expression vanishes to be replaced by an intelligent look of fascination. It's almost like she's saying, Great, an interesting case for a change. It's tempting to really get her going by telling her that it's a sheep or something, but you don't. You oblige by giving her the whole Johnny saga, how you bent professional ethics to give him the job, the weekend in Wexford, the events up on the disused railway bridge, the escapades in his house that Saturday afternoon, and the lies, the lies, the lies. The week on medication has provided you with a layer of protection. It's possible to talk about him without feeling that your heart is being ripped to shreds. The doc lets you go so far before she asks you to go back in time.

You begin to untangle the web of lies. Everything comes out, and as it does you feel your sanity creeping back to a state of relative equilibrium. Mr Calm-and-Control is being hoisted back up onto his throne wearing a new outfit. But you're telling her all sorts of crazy things, things you didn't know were still knocking about inside that head of yours. You tell her how, around puberty, you used to look up words like "homosexual" in the dictionary for a thrill. You tell her about the openly gay DJ on a pirate radio station you used to secretly listen to when you were about fifteen. How his exuberant voice had you thrilled skinny, simply because you knew that he was gay. It was like he was sending signals out to you. He was the only one who made sense. As well as playing the right music, he talked openly about his world, the places in town he went to, his friends. It was so exhilarating, you tell her, you often expected the radio to burst into flames.

"That's because of the lack of role models," she says.

But you don't tell her that you used to turn the radio volume down whenever anyone was around, because you were afraid that they might ask, Why are you listening to that queer DJ? Are you a bender? Anyway, you sense that she's heard enough about the DJ, that she wants to hear something a little more juicy.

So you tell her about the dances you went to in your youth, and of how you couldn't wait for the damn things to finish up.

"I'm not saying I didn't enjoy myself, but it was the constant pressure of having to pretend that I was interested in girls."

"Yes, I imagine that must have been difficult."

"I even used to pretend I suffered from headaches."

Miracle of miracles, this remark results in the faintest of smiles. She isn't made of stone after all.

"But why did you continue with this pretence?"

You left yourself open for this one.

"I don't know, I got good at it...and things got less hectic as we all grew up...I mean the whole cattle-herd scene diminished somewhat...and besides, the alternative didn't appear too appealing."

She observes you through hooded eyelids, as if to say, What the hell do you know about the alternatives? But it's clear she wants to hear something even a little juicier.

So you tell her about the three major crushes you had as a youngster. Names, the type of guys they were, what you liked about them, what they looked like, the works. You even mention the songs from those periods that remind you of those secret crushes and how, whenever you hear these songs on the radio, even now, the memories still flood back with amazing lucidity. You were the original teenager in love with no one to tell. Of course, overshadowing all of this was the crushing homophobia of your schooldays, the ignorance, the fear of difference, the lack of compassion from quarters you might have expected it, the lack of anything apart from a DJ with a dainty voice. Almost every message you received was telling you that you were wrong, that you didn't fit in. Suicide was a comforting option to wallow in, in a childish way you believed that it would teach everyone a lesson. But you knew you'd never have the courage to go through with it, so you reasoned that it was probably exactly what the bigots would like you to do. A stubborn streak emerged in the face of adversity. It was either sink or swim. So you pulled down the shutters, bolted down the hatches, buttoned up your lips and existed. And, ironically, you became known as a bit of a womaniser because you swapped girlfriends frequently to avoid anything serious developing.

"But it's different nowadays," you say.

"Why d'you say that?"

"Well, I mean, it's more open and accepted."

"It can still be a big problem if you're young."

After this, she asks you about your family, and you feel like a bit of a fraud while you describe your happy childhood. There's no doubt, there ought to be a bit of abuse or neglect thrown in for good measure. But the doc knows her stuff. It isn't long before she has you talking about the family's expectations. The aunts and uncles asking about the girlfriend. Christmas, debs dances, football club dinner dances, weddings, anniversaries, birthday parties, all the events to which you were expected to drag a female along with you. The fast-flowing rapids which were hurtling you towards that engagement ring, the big wedding, the babies.

"What if you had brought along a boyfriend?"

You erupt into spontaneous laughter. A hoarse, honking noise which sounds like a sea lion. She remains stony-faced, watching you as though you are some sort of imbecile. She waits until you stop before she speaks again.

"With time people would have grown to accept it."

Again, you laugh. "It isn't even worth thinking about."

Her eyebrows flicker, like she's met hoards of blokes who drag the boyfriend along with them on family outings. "Well, wouldn't it have been easier then to have gone on your own to these functions?"

"Probably, but I didn't want to be considered...you know, a loner." You lower your head and smile.

"You mean you didn't want people to think that you couldn't pull a woman."

You shrug, but the give-away flush rises to your cheeks.

"What you've done is adopt a lifestyle which is not innate to you and when we do this, sooner or later, we discover that nature cannot be forced."

For some reason, you think of the elderly man who you witnessed miscalculating the turn into his driveway, and how he subsequently tried to ram his car through the pillar.

In response, you start to talk about the alternative lifestyles, the life of the next thrill. You get into the sleaze factor. The men who slip into public toilets and don't re-emerge, the midnight cruisers on the seafront, the muscle-builders in the leisure centre, the ones who speak and act like Design Joe. Are you really telling her this? Seems like you are. Seems like you're trying to impress her. Let her know that you're aware of these subcultures, give the impression that you're a man of the world. A frown has crept over her face, so you change tack and tell her that this world never appealed to you because of the lack of permanence, the lack of self-dignity. She shows no obvious sign of interest. Maybe she's fallen asleep. Maybe she's heard this story hundreds of times before. Or maybe she's guessed the truth, that you never dipped into the "alternative lifestyle" simply because you just never had the nerve.

She deflates you by reminding you that you said your love for Johnny was stronger than any love you had ever experienced, that nothing could ever compare to it again. She's got you there. So, once again you change tack and tell her that you have your career to think about. That the business world isn't the sort of world in which you want to be branded as gay.. To make your point, you tell her that if she was an openly gay doctor who discovered a cure for cancer, people would know her as the gay cancer-curer.

"So?" she says.

"Well, they'd say it in a derogatory sort of way."

She shrugs. "Not if they had cancer, they wouldn't."

There's no flies on this doc.

But her interest level perks up noticeably when you attempt to explain how you think you are actually still in love with Anne. How she's the anchor in your life, your best friend, the one you talk to. Such lies. Dr K says nothing, she just sits there looking at you, disguising any scepticism she may be experiencing. And the more you say, the clearer the picture of how you've wronged Anne becomes. What a bastard you've been. What an absolute bastard. It's too painful to let your thoughts wander down this track so instead you tell the doc that, in spite of your close physical relationship and your friendship, something always seemed to be just that little off-kilter between the two of you.

"Emotionally, things were never quite right, were they?"

You hesitate a moment, and then shake your head.

"That's to be expected."

"Do you encounter many others like me?"

She shifts in her seat. "Indeed we do," she says, and you feel like asking her to hand over the list of names and addresses, pronto. Then, she directs an almost benign look at you. "Have you ever thought of telling Anne?"

Now there's the question that earns her her crust. You can't help admiring the neat way she slid it in. That's what they call professionalism. You close your eyes, but then open them again, conscious that she's probably watching for even the slightest signs of madness.

"I have and I haven't, if you know what I mean."

She lifts her eyebrows to let you know that she considers this to be a crock of shit. "You should think about it," she says, before she stands up and gathers her notes together.

"When I married her I thought I'd change...Like, I thought by being with her I'd forget about the other attractions, that I'd be worn down by her charm."

Dr Kelly glances at her watch, she's had enough of you. And then, almost as an afterthought, she jots down a telephone number on a scrap of paper, hands it to you, and says, "This is the number of a gay married men's help-line."

"Thanks." You don't say it, but all you can think is that they're probably just a bunch of pansies who prance around someone's living-room in the nip. People who you'd have nothing in common with. Then you think, the brainwashing really has been thorough.

"It'd be a good opportunity to meet others like you."

"Yeah."

She's on the phone, arranging to have you taken back to your ward.

After this, everything changes. You've emptied out the garbage. The puss has oozed from the sore and a resolve of steel enters your heart. Never again, you decide, never again will you allow something like that to happen to you. You discharge yourself from the hospital and catch a taxi home. Anne is startled to see you, and you're certain she's keeping a wary eye upon you, and the kitchen table between you, as you pour yourself a cup of coffee. All she can think of saying is that the health insurance will cover the hospital costs. All you want to do is see the baby.

Chapter Eleven

There are strange looks cast in your direction on your first day back at work. No doubt the circular tearoom played host to numerous discussions on your plight. No doubt they all agreed they would pretend that there was nothing amiss if you strolled into the same tearoom wearing your shoes on your hands and your socks on your ears. And no doubt Andy often entertained them by entering the tearoom with a wild-eyed look, muttering to himself, and no doubt they all laughed until they felt guilty about laughing. After all, sad things can be the most amusing.

When you do walk into the tearoom, all conversation dies instantly. It's like you're the strict teacher entering a boisterous classroom. It's one of those situations where you want to say, Hey, I'm not mad, I'm the same old bollox you always knew. But if you do this, they will all say, Oh yes Paul, we know that, while privately, it will simply serve to confirm their worst suspicions.

Teresa screens all business calls from you for the entire first day, and gradually drip-feeds them through after that. She treats you as though you've suffered a bereavement, which makes you suspect that she's guessed what you've been through. On the way home one day, you're listening to a news report on the car radio about a man who shot dead another man because he stole his girlfriend. This fellow drove seventy miles across country, pointed a shotgun at his rival Casanova, and blew him away. You sit in the car in the driveway until the report finishes. A tiny gap appears in the net curtain and there's Anne, peeping out at you, more than likely wondering if you've gone nuts again. Even though you pretend not to have seen her, to alleviate her fears you tell her you were listening to an interesting item on the news. She asks what it was, and you tell her that it was the business news. Something about a company you have shares in.

Friends call you up and ask you to join them for lunch, but things are not the way they used to be. The scent of madness

173

makes them uneasy. There's a tentativeness. They don't say it, but they do think that you've gone a bit soft in the head. Flipped the lid, gone cuckoo, and you get the impression that they seem fearful that it might rub off on them in some way. That whatever aura or psychic vibrations you give off will seep through their skin, implant themselves in their genes and they will end up producing lunatic children.

On Dr Kelly's instructions, you don a tracksuit after work every day and take yourself off for a vigorous walk. To avoid the curious neighbourhood eyes, you drive to the relative anonymity of Killiney Hill and walk the twins peaks, sometimes taking in a trek down to the beach at Whiterock. On these walks, you are reminded of the times when your father took you up here as a child, and how you would shelter your eyes from the sun and see if you could see the coast of Wales. And then, on one of these walks, you think of the time Johnny said that your parents and his grandparents were probably arguing together up in heaven over which of you was the biggest ponce. This memory stops you in your tracks, and an approaching female jogger slows up apprehensively before she changes direction and increases her pace. You're only fooling yourself, there is no way on earth that you can go without seeing him. If it rains, you are reminded of a time it rained when he was with you. The same happens when it's sunny or windy. And aside from the weather, there are people, places, music, things he said, things you both laughed about, and even the smell of those cigarettes he smoked. Reminders lurk everywhere. What a perfect time it really was.

And, as though by telepathy, he phones that very same evening. He tells you that he called you at the office for a chat and was surprised to find that you had left early. This simple revelation sends your spirits skyrocketing. It turns out that Teresa gave him your home number, as well as telling him about your recent hospitalisation.

"So what were you in for?"

He listens sympathetically while you play down the mad card, and tell him that you were just feeling a little stressed.

"You? Stressed?" He is quite surprised. Amazingly, he doesn't appear to link it to himself in any way.

"Well, it was a little more than that."

"How d'you mean?"

There's the familiar awkward silence while you talk about the depression. Even saints like him aren't too keen on this sort of thing. Or maybe it has occurred to him what the cause was.

But when he suggests you meet himself and Derek for a pint in town that night, the rush you experience is something akin to the excitement of your first meeting.

"I'll just warn you, this ain't no ordinary pub," he says.

You laugh like an imbecile. If the pub was underwater, you'd invest in a submarine.

* * * *

The red sun is dropping from sight behind the mixed skyline of old-world rooftops and square office buildings. The warm doughy fragrance of fast food wafts through the narrow streets off Grafton Street. Young people spill out onto these streets, moving in different directions, beer glasses in hand. They shout back and forth, ignoring the cars that blow their horns at them. Clusters of them are already sitting on the pavements. Everyone is pumped up, ready to go. You feel like the odd man out, the madman in their midst. The old-timer out for a good time.

And by the time you get to George's Street, the anxiety that grips you is akin to those few seconds of hesitation before plunging into the sea for the first swim of the year. Standing across the road, you watch the pub. People don't drink on the street outside, but there's nothing really clandestine about the people going in. None of them appear to be attempting to conceal their identity the way you imagined they might. A passing youngster asks you if you, "Wanna buy some E?" You shake your head, but there's no doubt, this simple offer makes you feel young and invigorated. So you cross the street, comforting yourself with the knowledge that if anyone you know does see you, your recent visit to hospital is the ideal excuse. Anything is possible when people think you are crazy.

The doorman nods and, without any great trepidation, you

take your first step across the threshold into this other world. Inside it's a blur of music, chatter and faces. It's packed; finding him is going to be an ordeal. You wait for your breathing to settle before you move through the din. There are quick glances cast in your direction, but you no longer have the youthful appeal that might make these glances linger. Aside from the odd kissing, same-sex couple, it's so ordinary, you could be inside any old pub. Then you notice that there's an upstairs. That looks like the place to be, and that's where he'd go. Everyone can see you on the stairs, so you latch onto a group of people and mingle with them on the way up.

A cavern-style bar unfolds in front of you. Dark and smoky, with a Sistine Chapel-style mural of scantily-clad men adorning the ceiling, it oozes with possibilities. A tall, painted transvestite, who in other circumstances might be mistaken for a Zulu warrior, says "hi", and you say "hi" back, acting like this is all a regular occurrence. You push on, the trail of tranny perfume lingering in your nostrils. You wonder if this is the same transvestite who entertains on the business circuit. It would be quite something if 'she' were to say "Hi, Paulie Baby, fancy meeting you here," to you in front of Carney, Ronnie Burke and the rest of the executive crew.

You strike up a determined pose, squinting, furrowing your brow, trying to give the impression that you're a journalist researching an article on gay nightlife in the capital. You order a double tequila, "With ice," you say to the barman who seems to be making a point of avoiding unnecessary eye contact. Perhaps it's a clause in his contract. No flirting with the customers. Or perhaps it's because he's sick and tired of being eyeballed. You wipe the rim of your glass clean when no one is looking. Better safe than sorry. If you told certain people you had done this, they'd give out yards, but what's the betting they do the very same thing themselves. Survival is the key.

The taste of the tequila makes you wince and your eyes water. It's not a taste you appreciate, but it will provide the kick to get the night moving. While your eyes are adjusting to the dimness, you lean against the bar, trying to look bored. Up here, fashion seems to be the key. Neat dress is not essential. Fortunes have been spent by people trying to look downbeat, and fortunes have been spent by people trying to look upbeat. Heads are shaved to the point of uniformity. Men and women, all making statements. It's also dangle city. Earrings, nasal-rings, eyebrow-rings. Some of the dangling objects wouldn't look out of place in a modern art gallery. Two guys nearby are conducting a conversation, and both of them sound like they're imitating Design Joe. They speak the universal accent which smacks of new identity that stems from understandable low self-esteem. Like any night-club, it reeks of falseness, drips with tackiness, and here you are in the middle of it all, wishing you could meet someone who, like yourself, feels that they don't really belong here.

And then you see him. You're in the middle of picturing the reaction of the crowd in the tearoom if you arrived in with your head shaved, a chandelier dangling from your earlobe and your nose split by a decorative steel bar, when he falls into your line of vision. The surge of joy ebbs away when you see old Beaker Nose sitting alongside him with his hand resting on his thigh. A high-pitched sound escapes from your throat. A great sadness paralyses you. It's like someone has scooped your insides out and left a hollow void. If you were certain that you'd never be caught, you would murder Beaker Nose. Slip a kitchen knife into his gut. Spill all his belly slop out onto the floor. What would Dr Kelly say to that? She'd hardly encourage you to order another double tequila and knock it back in one. This manoeuvre earns a look from the non-looking barman. He's probably waiting for you to cause a disturbance. The alcohol molecules are cruising through your bloodstream, male molecules with male molecules, female molecules with female molecules, all holding hands while they dance their merry mad way towards your brain. The night is shifting gear. You're beginning to feel omnipotent, pumped up, ready to go. If you had a gun, you'd whip it out, fire a few shots in the air and shout "yahoo". And after that, plug a hole in old Beaker Nose.

And then it happens. Johnny spots you. The immediate signs are promising. He smiles, stands up, crosses the bar and hugs you.

It's too much. It's not all sympathy. Definitely not. There's a buzzing sound inside your head. It's either a simple case of hyperventilation, or else your emotional machinery is incapable of dealing with this overload.

"Never thought you'd come in."

"Would I..." You stop yourself. The golden rule is not to say anything that might drive him away.

"What's that you're drinking?" His hand touches yours.

"Lemonade and Ribena."

For a moment, he believes you. The stay in the hospital has altered even his perceptions of you.

He sniffs at your drink. "Yes, the lemonade and Ribenas smell excellent tonight," he says, and you can tell that he's delighted that you're back on song.

He leads you over to the table, where Derek vacates his seat. He switches to sit at the outside, where the passing throng continually bump against him. He's letting you sit beside Johnny. He even buys you another tequila. Maybe you'll hold back with the kitchen knife for the time being. There's an awkward silence, until Johnny turns to Beaker Nose and asks him to tell you the story about the fire in the sauna. While you listen, your face is fixed in a half-smile, but beneath that surface there's desolation. What sort of lifestyle has Johnny adopted? Gay saunas? But gradually you realise that neither of them were actually there, that it's just a story they heard. According to Beaker Nose, when the fire started the sauna-users spilled out onto the street in the early hours of the morning, clad only in miniature towels and flip-flops. The guards advised them that they had two choices; they could either wait around until the fire was put out to collect their clothes and belongings, by which time, the guards warned them, there were sure to be a posse of unscrupulous journalists and their sidekick cameramen sniffing around for a scoop; or alternatively, they could jump in a taxi and go home. The street was awash with men in white towels hailing down taxis.

It's difficult to concentrate. All you want to know is whether or not Johnny stays overnight in Beaker Nose's dingy bedsit, which he refers to as an apartment. And besides this, there's something of a mini-riot going on inside your head. It feels like a rowdy band of little tequila men have been let loose, whooping, shouting and turning somersaults. The music has been cranked up to a volume which renders conversation virtually impossible. Johnny's lips touch against your ear when he speaks to you. His raised voice causes your eardrums to vibrate. How you resist the urge to kiss him, you'll never know.

"C'mon," he says, "We'll find someone for you."

It's like a blow to the stomach. A knee in the balls. The wind is knocked out of you. A few simple words like that and you're nearly on your way back to Doc Kelly and her crew. The best thing for you to do would be to stand up, say goodbye, walk right on out of this place and break off all contact with him. But you can't. Not yet anyway. It's almost like you want him to hurt you, to kick your heart around the place until you finally get the message.

Next thing you know, you're following them through to the other side of the cavern-style bar and down a few steps to a dance-floor, where the music is so loud, your teeth vibrate.

"It's really jumping," Johnny shouts in your ear, and you nod, watching bubbles of psychedelic light wobble their way across a mirrored wall. Out on the dancefloor, the dancers move in a mesmerising trance between the pencil-beams of ultraviolet light which scour the place like searchlights over a prison exercise-yard.

Aside from him, there's no one else on the planet who could coax you out onto this dancefloor. You feel like a complete fool. These people can really dance, and you are moving about like a participant in a three-legged race. And to make matters worse, there's the added stress of constantly tracking him around the place and willing him to not to go too close to Derek. And, of course, all this activity has you soaked in an uncomfortable lather of sweat. Under your jeans, perspiration is trickling down your legs. This reminds you of one hot, humid, summer day in New York City when the subway you were travelling on broke down somewhere deep in the bowels of the city. The air-conditioning went off and the sweat poured. It ranks as one of the most uncomfortable moments in your life, and this is running a close second, but this is supposed to be fun.

And as though to mark the occasion, the strobe lights come on, the dentist-drill dance music steps up a beat, clouds of dry ice waft out from somewhere, and everyone seems to be moving in slow motion, like a succession of black-and-white snapshots. You let yourself go a little, convinced that your unique style of dancing isn't quite so noticeable under the strobes. Life is too short for such concerns. These pulsating rhythms could trap even the likes of you in their hypnotic spell. And with the assistance of the tequila, you have very nearly achieved a neutral state of not caring, until you spot three guys on the edge of the dancefloor, watching you, and clearly deriving great mirth from your performance. It's time to tone down the Big Bird imitation and wiggle and shake your way after Johnny through the forest of bodies, way back into the interiors of the nightclub.

You lose sight of him momentarily and panic sets in. People are bumped out of your way. There's no doubt, you would trample over pensioners to be near him. When you do locate him, a surge of hope rises up within you. There's no sight of Beaker Snot. Maybe he's given him the flick. The two of you are alone. You tap him on the shoulder to make it appear like you just happened to be in the neighbourhood. He's sniffing from a small bottle of poppers. This saddens you. It's another move away from you. He thrusts the small bottle into your hand and tells you to try it.

"It's poppers," he says, and you act like you are shocked.

Hesitant, you take a precautionary sniff. There's no discernible effect. You attempt to convey this bit of news, but his eyes are like glazed glass. You might as well be talking to the bottle. He's in another world and you want to join him there. "Check out the moonbeams," is what he appears to say, and you gather that he's away in another galaxy now. But you will look after him, that's your purpose on this earth. The latest dance number on the turntable has one lyric, and as far as you can make out, it's "Give me love". The female vocalist sounds pretty frantic about being given love. Her voice hits the note of pure angst that so appeals to the young, and to the heartbroken like yourself. So, with the reckless exhilaration of love, you pin the small bottle to both nostrils in turn and sniff the contents like there's no tomorrow. You're slipping into a morass of drug addiction, but you don't care. Euphoria is the name of the game. The tequila men are on the rampage. The two of you are dancing. People around you are jerking about like someone had slipped ice-cubes down the back of their T-shirts. The night is lifting into orbit.

It takes a few moments for the effect to manifest itself. You touch your neck and feel the forceful thump of the artery. A pressure cooker is firing up inside you. Your blood-pressure rockets, your knees buckle, your heart seems to be ripping through the fabric of your fashionable shirt. Even the rowdy tequila men have been caught unawares; it feels like they've been left hanging from the chandeliers inside your skull. The tinsel world has been shattered. It's a struggle to reach the edge of the dancefloor, to grasp onto an immovable object, which turns out to be a railing. Then there's the frightening sensation of losing control, of sinking down. Everything is in free-fall. A blurred world of swirling lights. Johnny is by your side, telling you not to worry, that it'll pass in a minute, but you're not so sure. It feels like you're going to die. Your metabolism has gone haywire. You clench every muscle and breathe in and out. All it takes is the slightest weakness in the ticker and your number's up. A burst artery could spray the place in blood and no one would even notice. Bloody Marys on the house.

Fear of death urges you to try to remember the words of those forgotten prayers. The female singer sings, "Give me love" in her computer-distorted voice. Everything is distorted. The dancers continue to move to the repetitious thumping beat. No words emerge from the labyrinth of your memory. Your entire body seems to be expanding and contracting with every beat of your heart. Surely people must notice. You want them all to stop, to turn the music off, switch the house lights on, and acknowledge your plight. Johnny has his arm around your shoulder, but it means nothing to you. Survival has pushed such simple pleasures aside.

It seems like an hour, but you suspect that it's only a minute or two before your system has normalised itself. An overwhelming sense of relief gushes through you and you want to tell him that you feel like you've been given a second life, another chance, that it must be an omen for the two of you. He leads you away from the dancefloor and as you pass by tables, you see that people are wary of you, as though they're convinced you're about to disgorge the contents of your stomach over them any moment now. You want to stop and whisper to them individually that they should keep their hopes up, that they could meet the love of their life here tonight. What a thought. And if Johnny wasn't looking, you would point to him and say, See him, he's the love of my life.

This tiny flicker of hope is promptly quenched when Derek appears, with his face contorted into an idiotic trance-like smile, his eyes focusing on the middle distance like he's trying to give the impression that he's some sort of mystic. But he doesn't stop, he just waves and dances his way past, out onto the dancefloor.

"He's on E," Johnny says.

This surprises you, and it must show. It's all very well reading about this sort of thing, or hearing about it on television, or having someone try to sell it to you on the street, but to actually meet someone on it is an entirely different matter.

"Have you ever taken it?"

Johnny shrugs and looks at the floor. "A few times. I've given it up though."

You say nothing for a moment. A reproachful fatherly frown is all you can manage. This really hurts. He used to copy everything you did, but now he has a new role model. And you have to pretend that it means nothing to you. Nor should it matter to you if they are sleeping together, so you enquire, as casually as you can, what Derek's like in the sack.

"It's like being in bed with an octopus," he replies, before he realises that his answer should have been to tell you to mind your own business. And now you wish he had.

A word has yet to be invented to adequately describe the intensity of the jealousy you are experiencing. He looks guilty when he sees how upset you are. You try to hide it but you can't. There's such a difference between suspecting and knowing. Now it seems so pathetic that you had actually deluded yourself into believing that they shook hands every night, said goodnight, maybe pecked one another on the cheek, before heading off in their separate directions. Two hormone-frenzied twenty-three year olds who could think of nothing better than sleeping alone. It seems so pathetic now, you want to break down and cry.

"Things aren't going that well between us though," he says, and you experience such a flip-over of emotions you feel faint. And when you clasp onto a counter for support, a thought occurs to you. Maybe he's saying this to humour you. But why should he? He doesn't lie. Maybe he is just this once, in case you go mad again.

"How d'you mean?"

"Well, he's doing a lot of stuff."

Get out quick, you want to say, but you hold the reins.

"Not a good idea," you say instead. It really is difficult to contain yourself.

"Also ..." He takes a look around him. "Promise you won't say a word to anyone."

"Of course." You might not be a lover, but you will gladly slide into that trusted friend role.

"He watches videos."

"Hah?" You play the innocent.

"Videos. And I ain't talking about Disney videos."

Now you pretend to have just twigged what he's talking about.

"I mean once in a while is all right, but he's obsessed. He must have over fifty of them."

Outwardly, you're shaking your head, making tut-tutting sounds of disapproval, while inwardly, you're already planning how you might orchestrate it so that you can get your grubby hands on a sample of these grubby videos.

"They're so degrading."

Of course, this moral stance only serves to further enhance

your opinion of him. Anyone else would be simply disregarded as a goody-two-shoes Mary Poppins, but not him.

"And I'd say they're repetitive."

Johnny nods. "He's promised to get rid of them for me."

A tiny dart of pain shoots through you. Little promises between them are enough to make you want to puke.

That's enough for you. It's two o'clock in the morning, the night has turned the corner into utter fatigue, so you tell him you're off home, with, it can't be denied, the slender hope that he will say he's sick of the pornographer and he's coming with you.

"Make sure you take a taxi," is all he says before he pecks you on the cheek like some sort of common everyday acquaintance.

* * * *

Anne doesn't ask questions when you go out anymore. After the roar you let out on that black night, and after your subsequent behaviour, it's not surprising really. If the truth be known, she's probably glad to see the back of you. Things have altered between you since the black night. Whether she believes what you say is another matter entirely. You've told her that you've taken up chess again, joined a club. Good for the mind, you actually said. What she doesn't know is that Johnny and Derek are the only other members of this fantasy chess club, where chess is never played. Like a pathetic fool, you have started to meet up with the pair of them on a regular basis. It's impossible to survive without the fix of seeing him. And you've convinced yourself that it's only a matter of time before he sees sense and gives old Beaker Nose the heave-ho.

The highlights of these nights are when you're left alone with him. Those precious moments when Derek goes off to the loo, or up to the bar, or best of all, when he goes off to chat to people he knows. You live for those moments of almost furtive one-to-one conversation. You're like a magpie, searching for those valuable little nuggets. But you're also like a cuckoo, planting the subtle seeds of doubt. However, you obviously aren't quite as subtle as you think because, one night, you push it too far, and Johnny puts an end to it.

"I think you've got Derek all wrong," he says.

"No, I don't, eh..." You're tongue-tied, and that stinks of guilt.

"He's a sound bloke."

Immediately, you remove the blocks from behind the wheels and blindly backtrack your way back down along the slimeball path you came.

"Of course I know that Derek is sound," you say, spinning about in mud slime, "you must have picked me up wrong. It wasn't Derek I was talking about."

You will say anything to slither your way out of his bad books. Of course, you're convinced that he's being held against his will, and that's why old Beaker Nose always has to come along to these social outings. He probably has a gun stuck into Johnny's ribs to make sure that he doesn't say anything out of turn like, "Call the cops". However, during rare moments of lucidity, you almost admit that things are quite the opposite. If anyone's doing the chasing, it's Johnny. He's always been mad about Beaker Nose, and he's only letting you see this now because he thinks you can cope with it, that you're comfortable with it. After all, if you weren't, you'd hardly be going out with them, would you? That's what he logically reasons. That you'd never be so mad as to come along and sit with them and endure the horror of watching the one you love go home with someone you're pretending to be pally with. The words pathetic and desperate spring to mind.

Most of these meetings take place in pubs in Ranelagh, close to Derek's flat. In some way, you sense that they'd prefer to go into the gay pub in town, but that they're making allowances for you. You've told them that once was enough. The real reason you don't want to meet them in town is that, in there, they can openly hold hands, kiss and touch one another, and if that were going on in front of you, and you had sufficient alcohol in your system, it could conceivably lead to a murder trial. And besides this, it appears that Derek is the one who most likes going to the gay pub, so any strain between them is good strain. How devious we can be when the moment demands.

Derek's flat isn't dingy at all, in fact, it's quite the opposite. It actually is an apartment, which leads you to suspect that he may be earning extra income from a dubious source, such as drug dealing or pornography distribution. This possibility fires up your pistons. A simple anonymous phone call could have him locked up. And you'd even pop into prison to visit him. Along with Johnny, of course. And you'd leave with Johnny and he'd have to watch you go, the same way you have to watch the pair of them go.

You're alone in the living-room, sipping a mug of coffee, listening to a Radiohead song called "Creep", while the pair of them are out in the kitchen making toast. If you weren't so preoccupied, you might suspect that this song is Beaker Nose's subtle way of getting at you. With the intention of flicking through the rack of CDs, you go over to the sound system, and discover a pile of video tapes concealed behind an armchair. Their lurid titles leave nothing to the imagination. After a quick check that the coast is clear, you take the one with the meatiest title and shove it into the inside pocket of your jacket.

*　*　*　*

It's 12.30am when you slip the same video into the VCR and press play. The anticipation has your hands shaking. Anne is asleep, the baby is asleep, the entire population of Legoland seem to be sleeping. What follows is a blur of naked males performing extraordinary tricks and manoeuvres. But their perfunctory performance is such that you get the impression that they would probably wear the same bored and detached expressions if they were sweeping floors in a fast-food restaurant. It's difficult to switch the rational side of your brain off and take a ramble down into the sewer department. The paucity of plot amuses you, as do the shadows of the camera crew, the continuity blunders and the role of the dialogue editor. The only major concern seems to be to keep this threesome rolling. Does Piggy-in-the-middle get paid extra, you wonder. And what do these actors do in their spare time? Do they socialise together? Pop into porn stores and watch videos of themselves in action? How would they react if someone posted their elderly aunts a copy?

However, soon after you're operating on that base, uncomplicated level of raw excitement. Primitive animal nature has taken over. The reins have been loosened and your imagination has raced off into the sewer pipe. The threesome on screen have been joined by new stars. The expression, 'at sixes and sevens' takes on an entirely new meaning. You're there with them, pumping away with energetic zeal. Should you hold yourself back and go upstairs to Anne and let her see what a horny boy you are tonight, you wonder. But you don't. You can't. You hold your breath and let fly. It overshoots the kitchen-roll runway and reaches the top button of your shirt. Immediately you imagine Anne asking how that got there. Was it Teresa? The men on the screen shoot onto Piggy-in-the-middle. He's smiling, licking the hot spunk that's trickling down his face. It's not the sort of starring role his elderly aunts would relish viewing.

Ultimately, it's dissatisfying. You're left with a frustrating feeling of being cheated. It reminds you of how, as a youngster, after you had reached those self-induced climaxes, you used to convince yourself that it was thoughts of women which brought on the climaxes, and how just thinking that lifted your spirits and made you feel the omnipotence of youth. A psychiatrist would have had a field day tinkering about with your mind, and probably still would.

After rinsing the shirt in the kitchen, you pop it into the washing-machine. If she asks, you can tell Anne that you spilt sour cream on it. Upstairs, when you slide into bed, she makes a mumbling sort of sound and turns to face you. If she wants bed action now, you're in trouble. Imagine her face if you told her to control her passions, that you've just indulged in a little bout of auto-eroticism, as the churchmen so euphemistically put it. That's an area you don't talk about. Too juvenile, she would say, but really it's something else. The discomfort with sex still prevails through the genes. The legacy of those censorious clerics lives on. The legacy of, That which we say we'll never do is often what we want to do most.

Her breathing is steady. She's asleep. You experience a sudden urge to place your ear to her stomach and listen for the tiny heart-beat of the growing foetus. This is followed by the uncomfortable concern of how the same baby might be affected by the thoughts you were having around the time of its conception. This doesn't bear contemplation.

And you are slipping away into the land of dreams when you remember that you left the video in the VCR. A sudden cramp knots your stomach. Thoughts of Anne and her mother sitting down to watch an afternoon film and switching on the video by mistake. Oh, I've seen this fillum before Anne, it's *Spartacus*, isn't it? Oh Mummy, you're a walking encyclopaedia when it comes to films.

Down the stairs you go, two steps at a time, convinced that the Family Values group are going to greet you in the living-room, their faces contorted in looks of horror. You lock the video in the drawer in your study. The lock is supposed to keep the baby at bay. Ha! The Family Values group will be rapping at the window. Hand over the *Spartacus* video, they'll shout. I'll have to watch it just to see how repulsive it actually is, their duplicitous leader will insist.

*   *   *   *

The circular speed-limit sign at the entrance to Legoland has been altered to 1,100 MPH. The gawky teenagers are looking for attention. There's a brand new Jaguar parked outside the house. Either some lucky neighbour has struck gold in the lottery, or some distant relative has called to leave you their fortune, or else Anne is having an affair with an oil sheikh. You swing the car into the driveway. It's such a snug fit. The nose tips the garage door, the rear is centimetres inside the driveway. The architects certainly didn't cater for Legoland residents breaking into the world of stretch limos.

In the movies, the man pushes the front door open and

announces, "Honey, I'm home", and a bunch of healthy, freshly-scrubbed kids rush to greet him, shouting, "Daddy's home! Daddy's home!" And daddy listens to all their breathless stories, but everything stops and the children's faces glow when Mammy and Daddy kiss. With you, it's all about sounds. Sounds signal your mood. If Anne hears you moving slowly, she knows you're irritable. If she hears you mount the stairs, she knows you're extremely irritable and should not be approached. A good mood is signalled by a beeline for the kitchen door. You've only had one or two minor Johnny attacks during the day and have no particular reason to be in bad form, so you go into the kitchen and discover that it's empty. Signs of recent life all right, but empty.

"In here, Paul."

You turn and see your wife's head sticking out the living-room door, beckoning you to join her. Something is up. A death perhaps. Her mother springs to mind, and you can't deny that you experience just the slightest wave of relief. Immediately, you reprimand yourself, but not severely because recently, there have been mutterings of her mother selling her house and moving in with you.

"This is Paul, my husband."

A distinguished-looking man with silver hair stands up to shake your hand. He has the embarrassed look of an inopportune visitor, but there is something vaguely familiar about him.

"Henry McLoughlin's the name, I'm really sorry for disturbing you like this." His gravely, well-tuned accent oozes with the confidence that goes with success.

Initially, the name means little to you, but when Anne explains that your name and address was in the address book belonging to this man's son, you have to call upon every reserve of self-control. Events are cascading out of control.

"You see, what we're worried about, my wife and myself, is that he might be taking drugs."

In your relief, you smile inappropriately, but Mr McLoughlin reads this to be a declaration of the ludicrousness of the notion of you being involved in drugs.

"But obviously it has nothing to do with that," he says, looking from Anne to you to the baby, who's watching the entire show from her buggy.

Poo poo, she mouths silently to you, and it's a struggle to contain your amusement.

"You can never be too careful," Anne says.

Mr McLoughlin sips his tea, he's relaxing now. "You see, we had a lot of trouble with him when he was younger."

"With drugs?" Anne asks.

"Well no..." Again, he spans the happy family, before deciding that he can confide in you. "You see, Derek is a homosexual."

Upon hearing the word homosexual, the tips of Anne's ears turn bright pink, and her eyebrows go into the incredulous loop they go into when anything like this is being discussed. Your own reaction is ambivalent. There's a sort of what's-this-got-to-do-with-me anger, but there's also the urge to say, Yeah, I know, I've got one of his porn videos upstairs in my study.

"Now I don't mind that, but when he was younger, he went a little wild...Like, when he was fifteen, the guards once called to our house and told us that he was frequenting a place on the seafront which was...emmm...what they call, a gay cruising spot."

"You mean for..." Anne can't say the word "sex", but it's pretty clear what she means.

Mr McLoughlin nods, and there's a deadly silence in the room. You reckon the guards calling to your house to report your sexual activities must be on a par with the other horror of a raunchy video being posted to a porn star's elderly aunts.

From the way she's glancing at you, it's pretty clear that Anne is trying to figure out how the hell your name and address have appeared in the address book of a young homosexual. The thought of running off to Tibet and signing up for an order of silent monks has a certain appeal. The years of practise are required because she is watching you closely. This is wedding day pretence-levels. But you really are an old hand at this stage. Nothing can phase you.

"I believe you know Johnny," Mr McLoughlin says.

"Who?"

"Johnny Lyons, he used to work in Carney Textiles."

"Oh that Johnny, right." You act like you're recalling an old school contemporary. This McLoughlin fellow certainly seems to have done his homework.

"Well, Derek is involved with Johnny."

"Involved?" Anne has crinkled her nose up.

"You know..." Mr McLoughlin grimaces.

"Is Johnny gay?" Anne asks you, bewildered.

"Is he?" You divert the question to Mr McLoughlin. This is perhaps the most bizarre conversation you have ever participated in. But what really concerns you is what Derek is liable to say to his father about you.

"Yes, it appears so, but, like I said, I have absolutely no problem with that...In fact, Johnny's a lovely fellow, and I'm sure he has nothing but a good effect on Derek – "

Anne cuts across him. "Did you know he was gay?" she asks.

You shake your head and shrug. "It had occurred to me that he might be."

"But you never said anything."

"What was I supposed to say? There's this guy at work and I suspect he might be a bit..." You swivel your hand in a circular motion.

"What I'm worried about is the drugs. I have a friend in the guards, and he was the one who gave me this address book. They had confiscated it from Derek." A flush rises to Mr McLoughlin's cheeks. "Oh, by the way, the guards may call on you, and everyone else in the diary."

Anne balks. "The guards?"

Mr McLoughlin squirms. "Just to ask a few harmless questions, like."

"Has your son been in trouble with the guards before in respect to drugs?" Anne asks.

"Ah, only a minor possession charge. It was for his own use so he was let off with a warning."

Anne then turns to you and asks the obvious question. "But how come your name and address are in his diary?"

You shrug. "Must've been through Johnny," you say, avoiding her gaze.

"But, have you seen this Johnny fellow since he left the job?"

"Emm, oh yeah, I bumped into him in town one day."

"I don't see why he'd want to give Derek your address." Anne is scratching her temple distractedly.

You lift your eyebrows. It's easy to guess what she's thinking now. She sees everything falling into place with eerie precision. Derek's been supplying you with drugs, and that's what caused your strange behaviour on the night of madness. This could be the escape hatch you were looking for. You could claim you were experimenting, that's all. It would tie up all the loose ends.

After Mr McLoughlin leaves, Anne asks you if Johnny went to Wexford with you for that weekend. The question unsettles you for those give-away few seconds. You knot your brow, like she'd just asked you to recite the alphabet backwards. Finally, you pretend to see the light and nod.

"Did he try to make a move on you?" She titters like a school-girl, and, in line with the serious type of person she thinks you are, you have to frown and give the impression that all "that sort of thing" is absolutely bewildering to you. But there's no doubt about it, the noose is slowly tightening.

Chapter Twelve

Not that you need much prompting, but the visit from Derek's father has given you a genuine reason to phone Johnny. He's not home, so you phone Derek's apartment. As always happens when Derek answers, you're tempted to ask to speak to Johnny, but you can't do that. You have to go along with the new friendship charade. Both of them are your friends now and they're a couple, so why should you want to speak to one more than the other? Unless you have ulterior motives. And you couldn't have Beaker Nose thinking this, could you. Anne is moving about in the kitchen so you hold the reins on the story of Mr McLoughlin's visit. He says they're going to the pub in town that night and that you're very welcome to join them. How kind of him.

So, when the moment is right, you tell Anne that the chess club are having a social get-together in a pub in town. She suggests the baby-sitter, and you do well at pretending that this is a good idea. But you know that her heart isn't really in it, and it doesn't take long to persuade her that the chess club crowd are a particularly dull bunch.

"I'll have to meet them someday," she says, and you agree.

Stepping over the threshold of the gay bar isn't quite the ordeal it was first time round. Derek assured you that it's much more pleasant midweek, that it's less crowded, and that it'll give you a better opportunity to "meet someone". That latter comment prompted a ferocious spasm of anger to flare up within you; it did cross your mind that the phone might melt in your hand.

The pair of them are sitting in the same place upstairs in the cavern-style bar. The music is playing at a volume conducive to conversation. There isn't the hectic weekend buzz tonight. Everything about the place seems to be just that bit slower and saner. Old Beaker Nose is talking about his experiences when he "came out" to people. It appears that he's encouraging Johnny to tell everyone about himself.

"Women generally don't tend to have a problem. Probably has something to do with them being the ones who have the babies and all that. Now, men who are fully heterosexual don't usually have a problem either. Their reaction tends to be, Hey Derek, just means less competition, man...It's the men who are further down the scale who have the big problems with it. It seems to stir those latent desires and this unsettles them, so they resort to all the usual name-calling et cetera."

"Yeah, I know the type." Johnny nods his head.

"You know, I'd love to go back to my old school and talk about this. I'd say, Right lads, if you're the dainty one, the cream puff of the class, and someone is jeering you, all you got to say to him is, Hey, why are you revealing yourself like this? You realise that this is simply a displaced manifestation of your own sexual insecurity?"

Johnny is laughing.

"And then I'd warn him to turn on his heels and run as fast as his little legs can carry him."

Both of them laugh, and you sit there, smiling, so tempted to tell Derek that he isn't as stupid as he looks.

Something else intervenes though. Johnny beckons you towards him and whispers to you to take a look at the guy standing at the end of the bar. Your eyes haven't fully adjusted to the dimness yet, so you have to squint.

"Eighties pop star," Derek prompts.

"American," Johnny adds.

You nod in acknowledgement, but you haven't the faintest idea who the pop star is. You had study to do back then. Johnny reveals the star's name, a name you've heard of, and it surprises you to find that you've been struck with a dose of fame-worship. Now you recognise him from the television, and remember that Anne has a couple of his records. How she would love to be here with you.

The star himself is chewing gum and drinking lager in sizeable gulps. His clothes are fashionably downbeat, his smile is one of studied irony, his hair is still cut in a style which was fashionable in the 1980s, but none of this can take away from the fact that his chin looks as though it could double-up as an ice-cream scoop. There's a woman at his side, her lipsticked mouth opens and closes at his ear like a skipping-rope. Judging by his lack of interest, it's obvious that she's a cover. You'll have to suggest marriage to him. Blow away all the suspicions. There are people buzzing around him, giddy just to be in close proximity, while doing their utmost to pretend that they haven't noticed him. Comments like "multi-millionaire", "genius"and "weirdo" float around. But there's no doubt, his presence has sparked an electric charge into everyone's night.

A bald, portly, middle-aged man passes your table and Johnny groans and says, "Wouldn't throw him out of bed for nibbling Weetabix." And when you realise that he's being serious, you want to pluck out your remaining hair and go on a diet of pizza and beer. You gloat at skinnymalinks Derek with his full head of hair, but he doesn't bat an eyelid. He doesn't appear to be even listening. He's probably stoned out of his head, and that reminds you.

He rolls his eyes up and laughs sardonically when you tell him about his father's visit. It's such an irritating laugh, you're tempted to box him on the nose. This is awkward. He's the type to say, Why should I lie? He obviously has dilemmas of his own to be concerned about. And the drugs have probably loosened a screw or two, made him unpredictable, dried up all those endorphins. It will take some delicate tinkering to get it across to him that he can't tell his father who you really are. The thought of arriving home to be greeted by Anne and Mr McLoughlin chatting about your secret love life over a cuppa, is enough to make you wish you had never met Derek. Then, you think, perhaps it's best to say nothing. By drawing attention to it, you're exposing your weakness. Naturally he's wary of you after all the tacit hostility you've aimed in his direction. If the roles were reversed, you would certainly be tempted to drop him in it.

Before you can decide either way, a hand touches your shoulder and a familiar voice shrieks, "Paul Cullen!"

Every head within a thirty foot radius seems to turn to look at you. This is the type of publicity you could do without. You turn to face Joe Corcoran from the design department.

"How's Joe."

Design Joe has his hands clasped to his face. "Gawd! Didn't expect to meet you here!" In his rush of the moment, he's letting his studied accent slip. Instead of sounding like a husky woman with a hair clip clasped between her teeth, he sounds like any ordinary man you'd meet in a bar. "And you're..." He's pointing at Johnny.

"JL, son of a gun," Johnny says.

"You worked in accounts, didn't you?" Design Joe sneaks a glance at your bare wedding ring finger.

"Well, I wouldn't go so far as to say I worked there," Johnny says, winking at you, "Let's just say I put in appearances there."

"But Paul, I thought you were married!" Design Joe says.

"I am married."

"Doesn't stop him coming in here," Johnny says.

"Oh like, you're not gay, are you?" Design Joe has retrieved his hairclip-between-teeth accent.

You say, "Whatever gave you that idea?"

Design Joe takes an exaggerated look at the mural of near-naked men sketched on the ceiling.

"Nothing would surprise me these days," Derek says, in a joking manner.

"I blame it all on MTV," Johnny says, in mock solemnity.

Design Joe kneels down alongside you, rests his hand upon your shoulder, his body language telling Johnny and Derek to make themselves scarce. If Ronnie Burke were to see you now, he'd probably go on the wagon.

"Come here to me, d'you think your man Andy from computers is gay?"

"Wouldn't surprise me."

"Andy Warhol, that's what I call him." Design Joe throws his head back as he laughs. "Anyway, I always keep an eye out for him in here." Design Joe smacks his lips and flutters his suspiciously long eyelashes. "I wouldn't want the dear boy falling into the wrong hands."

The image of Design Joe and Andy waltzing their way, hand in hand, across the factory floor is one to savour.

"Are you here on your own?"

"Me on my own! Not a chance!"

Behind the defence layers, there's just the tiniest hint of embarrassment which tells you that he is here alone. It is the sort of place you could come to on your own, but the fact that he lies about it makes you feel sympathetic towards him.

"I have, what you might call, a residency here."

"I must say, it's a really different place for someone like me to come to."

"You know that there's a gay married men's organisation."

"But..." You check that Derek isn't listening. "I'm not gay."

"Listen to her!" Design Joe slaps your arm.

"I'm not, Joe."

"That's what they all say."

"You don't believe me?" There's a note of desperation in your voice now. When it comes to office gossip, Design Joe can scatter stories quicker than machine-gun fire.

"Oh, I believe you all right." He winks at you as he stands up.

"You don't."

"No, I don't, but I can pretend I do if that's what you want me to do." He flicks his hair back with exaggerated femininity. "I know all about you married men and your little peccadilloes. Believe me, I've been around."

"Joe, I..." Your voice trails off. It's time to stop digging that hole.

"I just knew there was something going on between yourself and pretty boy there." This is his parting shot, and it leaves you winded. But you can't deny that you're pleased that he had noticed that there was something between Johnny and yourself. It's funny that something you are so anxious to hide is also something you want people to acknowledge.

It's like the changing of the guard. Design Joe heads away off into the forest of bodies and someone else approaches the table and asks, "Got a light, please?" The fact that someone should actually use this line fascinates you. In the dim light, you can't get a decent look at the face. He could be Adonis, or he could be Quasimodo. Johnny is watching you, and he's not smiling. This lifts your spirits. Maybe he's jealous.

"Sure," you say, and as you reach for the box of matches, you notice that Quasi Quasimodo is already holding a lit cigarette. It's a welcome boost for the ego, but you're in no sort of emotional condition for anything, so you act the sap, hand him the box of matches and tell him that he can keep them.

"Thank you," he says, moving away reluctantly, holding the box of matches like it's a piece of dirt.

"I gave them up," Johnny says when you offer him a cigarette from the first packet you ever bought in your life. You've been bumming too many off them. "Both of us have," he adds, pointing to Beaker Nose.

At moments like this, it's difficult to keep up the pretence. These "little things" they do together touch a raw nerve. To make matters worse, the song that reminds you of him comes on the jukebox. It's a struggle to retain your composure.

"If I wanted to kill myself, I'd use a gun, it's quicker and cleaner," Johnny says, pointing at your cigarette, and you extinguish what's to be your last cigarette.

When it's time to go, Johnny smiles and says he has something to do. He cuts through the crowd of liggers hovering in the vicinity of the rock star, calls out the star's name like he knows him, extends his hand and says, "Hi, I've been trying to avoid you all night, but I suppose I better say goodbye."

The rock star's shoulders shake with laughter. The lipsticked girl at his side frowns. The crowd of liggers watch in apparent awe, staring at Johnny, trying to decide if he's someone famous. Up close, you see the star clearly, and there is no doubting it, his sharp chin could cause dangerous lacerations.

"Going home alone then, are we?" he says.

"*Moi*?" Johnny opens his eyes wide. And with that he throws his arms around both your shoulder and Derek's shoulder, and proceeds to kiss you both on the mouth in turn. The thought of a newspaper man taking a snapshot curdles your blood. Johnny is kissing you right smack on the lips for the second time when, out of the corner of your eye, who do you see, but none other than Design Joe. His jaw drops open in a way that must have him worrying about dislocation.

* * * *

At work the following morning, there are stranger than normal looks being cast in your direction. It's not your imagination. These are people you've known for years and you know their behaviour. They looked at you oddly when they thought you were mad, but this is different. There's too many double-takes, too much hesitation. Even Teresa is struggling to act naturally. But being the loyal person she is, she can't keep it from you. She tells you that there's a story doing the rounds that yourself and Johnny were seen together in a gay bar the previous night.

"Design Joe?"

Teresa nods.

You sigh, but you can't stop blushing. "We went in there with a gay friend of his."

Teresa looks at the ground the way she does when she has something difficult to say. When you eventually catch her eye, you open your eyes questioningly.

"I'll just warn you Paul, people did think that Johnny was gay...And like, because you and him got on so well, and like, socialised together and what-have-you, some people sort of thought...well..."

"That I was gay?"

Teresa's nod is almost apologetic. Your laugh is unconvincing.

"Is marriage no longer a gilt-edged cover?" you joke, in the lilting hair clip-between-teeth accent.

She laughs, more in relief that you're taking it so well, you suspect, than anything else.

Your hands are shaking when you dial Design Joe's number. Seconds later, he pops his head into your office, says, "How's my friend", and, not for the first time, you suspect that you are capable of murder. You wait until the door's closed and he's seated in front of you before you ask him who he's yapped to.

"I only mentioned it to Ursula...in passing," he says, a liar's flush rising to his cheeks.

Anger rises up within you. Ursula is a motor-mouth. "Joe, what exactly did you tell Ursula?"

"That I met you in town last night."

"And what else?"

"And that you were with what's-his-name, Pretty Boy Johnny." He winces under your glare. "Well, it's the truth, isn't it."

"I was also with someone else, did you mention him?"

"No."

"Why not?"

"Well, because no one here knows him, but they all know Johnny."

"So that made it a nice juicy story?"

Slightly piqued, Joe flicks his hair back. "Well, you know yourself."

You bang your fist down on the desk. "Joe, you've got this arseways."

"Sorry, I – "

"I went there with a friend of mine who happens to be gay, now is there anything wrong with that?"

"No, no, of course not. But it's nothing to ashamed of."

You stare at him defiantly. "What's nothing to be ashamed of?"

His face has paled. "Being in a gay pub."

"I'm quite aware of that Joe, but I'm talking about something entirely different. I'm talking about someone going around blabbering to everyone that I was in there with my boyfriend. Your weary tone has unsettled him. Like everyone else, he likes to be liked. He shakes his head. "I didn't say that."

"Not in so many words, but you left no one in any doubt." You start to imitate his accent. "The two of them were sitting together in a gay bar, need I say anymore." As a finale, you let your wrist hang limp.

But Joe is obviously well used to this. "You never said not to mention that I had met you."

He's right, you didn't. And he did see you and Johnny kissing.

"Joe, I couldn't give a flying fuck who or what you are. I don't interfere with your life. As far as I can see, you're a man in his mid-thirties who still thinks he's eighteen." This is a low strike. His lower lip is quivering. "But the fact of the matter is that I'm a married man and, unlike you, I have responsibilities. Now you might think that the world is a simple place where everyone can go out at night and swap handbags or whatever, but that just is not the case, and the sooner you get that into your thick skull, the better. I realise you have your agendas and what-ever, but one thing I'll ask you, don't ever spread gossip or rumours about me again, please."

He starts to cry. Right there in front of you, he's reduced to a big blubbering baby. And you just want to burst out laughing. The situation is so ludicrous. Why are you berating him? For telling people about you and Johnny? The very thing you ought to be most proud of. You apologise for losing the rag, tell him that you're under pressure, blame it on everything from Carney to the monthly forecasts to the weather. The blubbering subsides with each new excuse.

Eventually, you judge that he's sufficiently recovered to send him back out into the outside world. To make matters even more ludicrous, he's actually thanking you for "lifting him out of it", claiming that he's had it coming to him for a long time now, and that he'll watch what he says in future. And you feel like saying, Joe, stop the bullshit, both you and I know that you'll be back to your usual tricks within half an hour. But you are tempted to use the moment to tell him to give up his habit of throwing his head back as he laughs, that people think it's easily the most false of all his false gestures. But he could retort that no one else in design acts naturally so why should he be the only one? That would stump you.

When you open the office door, his eyes are red and he's holding a wet tissue to his dribbling nose, and who should swing around the corner at that precise moment, but none other than Ronnie Burke. His reaction borders on the comical, his eyes bulge, a film of drink sweat glistens on his forehead, and there's no doubt that his palpitations have shifted into overdrive. He's like a child putting the last piece to a jigsaw. He passes by, aims a friendly nod in your direction, doing his utmost to pretend that nothing is amiss, but you'd want to be blind not to see the well-that-just-confirms-it look in his eyes.

Later that morning, the Phantom emerges from his office, spots you, performs an immediate about-turn, and scuttles back into his work-lair like some sort of demented cockroach. It isn't difficult to know what he's thinking. If people see me talking to that fellow, they'll think I'm bent. If it weren't so sad, you would laugh. Perhaps if you ignore it, it will all fade away into the haze of used office stories. A new scandal will soon replace it.

*   *   *   *

That evening, the moment you step into the changing-room at the leisure centre, you know the lads have heard. The story has spread its tentacles. The silence is the give-away. The unwillingness to catch your eye. There is only one possible source and that's Jason from the post-room. Six months ago, one of the regular five-a-siders decided to retire and you invited Jason along to replace him. Now you see the error of your ways. Work and play should never mix. It's a surprise that Jason told them, but then he is only eighteen, and he likes to impress the older lads. But it's these older lads, your friends, who really disappoint you.

For six years now you've been togging out and showering with the same group of lads. Now they hear that you've been spotted in a gay pub and everything changes. Suddenly, you're going to try and rape the lot of them. You're a monster. No male is safe. Funnily enough, it's the ugliest of them who are taking most care not to expose themselves. And what about Maurice and Gerry? Both of them are bachelors, well into their thirties and, as far as you know, neither of them has ever had a steady girlfriend. It's a classic case of the difference between suspecting and knowing. It's like you've stepped across some invisible line. Honesty is certainly not the best policy when it comes to the practicalities of male-bonding.

During the heat and passion of the match, they forget that they've got a "guy who was seen kissing another guy in a gay bar" in their midst. The battle of competitive spirits takes over. This is war. And with the release of endorphins, they actually speak to you, and get back to treating you the way they normally do. After the game, it's tempting to slip on a tracksuit and shower at home; but you don't, you make a point of stripping off and walking into the open-plan showers, letting it all hang out. But you get the impression that, by this stage, they're all too tired to care. But one thing seems certain, unless you can round up a posse of gay footballers, this probably signals a premature end to your footballing career.

* * * *

At lunchtime the following day, the fashion terrorists are out in force. Grafton Street is awash with the marching suits. The swaggers that go with the new confidence of boomtimes. You lose yourself among the intimidating clusters of four and five marching in straight lines, like soldier ants, some wearing Raybans, others yacking into mobiles, others letting their jackets flap in the breeze to reveal their expensive labels, and others with nothing better to do than flash contemptuous looks at those they consider to be beneath them. Somewhere in your mind, you pore over an illustration from a book you read as a child depicting hideous creatures. And you are now weaving your way through their descendants, sheltering your eyes against the slants of blinding sunlight, all the time keeping an eagle-eye out for undesirables.

Autumn is hardly in the door and already the big ship Christmas is sitting out there on the horizon, firing long-range salvos onto TV screens everywhere, causing this panic on the high streets. The shops are all hustle and bustle. These are affluent times to live in. Everybody has cash to spend.

Outside Bewley's, an awkward dilemma presents itself. People are smiling as they approach. Something is amiss. Something about you is amusing them. But what? With a casual sweeping motion you check that your fly is shut. Then you rub your hand across your mouth to wipe away any remnants of lunch. It soon becomes obvious that the object of their amusement is behind you. A quick glance at your reflection in a shop window confirms this. A mime-artist is three steps behind you, imitating your walk in a wildly exaggerated manner.

Pretending to be unaware of this public embarrassment, you duck into the sanctuary of HMV and turn to see the idiotic mime-artist select a new victim.

"Hey there stranger," a vaguely familiar voice addresses you. A hand rests upon your shoulder. You spin around and you feel like biting this hand when you see that it belongs to none other than the Wax Hennessy.

"Oh, hiya Dave," you mutter with little enthusiasm.

"This is my number two. Ray Colgan, Paul Cullen. Paul Cullen, Ray Colgan." The Wax behaves like he's introducing international diplomats.

You shake hands with the six-foot-four inch giant, who has the eager-beaver face of someone about to strike a multimillion pound deal.

"Still with Carney's?" Hennessy asks.

"Yeah, and yourself? Still with..." You can't remember.

No worries, Hennessy is only too glad to fill the gap. And with that, he proceeds to give you a quick résumé of his high-flying career in the dizzy world of super-high finance. At last he has the opportunity to tell you about his recent promotion.

"Got promoted myself last month. Director."

Do people like this exist? Apparently they do, because you are talking to one right now. He has a drip-dry face, and his emotions are more than likely controlled by the stock market, house prices, his bank balance, and various other mystery ingredients such as the multiple uses for molten candle wax. Something dreadful must have happened to him during his childhood. It's the only explanation.

Satisfied that he now has you suitably impressed, Hennessy launches into his less-than-subtle game of comparing respective successes.

"So what're you driving these days?"

"A car."

The Wax stares blankly at you; you would find more humour in a block of wood.

"530."

He nods. He knows you are lying. But what's a litre between enemies? "Nice motor," he says, waiting for you to reciprocate on the question, but once he realises that you are not going to, he decides to change track, which means his car isn't as high-powered as your fictitious one. It's all so pathetic and immature. This is what boomtimes do to otherwise balanced people.

"So what kind of readies are they paying you now?"

Is this really happening? You glance up at Number Two to see if he's amused by the bizarre nature of his Number One's inquisition, but the giant isn't breaking ranks. Not a shred of irony to be found. The eager-beaver look has drained from his face now that he realises that he isn't involved in a multimillion pound deal, and his sideways glance seems to suggest that he suspects you might be concealing some class of threatening weapon under your jacket. Protect Number One at all cost.

"What is this? The first degree?"

This embarrasses the Wax, but he's quick to regain his composure. He can't let Number Two see him out of sorts. How you would love to just poke your finger in his eye and walk on.

"Heard Karen dropped another sprog," he says and you nod, slightly bemused by the information superhighway which carries such events around the network of undesirables which you have had the misfortune of encountering in your life.

"That was a while ago."

"Yeah, so it was."

"What about yourself?"

"Three. Two girls and an heir to the throne."

It's like a printer is spewing the details out of his mouth.

"Number four on the way."

Taste in music says a lot about people, and the Michael Bolton CD the Wax is holding tells its own story. The question is, why are you engaged in this conversation? Why didn't you feign amnesia or something? Hennessy? you imagine yourself saying in a put-on accent, all the while scratching your forehead in a detached manner, Sorry old chap, never heard of you. Or maybe you could dig up some college incident which would embarrass him in front of Number Two. You try, but you can't think of any. It strikes you that the Wax was one of those anonymous creeps who sat at the front right-hand side of the lecture theatre.

"See any of the old crowd?"

You shake your head absently and half-listen while the Wax lists off the amazing feats of certain classmates, the ones from the front right-hand side of the lecture theatre, people whom you really have no interest in.

You halt his progress by drawing Number Two's attention to the Wax's college days. "So, did he fill you in on his glory days in the candle factory?"

Number Two stares at you as if you've just told him that his entire family had been washed away in a flash flood.

"That's where he got the nickname 'the Wax'."

The Wax's face changes colour. Since college, he has worked tirelessly to lose this nickname, but the more fuss he creates, the more people persist with it.

But he has vengeance on his mind. Two can play at that game. And, at the last moment, you realise that he's been biding his time all along, waiting to deliver this sucker punch. A slimy, condescending look has formed on his drip-dry mug. "Hey, what's this I hear about you being a leading light in the gay community," he says, and you are out for the count. You really ought to have guessed that he would have heard. Those ears of his are like transmitters. Number Two's demeanour has altered dramatically. It's become almost defensive, like he suspects you're going to try and wrap your arms around his neck at any moment.

"Ah yeah, you'll have to call around and admire me in my tutu one of these nights," you say, moving away from them, ignoring the smirks.

The encounter leaves you drained, like you've just run a marathon. The afternoon is a dreary one until Kevin Daniels slips into your office, shuts the door behind him and sits opposite you, his face resembling one big long funeral cortege.

"How's Kevin."

"Paul, I just heard."

You crease your brow into a puzzled frown.

"About you and Johnny. I would never have guessed."

"Guessed what?"

"Listen Paul, I just want you to know that it makes no difference to me whatsoever." He persists through your attempted interruption. "None at all. As you know, the better half works in advertising, and through that we have many gay friends who we often have over for dinner and what-have-you."

What does he expect? A marching band to strike up a tune? A girl to burst out of a big cake, thrust her crotch into his face and pin a medal onto his lapel?

"Kevin, you shouldn't believe all you hear."

He stares at you, somewhat bemused. "You mean it's not true?"

"No." You avoid his gaze, a certain giveaway.

"Well, even if it were, it makes no difference to me."

"That's good to hear."

"I've always had nothing but the utmost respect for you, and no silly story, even if it were true, could alter that."

There's just the slightest twinge of guilt lurking somewhere at the back of your mind. Perhaps you have misjudged the man. Maybe he's not the world's worst after all.

"Well, thanks anyway Kevin, that's good to hear."

He hesitates, wondering what to do next. You've been too hard on him. How would he react if you told him that you had leafed your way through his diary? Or that you regularly entertained thoughts of murdering him?

"Better dash, work to do," he says, standing up to go.

And now, for the first time, you see a benign, comical side to his peculiar mannerisms. At the door, you thank him again, and then smile as he moves away like he has miniature hovercrafts attached to his shoes.

* * * *

The only consolation is that it has to pass over, people will forget, or assume that the story was made up in the first place. And anyway, most people are too busy worrying about themselves to be concerned about some piss-eyed tale of someone being seen in a gay bar.

Anne is asleep, the baby is asleep, all of Legoland seems to be asleep when you unlock the cabinet in the study and delicately lift the video out between your finger and thumb. Just the sight of it sends a tingle through your groin. Recent events are driving you to take refuge in lurid comforts.

This time, it doesn't take so long to immerse yourself in the primitive pool in your brain. And towards the latter stages of the video, things begin to calm down, probably due to cast exhaustion, and the action approaches something bordering on the erotic. There are only two participants and they actually have their clothes on at the outset of the scene. Such is your intense concentration, you're breathing aloud like a chronic asthmatic, and you don't even notice it until you reach the end of the first "erotic short". It's during the third one of these "erotic shorts" that you become aware of her presence in the room. A panic grips you. It takes too long to press the stop button. An age seems to pass before the two guys in mid-fuck disappear off the screen.

Anne is standing behind you, pointing at the TV screen. To say that she's flabbergasted would be an understatement. She seems to be experiencing difficulties with her breathing. "That was ...," she mutters, the way people probably do when they see alien spacecraft land in their back garden.

"I know, a porn video." Out of her line of vision, you fumble with the buttons on your trousers.

"But..." Her mouth is opening and closing.

"I'm sorry, I just wanted to see what they were like." You lean forward to press the eject button on the VCR.

"But, they were two men."

"What?" You address her like she has just made the most preposterous of statements.

"It was two men."

"No it wasn't."

"It was Paul, I saw it." This is the closest you've ever seen her to hysteria.

"I'm telling you, it wasn't."

"Put it on then and we'll see."

This is a new Anne, an assertive Anne.

"Don't be stupid."

"Why don't you? What've you got to be afraid of?" She moves sideways, all the time watching you like you're a burglar she's just rumbled.

"Look, it's late, let's go to bed and talk about this in the morning." You stand up and unplug the TV.

"You're bisexual, aren't you?" The starkness of the statement rattles you, but you suspect it's the fact that Anne, of all people, has used a word like bisexual, that really throws you. And in some crazy way, you see it almost as a lifeline, as though being bisexual isn't as bad as being homosexual.

"No, I'm not." It feels funny to be telling her the truth for a change.

"Are you gay?" There's a quiver in her voice. Events are falling into place for her. She once told you that her mother didn't know what a homosexual was until she was twenty-one. But these are different days.

"That's why that fellow McLoughlin called here! You and his son are...Oh, Jesus!"

"There's nothing between his son and me." You lower your eyes to avoid her gaze and you know that she knows.

"That Johnny fellow."

You look at her strangely. Something in you cannot deny.

Something in you wants to tell her.

"Did you sleep with him?" She holds her stomach defensively.

"What?" is all you can think of saying.

"Did you fucking well sleep with him? I want to know!"

The balance between you has been tipped. A strange guttural sound escapes from your throat. She's screaming about catching AIDS. She picks the wedding photo up off the mantelpiece and hurls it in your direction. As though in slow motion, you move aside and watch it turn round and round until it crashes against the wall. Slivers of glass fly everywhere, and when the photo lands, there you are, the two of you, arm-in-arm, together, smiling for the camera. Now Anne is jumping up and down on the same wedding photo. Somewhere in the background the baby has begun to roar.

A heavy weight seems to be pushing you down into the armchair. Anne has left the room. Little white dots are swirling in front of your eyes. Sharing secrets doesn't always lessen burdens, that's for sure. Upstairs, the baby's cries have changed to a whimper of self-pity. The poor little thing is shocked that mama and dada haven't arrived to see what's wrong with her. Strange rummaging noises emanate from the direction of the kitchen. Then you hear Anne's footsteps approaching. And before you can react, she's standing behind you, tipping the contents of a large refuse bag right over your head. Egg shells, soppy tea-bags, disposable nappies, empty tins, the oddest pieces of slop, and you just sit there, motionless, letting it all come to rest. Nothing is said. She leaves the room, her thumping footsteps lighten towards the top of the stairs. She goes into the baby's room, the key turns in the lock and she speaks the words of comfort.

Chapter Thirteen

It rains during the night, and it's no major surprise when you look out the window the following morning and see a dry patch where Anne's car had been parked. It's only when you look into the baby's empty cot that it hits you, a tremor of sadness shakes you right to the very core. A phone call to her mother's house confirms your suspicions. Anne is a creature of habit. She tells you that she's going to stay there while she thinks things over. It's a relief that she even speaks to you at all. You suspect that if you were her, you might not have.

So that's it, a long Sunday stretches ahead. Plenty of time to watch all the videos you want, but d'you think you do? Not a flicker of interest in Big Al and the other luminaries of the late-night screen now. Instead, you sit in silence and listen to the peculiar sounds of the house, sounds which are normally blocked out by the hum of domesticity. Seemingly inexplicable creaks and groans drift out from the strangest of quarters. Maybe a shopping-trolley has shifted its position in the foundations and triggered this litany of sounds. Maybe the house is about to crumble down around you. For all you know, there could be human remains down there. A fight after the pub. A drink-induced frenzy which results in one kick too many. Toss him into the cement, no one will ever find him. He married my sister and he's a queer. This thought triggers a chill of fear. What if Anne tells her brothers?

The doorbell rings, and you sneak a precautionary look through the spy-hole before you open the door. The harsh glare of sunlight on wet concrete very nearly bowls you over. There's a woman in her late thirties standing in front of you. She's kitted out in tennis gear; short white skirt, little ankle socks, sweatband, tennis-racket under the arm, scarf to hide the give-away neck and that eager wide-eyed look of someone who still believes she's a jolly seventeen-year-old.

"Hi, Paul."

"Oh, hi," you reply, not having the first clue who this person is.

"Is Anne ready?"

"Emm, has she a match today?" You point at her tennis racket.

"League," she says, like she expects you to drop everything and do a handstand in celebration.

"She must've forgotten, she's gone to her mother's for a few days."

"Nothing the matter I hope."

"Hah?"

"With her mother?"

"Oh no, nothing serious, just a slight dose of 'flu."

"Well, tell her I called."

"I will."

Before she turns to walk away she winks in a manner which suggests that all you've got to do is say the word and the miniature tennis skirt would be jettisoned and her firm thighs would squeeze every drop of air from your lungs. Or maybe you've just been watching too many smutty videos. Before you close the door, you watch the six-year-old girl from next door pass by. This young girl never walks, she parades. With her head held high, her shoulders back and her chest out, she always looks as though she's a part of a marching band. Just the sight of her is enough to brighten the dullest day.

An hour passes; an hour of listening to the hum of lawn mowers, the distant pok-pok of tennis balls and the cars heading off for the weekly drive. The sweet Sunday morning sounds of Legoland. Your resistance is weakening. The urge to phone that number, which must be high in the running for an engraved spot on your tombstone, is too great. As always, while you dial the magical sequence, your stomach flutters. But the flutter turns to a churn when his younger sister answers and says, "Yeah, hold on and I'll get him." There's definitely something to be said for adopting a stance of low expectation. Pinning the receiver to your ear, you hear her call, "Hogbreath, it's Paul for you." She's recognised your voice, which isn't surprising really. But she definitely called him without any hint of tomfoolery as regards your name. Maybe she's warmed to you, or maybe she suspects that you are the type of neurotic person who would pin the phone to your ear and listen out for any tomfoolery.

He's subdued, and you soon discover why. Derek has given him the old heave-ho. And funnily enough, you don't experience the sheer, unadulterated surge of joy you might have expected. His mood dampens celebrations. In your mind, he ought to be delighted to be rid of that drug-pedalling porno fiend, but he's not.

"I'm heading off next week," he says, and you have to swallow a couple of times to clear the sudden blockage in your throat.

"Where to?"

"States. I got a green card."

Placing a devious anonymous phone call to the American Embassy crosses your mind.

"Which part?"

"New York."

"New York City?" You stall for time. "Very dangerous place." Is that the best you can think of? You're the very one who repeatedly told him that you considered New York City to be the most exciting place on this earth. The debauchery is making inroads on the grey matter.

"I love danger."

You used to love me.

"Has the highest number of mental patients in the world." Boy, you can still whip out the big ones when you need to.

"I should feel at home then."

It's chilling to think that you could now qualify for inclusion in the mental club, so you change the subject and tell him all about the previous night's incident.

There's a silence when you finish. "I wouldn't mind, but she walked in during a part I wasn't particularly interested in," you say, anxious to fill the void. Now you wish there was some way you could've told the story without mentioning the porno video. His disapproval is seeping down the phoneline.

"And I thought I had problems," he says eventually. "So like, have you split up?"

"More or less."

"I'm sorry to hear that, but I'm sort of glad she knows. Like, I don't care if she's the Wicked Witch of the North or the Prize Bitch of the South, it's just not fair to do that to anyone."

You imagine a halo shimmering above his head.

"Yeah, well...So listen, what day are you heading off?"

"Friday."

"Maybe I could drop you out to the airport?"

"Ah, my family are coming out with me."

You hold onto yourself. These are uncomfortable reminders of your place.

"Hey, wanna come to the States with me?"

How could he pose such a question in such a throwaway manner? Does he not realise? But there's no stopping an image of the airport departures terminal springing to mind. And there you are with a rucksack slung over your shoulder and a bandanna covering the Gobi Desert, slinking behind pillars, wearing dark glasses to avoid detection by his ever-vigilant brother and sister.

"What's there to keep you here now?"

What if you did just go and do it? Cash in the pension, the life insurance plan, the share options. Split the loot with Anne and skidaddle across the Atlantic. Now you're talking real palpitations. This is what they mean when they say, *really living*. How did that greaseball author on the TV put it? You rot if you stay too long in the one place. Everybody needs change.

"Johnny, are you serious?"

"I wouldn't have said it if I wasn't. It's just, I wouldn't mind having someone I know with me."

The blood is thumping against your temples. Air is flushing through your nostrils, cruising up the direct highway to the endorphin-release department of your brain. The taste of elation is in your mouth.

"Well?"

"I just might, you know."

"You can stay with me in my cousins' till we find a place to live. You'd get a really good job over there."

The word responsibility somehow manages to wriggle its way to the front of your consciousness and hold a policeman's hand up to those escaping endorphins. The system calms itself. A look in the mirror confirms that you are a man hurtling towards middle-age. Touching down in New York City with a rucksack slung over your shoulder is something you ought to have got out of your system years before. But when he suggests that the two of you should talk, responsibilities are once again shoved onto the back-burner. Seven o'clock that very same evening is the agreed rendezvous time. The hands on the wedding-present clock won't move fast enough.

After lunch, for want of something better to do, you head into the office. There's monthly projections you were supposed to have ready by Friday. The volume of traffic is a surprise, Sunday seems to have become the day to drive into the city and look around the shops. *Affluenza* is what Anne calls this compulsion to shop and spend money.

Ned is sitting in the reception area reading a tabloid newspaper. He doesn't become aware of your presence until you slam the heavy front door shut.

"How's Ned."

He stares at you warily, like he expects you to suddenly lunge at him and plant a love-bite on his wrinkled neck.

"Yer man Gorgeous Gus is in," he says, after he's recovered from the shock of being alone in an enclosed space with someone like you. Touching seventy, he's too old to change now. In his world, homosexual people were always odd-bods and freaks. Homos and queers. There will be none of the usual chat about the football results today. Manly games and queers don't mix in his thinking. So you give him a friendly nod and head towards the lift.

There are strange people in this world, but few are as strange as the Phantom. You stop outside his office to listen to his off-key rendition of "The Boxer". Strumming his recently-acquired guitar with a beginner's less-than-nimble finger movements, you hear him simulate the soft "tsssh" sound of the high-cymbal at the end of every "li-li-li". For such a reclusive man it's quite a performance. It isn't difficult to picture his face, screwed up in concentration, delighting the rapturous million-plus crowd packed into Central Park for that famous last concert. There's a million-plus lighters being held aloft in that office of his. TV cameras from all over the world are zooming in on him. It might be Sunday afternoon in Stress City for some, but not for the Phantom.

You tiptoe away down the corridor. If he were to find you loitering outside his office, it'd probably be as embarrassing for you as it would be for him. You open the door to Johnny's old office, and close it again before you're overcome by a wave of nostalgia. His replacement has rendered it unrecognisable. Fifteen minutes later, you are buried in your work when the door to your office opens and the Phantom glides in. Instinctively, your eyes open wide to register surprise. This is the first visit from the Phantom since the news broke. It occurs to you that Ned must have phoned him to tell him you were in. Did he warn him to be careful, that there was *one-of-them* on the premises?

He sits down opposite you and proceeds to discuss the previous day's football results. He's a lifelong supporter of Huddersfield Town, so, of necessity, he's developed a humorous attitude towards the game. As expected, the real purpose of the visit soon forces its way out in the open.

"Listen, Paul, I presume you're aware of what people are saying about you."

You nod, rolling your eyes up to give the impression that it hasn't caused you a second thought.

"Well, I just wanted to say that I think it's reprehensible that such rumours should be spread around." He shakes his head incredulously. "Especially about someone like you."

Oh, clever manoeuvre. He's pretending that he doesn't believe them to be true.

"Thanks Gus."

He's pulling at a piece of slack skin on his emaciated jaw and it puts you in mind of a scrawny chicken.

"I don't know why people invent stories like that."

He appears to be genuinely annoyed. Maybe he does believe what he's saying, or maybe he's conned himself into believing it. How would he react if you were to tell him the truth about Johnny and yourself. How much in love you were. He's a grown man, he ought to be able to understand that these things happen. He might even admit that he's gay as well and expect you to hop into the sack with him. Perish the thought.

"Jesus, it's a laugh that they should think that someone like you is bent."

Maybe you're wrong. There are obviously years and years of denial and repression to unravel here. As far as you know, he deals with Design Joe by simply pretending that he doesn't know that he's gay. Maybe it's time to change the topic.

"Did I hear a radio on in your office?" you ask, and he prattles on about the teach-yourself-how-to-play-guitar book he's working from. He tells you that when he was living in Huddersfield during the 1960s, he saw both The Beatles and The Stones play live in concert, but that Eric Clapton was his real favourite. The meeting with Johnny that evening comes into your thoughts, your spirits lift, and you allow the Phantom to warble on uninterrupted. After all, aside from Ned, you're probably the first person he's spoken to this weekend.

* * * *

In the off-licence section of the supermarket, you get stuck in the queue behind an elderly man. He waits until the shop-assistant has totted up the amount owed, and has packed his meagre two bottles of Guinness into a plastic bag, before he reaches into his pocket and pulls out his chequebook, which he keeps in a protective plastic cover. A further delay ensues while the shop-assistant searches for a pen.

"To whom shall I make the cheque payable?" the old geezer asks, in a tone which suggests that this is one of the highlights of his week. You are tempted to tap him on the shoulder and urge him to put a shilling in the meter.

The shop-assistant says something you don't hear and the elderly man picks her up on her grammar and makes her repeat the sentence correctly before he puts pen to paper. By this stage, you're not the only one in the ever-lengthening queue to take an exaggerated look at your watch. You see them in the wall-mirror, and you see the contemptuous look in your own eyes. But this old geezer doesn't bat an eyelid, he seems to thrive on raising stress levels.

To lessen your irritation, you imagine yourself sliding a sharp kitchen knife between the old man's ribs and announcing to all present to stand clear, give him some air, the old geezer has fainted. After this, you would tip him into your shopping trolley, run him down the aisle and out the back door, where you'd toss him into one of the rubbish dumpsters which churns everything up with its shark-like teeth. But when the old man starts to ask the shop-assistant about the details of some free gift scheme planned for Christmas time, your toe is twitching in your shoe.

"Sorry for the delay," he says to you, and you see him as he is, a harmless old man with a zest for Sunday shopping.

"That's no problem." You smile at him, quite shocked now by the intensity of your anger. Recent events are taking their toll. "No problem at all," you add, giving him a friendly pat on the back to compensate.

His attempt to engage you in further conversation is halted by the arrival of Bob and Karen and their three kids, the youngest of whom is sitting in the shopping-trolley seat. The moment they catch your eye, you know that they've either been talking to Anne, or else Bob has told Karen about the incident in the toilet cubicle. You pay for the booze, and there's no doubt that the pair of them are a little taken aback by the number of lager cans heaped into your trolley. Twenty-four to be precise. Quite a stash. But how could you explain that your purchase is to mark Johnny's upcoming twenty-fourth birthday? And yes, he's the one you saw me snogging in that cubicle.

"Anne phoned us," Karen says.

"Oh, right."

Bob says, "Listen, emm, if there's anything you want us to

do, you know like, be sure to call."

Karen says, "Even if you just want to talk...Like, these kind of things happen in every marriage."

What the hell has she told them?

"Thanks, appreciate that."

The youngest child is growing restless. Cranky tiredness has set in. He's whinging about going to Nana's house. It's a ready-made distraction. The relief is palpable all round.

"Better head to Nana's gaff," you say, and the youngest child turns to look at you. You touch your finger against his button nose and he bursts into a ruddy-cheeked wail. It's always disconcerting when a small child doesn't warm to you. People believe that small children can cut through masks and see into hearts. And men, in particular, who make babies cry are to be treated with suspicion.

"Listen, give us a shout for tennis," Bob says.

"Will do."

The two older children are staring at the twenty-four cans.

Before they go, Bob tells you that they bumped into the Wax Hennessy, and almost immediately you see that he regrets mentioning this. Karen rolls her eyes up and remarks that the Wax is still "such a jerk", which obviously means the Wax said something derogatory about you. One last friendly wave, another promise to meet soon and you're on your way, comforting yourself with the thought of heading up into the clouds on board that jet bound for New York City.

*　*　*　*

After showering and shaving, you rub on a fair dollop of the expensive anti-ageing face cream, cross your fingers and hope it works its miracles. You can't drive fast enough to collect him. Irrational fear conjures up the situation where you arrive one minute after he's decided that you're not coming. And what if you get a puncture, or the car breaks down? Nothing unexpected happens, and he's waiting there in the prearranged spot at the end of his road. His smile rouses the familiar glow inside. Things are looking

219

good. The gods are smiling down. He tells you about the latest antics of his younger sister and brother. How they've taken to recording conversations with concealed tape-recorders.

"Another Watergate," you say, and his silence tells you that he's never heard of Watergate.

The traffic lights at Loughlinstown are out of order and there's a middle-aged guard directing traffic. He holds his hand up to stop you. Beside you, Johnny makes a purring sound and says the guard's "a bit of alright". To your eyes, the guard is certainly not "a bit of alright". The money spent on anti-ageing cream was a waste. Ageing cream would have been a better purchase.

"Imagine if I walked over to him right now and just pulled his trousers down," Johnny jokes.

"That might cause some interesting traffic problems."

"D'you know what Derek did as a laugh once. He sent this ad into *Hot Press*, saying: 'Small, bald and fat looking for tall, dark and handsome for deep meaningful relationship. Looks not important'." His smile vanishes when he notices how sombre you've become.

"Did he get any replies?"

"Ah, I don't know."

He does, but he's changing the subject for your sake. He pities you, and you were the very one who told him to only feel pity for those who pity themselves. One of the neat little Readers' Digest quotes you picked up in some dentist's waiting- room.

When you reach Legoland, you imagine every beady neighbourhood eye is trained on the pair of you. As it always is with guilt, you're convinced there's a flashing neon sign above your head declaring your intentions to the world.

In the kitchen, he opens the fridge and remarks that the insides look like a shrine to the god of lager. The twenty-four cans fill the top two shelves. All the food has been crammed onto the bottom shelf. He takes two cans out and pretends to gulp them both back simultaneously.

"Have a drink, why don't you."

"I could think of nothing worse," he says, replacing the cans and shutting the fridge door. Twenty-four cans for his birthday and he doesn't want a drink. You are such a high-grade sap. Nothing you learned at school or college taught you how to deal with this.

In the living-room, the song that reminds you of him comes on MTV, and what does he do? He points to the TV and says that he loves the song, and then he proceeds to sing along with the very line that you feel was written for him. *You've got the most stumbling blue eyes I've ever seen.* And holding an imaginary microphone, he moves right up to you and inspects your eyes. "You've got hazel eyes," he says, and you cross your eyes for want of something better to do. Why hadn't he noticed the colour of your eyes before now? Are you the only fool who really falls in love? Something is going on inside your head. It's like that heightened sense of agitation a repetitive task often brings on. It's imperative that you speak before you lose touch.

The song finishes, and whatever effect it has on him, it certainly provides the icebreaker.

"Listen, Paul, I really want us to stay friends. Like, you're very important to me."

From anyone else, this would sound like a crock of shit, but not from him. He actually means what he's saying. He has none of your cynicism, that's what makes him all the more endearing. And it's also what makes this all the more difficult. It would definitely be a lot easier if he was feeding you all the usual bullshit that goes with this territory.

"And even if you don't want to stay friends, I'll always remember you."

"Of course I want to stay friends."

He leans forward and kisses your forehead. His familiar breath lingers in your nostrils. The urge to hug him is too great to resist, but he slips away from your attempted grasp, and frowns.

You say, "Would you mind if we went upstairs to talk?"

"Upstairs?"

"To bed."

A pained expression comes over his features. It's like the anguished look of a parent whose child has done something he swore blind he wouldn't do.

"For old times' sake," you add, rather pathetically.

"I'm really not in the mood right now."

"Just to talk, nothing else. I just want to lie down beside you."

His reluctance lessens somewhat. "Okay, but only on one condition."

You nod, the way you imagine a concerned counsellor might nod. Grave and sincere. Name the price.

"And what's that?"

"We keep our clothes on."

So there it is, you've succeeded in hammering out a deal and you're on your way up the stairs, regretting that you hadn't left the curtains drawn that morning. He insists that you don't use "the marital bed", so you lead him to the guest-room, where Anne's mother often stays. The lingering fragrance of her eau-de-toilette isn't exactly an aphrodisiac. You both climb beneath the duvet, and for some reason, you can't stop shivering. Your teeth are clacking, the shivers won't stop even when he rubs you to warm you up. It's like you've caught a sudden fever. Anyone else would no doubt have suspected that your shivers are a ruse, but not him. He doesn't have a suspicious bone in his body, and thinking of this only accentuates your feelings of loss, and this in turn makes the shivers worse. He blames the nippy spell of weather and you're only too glad to agree.

"Just as well you kept your clothes on," he says.

You want to tell him about all you went through on account of him, that he's the first thought to enter your head every morning, that you've read his horoscope every day since you met, but you're afraid you'll frighten him off completely if you do. Eventually, you settle down, the shivering stops, but it's not the same between you. Once trust is broken it can never be mended. He's never going to open up to you the way he did the first time. The moment has passed. The magic is gone. He might create a fair impression of things being as they were, but they're not, they never will be.

And you almost believe this until you lift your head to look at him. It's a moment that shakes you to the very core. He's lying back, with his arms outstretched above his head, his hair upon the pillow, his eyes lost in thought, his mouth open.

"Don't go."

"Hah?" He looks at you, like he's just awoken from a deep sleep.

"Don't go to the States"

He sighs and turns to look out the window.

"I have to find a place to live, and I'd like it if you moved in with me."

A long silence follows. Could it possibly be that he's going to say yes?

"Thanks, I appreciate that, but I really need some space right now. And, like, I know I said on the phone that I'd like you to come with me, but now I don't think it'd be a good idea."

The bombshell explodes somewhere inside you, more than likely in the environs of your heart.

"I just need to be on my own for a while, and if I don't go now, I'll never go."

"Yeah, I suppose you're right."

And somewhat spectacularly, the mask holds firm while you dispense big-brotherly advice. It's like you've stepped outside yourself into another being, the very same way you did on your wedding day. You may never see him again, and somehow you manage to hold the walls of your sanity intact while you watch him pat his hair into place in front of the mirror.

After you return from dropping him home, you pour the contents of a can of lager into a pint glass and swallow the lot in one long gulp. How foolish you have been. You'll have to let go. Forget about him. It was a good experience while it lasted, but you've got to move on. Time will heal. The world's a big place. More fish in the sea. There are so many soothing clichés sloshing about in your head, you almost succeed in convincing yourself that they can't all be so far off the mark. Lager number two and three get you into your stride. Spread out across the table in front of you are the photos you took in Wexford. Needless to say, he's in every single shot. The other weekend revellers who happened to wander in front of the camera are posing like they really believed you wanted a photo of them. Little did they know. On lager number five, the song that reminds you of him comes on the radio and you shove one of Lia's storytime tapes into the tape-recorder and press record. With the volume up loud, you replay the song over and over again. Any sharp-eared neighbour will have you marked down as an obsessive.

There's a notepad in front of you and your hand is guiding the scratchy pen across the page, telling the story that has to be told. Approximately every three minutes, a stumble takes you to the tape-deck to press that rewind button. The segment of tape will probably wear out and snap. It represents the last few months of your life. Since that fateful day he walked into that interview room and turned your world upside down. What were the chances of never meeting him? Very high. Would it be better if you never did? It'd be nice and comforting to be able to say yes, but that just isn't the truth. That irritating twerp of an author on the TV was right. Life without passion isn't living.

There are blurred shadows moving about inside your head. Shadows from the past, voices from the past. There's that pleasant time in primary school when all you cared about was the game of football in the yard at lunchtime. Whacker, Jinks, Specs Doyle, Nipper Healy, Hen Clarke and his little brother Pecks, all the names and faces return. That was when you were very young, and back then you were more worried about death than you are now. You used to be convinced that your mother and father were going to die. But you had contingency plans drawn up. You were going to take your sister away to the country where the two of you would live in a treehouse. No orphanage would get its claws on you. And look at you now, lurching towards the lager shrine for a refill. And where's your sister? Off in Australia with her Aussie hubby and her Aussie kids.

Faces and voices from another era drift in on the fog of music and lager. It's after you had turned fourteen and fallen in love for that breathtaking first time. Speaking aloud to an imaginary camera, you reminisce on how close you came to saying something to Eamonn O'Neill. How could you ever forget that name. The pair of you were inseparable, the purest of friendships. You've never had a friendship like it since, and something tells you even now that he was as much in love with you as you were with him. Anything that happened, your first thought was of telling him, of watching his animated reaction. And it was just after that fourteenth birthday when his family moved house, away down to the west of Ireland. One hundred and sixty miles away to be precise. The night before he left, the two of you kicked a football around on the road with all the others, the same way you did any summer night. At ten o'clock, with the long twilight turning to darkness, he said goodbye, and before he went into his house, he stood in front of you, neither of you knowing what to do or say. The moment is still so vivid. There were others around, but they seemed to be in another dimension. How were you to know that you would never look into those eyes again? The opportunity slipped by, you didn't have the words to say. And you went to bed and cried yourself to sleep.

Growing up meant you didn't cry, but you are openly crying when you make another raid on the lager shrine. All you can think of is that you may never see Johnny again. Change the music to music from your youth, your Eamonn song, "Find My Way Home" by Jon and Vangelis, and especially the one line that goes, "Your friend is close by your side." And with that, you dance around the room the way a youngster would have done back in the early eighties. Shuffling the feet, slouching, acting cool, flicking that fringe back, and keeping a constant look out for a mirror. Idiotic isn't the word for it. There are other songs to hear, songs that span the years, songs that pinpoint exact moments in time for a sentimental old fool. The dusty record collection is raided. Tracks are selected with loud, tearing scratches. Apologies are made to circular chunks of vinyl. But the music doesn't lift your spirits the way it used to. So it's on to the classical music phase of your college years, and if any neighbour happens to peek through a gap in the curtain, they'd certainly get the impression that there's a madman on the loose. To see someone standing in front of a mirror, conducting a conversation with absent friends from their college years, to the background music of Schubert, would be enough to spur anyone to place a call to the relevant authorities. And when you stumble back into the armchair, through the swimming half-light, you see that, in the broken and trampled wedding photograph, a jagged piece of glass is running right across your neck. And all you can do is point at the photograph and laugh.

* * * *

It feels like you are a ship, being tossed about on a wild sea, decks awash, winds howling, drunken passengers sliding the length of the beer-sodden bar floor. It sounds like an old-fashioned fire-engine is motoring its way along the top deck with its clanging bell ringing out the emergency across the waves. Are we on the Titanic? you hear a voice ask. Your eyelids are crusted together and it feels as though your eyeballs have been rolled in sand, that once familiar post-all-night-party sensation. Layers of scum have congealed inside your mouth. The top of your legs feel numb. You try to remember if you've been paralysed, if you are lying in a hospital bed. But you don't seem to be lying down. And who is it that's ringing that bell inside your head?

Finally, you manage to prise your eyes open and the glare of bright morning light sends a dull throb through your hollow head, right down the back of your neck. This is the most frightful of hangovers. If you move your head, it will cave in. That much you know. It becomes clear that you're actually sitting in an armchair in the living-room, and that's the trigger for the previous night's escapades to flood into every crevice of your memory with alarming lucidity. It's like pouring salt onto an open wound. The pain is overwhelming.

It's then you realise that the ringing sound is coming from the hallway. No, it's not a fire-engine on board a ship, it's definitely the telephone. But how long has it been ringing? And will it ring off the moment you leave the chair? The effort involved in actually standing up saps every ounce of your strength and you have to sit back down for a moment. The seat is wet beneath you. The shape of the damp stain on your trousers puts you in mind of a big head of cauliflower. Then, with a blinding dart of pain, it occurs to you that it might be him on the blower, calling to tell you he's changed his mind again. For beautiful people, a change of mind is always tolerated, almost expected.

A lurch is followed by a stumble and you're down on the ground, entangled with the coffee table. The wedding-present clock on the mantelpiece reads ten o'clock, and you can only assume that it's talking am. It's becoming a little like an army assault course. You are dragging yourself across the living-room floor with the coffee table and a rug attempting to haul you back, and with chairs and other assorted items of furniture jumping out in front of you, making vain attempts to halt your progress. In the hallway, with your tongue jammed in the side of your mouth, you reach out and lift the receiver. It's like you've just grabbed the last lifejacket.

After a fumble, the receiver is at your mouth but you can't speak. No words will come out. It's as though a thick layer of crusty late-night grunge has solidified on your vocal chords. Eventually, the woman on the other end of the line decides to break the silence. "Hello, could I speak to Paul Cullen please."

It dawns on you that it's Sophie, Carney's secretary.

You finally manage to utter a croaking noise, which was supposed to be, "Speaking", but which emerges as a gurgling roll of Rs.

"Is your daddy there?" Sophie puts on the childish voice people often do when they are speaking to children. What age does she think your daughter is?

With a scraping cough, you finally manage to clear your throat and say, "Sophie?"

"Paul, is that you?"

"It's me."

"God, you sound like you're dying."

"'Flu."

"Yeah, there's a terrible dose going around."

If you had told her that a comet had hit the house during the night, you suspect she may have agreed that there's a terrible spate of house-hitting comets flying about.

"Listen, I'm sorry for calling you at home, but Mr Carney's off to see the bankers now and he needs next month's projections."

She scribbles down the details of how to access the file, and while you are calling them out, you remember that you were supposed to accompany Carney to meet the bankers.

"Emm, Sophie, will you tell the Fat Man that he should take Janet along with him?"

"Yeah, he's taking her with him."

Now you can picture yourself, standing on the street, crystal-bowl in hand, jobless.

"Listen, Paul, I'm under pressure here, so I'll just wish you a speedy recovery and hopefully we'll see you back soon."

"Yeah, thanks."

She's hung up before you've finished your sentence. The joys of pressure.

Now you see the living-room in all its glory. There's evidence of a wild night scattered about all right. It looks like someone used a bulldozer to clear out the fireplace. And whoever was in that bulldozer must have been tossing crumpled beer cans about all night, and not only that, he was obviously a music-lover who doesn't believe in returning CDs, tapes or records to their covers. And then there's that beer stain on the carpet. If you look at it from a certain angle, it's actually in the shape of a long penis. Those videos have polluted your mind. But you can hardly blame the bulldozer man for the pages of barely-legible nonsensical scrawls, which, you suspect, it would take a team of psychiatrists to decipher.

* * * *

The following day, traces of the mammoth hangover still remain. In the tearoom, the reaction to you is definitely muted, and you suspect it will be some time before they make those jovial remarks like, "Sssh, here he is now", or the usual comments about imaginary sightings of you during your 'sick' day off. *Hey Paul, you looked very ill indeed while you were playing that backhand shot in the third set.*

But today, Doreen has a story worth telling, nothing is going to stand in her way. On her way home the previous evening, she stopped at a red light in the city centre, and quick as a flash, the front passenger window was smashed in by a chain.

"I caught a glimpse of one of those toothbrush heads reaching for me bag," she says, glancing at Jason, who immediately flushes bright crimson. "So I just pushed me foot to the floor and took off like the clappers through the red light.

This is greeted by gasps of approval and awe.

Bernie, who's sitting alongside Doreen, joins in. "And when she got home, what d'you think she found on the front-seat beside her." Bernie wants to let everyone know that she's already been privy to the story. "Tell them Dor," she says.

"One of yer man's fingers," Doreen says, and a collective gasp of amazement circles the tearoom.

"Jaysis," Tom says.

Others congratulate Doreen on her quick thinking. Everyone sneaks a quick glance down at their fingers.

"Fish-fingers for lunch in the canteen," Andy says.

"I'll send it down to them," Doreen says.

"Hope he washed his nails," someone else says.

"That'll make them think twice," Tom says.

Andy looks at him. "What will? If they got a dirty nail in their fish-fingers?"

Tom is flustered by the laughter all around. "Jaysis, what's he on?"

And just when it seems that they've all forgotten about your presence, Sophie sticks her head in the tearoom door, points to you and says that Mr Carney wants to see you. A hush descends on the room. It's like being back at school, and you're the one who was seen attempting to burn down the school over the weekend. Every step you take towards the door seems to be in slow motion.

Carney peers over the top of his half-frames. His expression appears to be a benevolent one. He pours a cup of coffee for you and thrusts a plate of biscuits in your direction.

"Paul, I'm not going to beat around the bush. I've heard the stories that are circulating."

You lift your eyebrows.

"Look, you know me, I'm just a big country lad at heart, but I'm also a man of the world...What I'm trying to say to you is that I don't give a damn what someone does in their own time. Like, I don't give a flying fuck if you want to have it off with fish, so long as you don't drag your aquarium into this office with you." His eyes bulge comically. "All I care about is your performance here."

You ought to say something, but there's nothing appropriate you can think of saying. However, you do sense that it's unnecessary to start denying now.

"You know me son, Cliff?"

You nod.

"Well, he's gay."

You contort your features into what you hope is a noncommittal sort of expression.

"What would you expect if you christen a young lad with a name like that."

You can't prevent a rush of air from escaping down your nostrils.

"It was the missus chose the name. Loved Cliff Richard, so she did."

"That's always the way." For some reason, you speak in a much deeper voice than normal.

"He told me when he was eighteen. Fine lad. Met his pals too, so I have. Although to be honest, it's all a bit of a puzzle to me. You see in my day, it was simple. The gay lads either went off to live abroad or else they joined the clergy and that was that. Everyone knew it, but no one would ever dare to say it."

He's crass, but you can't deny he makes a certain amount of sense.

"But nowadays it's different. Cliff has opened me eyes up, and I have to agree with him, it's senseless that it should make a difference. After all, we've had many fine clergymen in this country, haven't we?"

Again you nod, thinking of Johnny's cross-country coach, aware that Carney is becoming slightly exasperated by your silence. He's making all the running. But what does he expect you to say?

"Look, Paul, you know I've been very happy with the level of your performance here since the very first day you joined us. You've revolutionised our systems, dragged us kicking and screaming into the twentieth century. But more importantly, I like you as a person. I like to think we hit it off together, and because none of me own kids were bothered to come into the business, I've always seen you as a sort of adopted son."

This certainly throws you a little. And as far as you can tell, it isn't whiskey-fuelled.

"Thanks Mr Carney, I appreciate you saying this."

"Not a word to anyone else about Cliff now."

You draw an imaginary zip shut across your lips.

Carney takes a swig of his coffee. "Listen, strictly between ourselves, Paul." He lowers his voice to a whisper. "I'm letting Ronnie go."

You register an expression of surprise.

"To be honest, I should've gotten rid of him about five years ago, because it was around that time he became an incompetent gobshite."

You can't deny a certain feeling of elation. Ronnie Burke is hardly one of your favourite people.

"He's much too fond of the sauce." And with that Carney holds an imaginary bottle to his lips and makes a squeaking sound that puts you in mind of a hinge that needs oiling. But he also seems to have read your thoughts. "I know I'm fond of a drop meself, but I'm nowhere near Ronnie's league."

You nod eagerly to confirm this fact. "But what about the ...?" You rub your thumb against your fingers.

"No worries on that score, he was done for drink-driving three weeks ago."

You open your eyes wide.

"Tried to bribe a garda, so he did."

"You're joking."

"Offered him a tenner."

"A tenner!"

"Ten whole pounds. Always had style, our Ronnie."

Both of you snigger aloud, like two schoolboys sharing a smutty joke.

"And as you very well know, attempting to bribe a member of the police force is a resigning matter for a company director." Carney shakes his head. "He could even be looking at a jail sentence."

You emit a low whistling sound.

"What's most annoying is that I've also discovered why the old bollox was so adamant we buy that damn computer system. A little birdy filled me in, and I can tell you, he didn't have the company's best interests at heart."

Good old kickback Ronnie. It is a puzzle though as to how it took Carney so long to discover this.

"As soon as he's gone, I'm going to promote yourself and Kevin Daniels. I want dynamic people like the two of you running the show. And I'll be asking you to take control of Ronnie's brief on the manufacturing side of things."

After the meeting's over, you become aware of a damp sensation in your armpits, so you head off to the gents, slip into a cubicle, unravel lengths of toilet-paper and stuff them into your armpits. A worrying thought occurs to you. What sort of reaction will you encounter on the factory floor? If you ask someone to do something, will they turn to you and say, Do it yourself, Fairy Cakes? How would you react to that?

Your system has just about normalised itself when the toilet door opens and someone with light footsteps goes to the urinals. Moments later, the door opens again and you hear Ronnie Burke's voice.

"Ah, it's the man himself."

Obviously, a silent greeting is exchanged between them. You hold your breath and listen.

"Well, the question now is, who isn't queer?" Ronnie laughs and so does the other person. But the mystery person's laugh is restrained, almost reluctant.

"I'll tell you, I knew immediately that yer man Johnny was as bent as a thruppenny bit."

Whoever's with him laughs again out of politeness, but it's still difficult to pinpoint his identity.

"But I must admit, Cullen surprised me a little."

"Ah Ronnie, I don't think he's bent."

It's the Phantom.

"Ah, will you go 'way out of that Gussy, of course he is. I've been around long enough now to be able to spot a brown-nob from half a mile away."

A silence follows. Now you really take comfort from imagining Ronnie Burke's reaction to his impending dismissal.

"Well, better get the nose back to the grindstone."

"Okay, watch yourself out there now Gussy."

"Hah?"

"One of the boyos might hit on you."

The Phantom utters an almost hysterical, giggly laugh before his footsteps retreat and the door closes behind him.

You hear Ronnie Burke release a condescending rush of air through his nostrils. This is followed by a loud fart and a sigh of pleasure. Then there's silence, and it's odds on he's noticed the locked cubicle. Automatically, you lift your feet off the floor and look upwards, waiting for his face to appear over the top of the partition. The ludicrousness of the situation does occur to you. Maybe you should simply flush the toilet and walk right out there and watch Ronnie squirm. The hand-dryer shudders into action. This is followed by the click of Ronnie's footsteps and the toilet door closes. He's gone, but you wait another ten minutes before you leave.

Chapter Fourteen

It's Saturday morning and you're sitting out on the apartment balcony, smiling wryly as you find yourself glancing through the engagement notices in *The Irish Times*. Old habits die hard. Names of contemporaries pop up, together with the proud trailblaze of qualifications. Across the bay, Howth Head is shimmering in the heat haze. Sail boats dot the blue ocean, seahorses gallop towards the shore, cloud shadows speckle the water. Behind you, you become aware of a commotion. Lia is on the loose. Through the sliding-door you see her rush through the living-room with Johnny close on her heels. She knocks over a plant and chortles. Mayhem is written all over her features. She's grown into a two-and-a-half-year-old with no shortage of wild spirit. She can't believe that her dada and Donny still don't leave things out of reach of her marauding grasp. She shrieks when Johnny closes in, grabs hold of her, turns her upside down and blows air into her stomach. It's the fart-like sound that really gets her going.

"You'll waken the baby," Johnny whispers.

"Him's bold baby," she says.

"No, him is good baby."

"Silly billy Donny."

Contorting herself into a slippery eel, she wriggles free, delivers a sharp kick to Johnny's shins and bolts her way out onto the balcony. Once she's by your side, she turns to stick her tongue out at Johnny.

"Oh, wait'll your mama hears about this." Johnny is pointing at her, his eyes open wide, his hand covering his mouth.

She sticks her tongue out once again, shoves her thumbs in her ears and wiggles her fingers.

In reply, Johnny pretends that by twisting his ears back he is making his own tongue dart out.

She howls with laughter.

You say, "Lia, the baby is asleep."

"Baby asleep," she whispers, placing her finger to her lips.

Johnny wags his finger. "Don't be annoying your dada, he's nearly thirty now and Donny beat him at tennis again last night."

"It's the best of three."

Johnny speaks to Lia as though you are not present. "Even though your dada keeps changing the rules, he still loses all the time."

Lia plucks a potted plant from the ledge and tosses it out over the balcony wall. Immediately, Johnny and yourself look down, relieved not to see one of your fellow apartment dwellers lying poleaxed on the grass.

"Lia, that was one of my favourite plants," Johnny says, lifting her up and touching his nose against hers.

She grabs hold of his nose and twists it so sharply, his eyes water.

"Waah, Donny cry."

She pats his nose and then plants a kiss on it.

"Betta?"

"Donny betta now."

"I get you new plant," she says in her soothing motherly voice, tilting her head sideways in a manner which never fails to amuse you.

The intercom buzzer sounds and Lia jerks like she's been touched with an electrified cattle prod.

"Mama!" she shrieks.

"No, that's the eggman," Johnny teases.

The excitement of a caller has got the better of her. She stumbles her way across to the visual display monitor, where you have to lift her up to let her see her mama's face on the screen.

It's not her mama, it's Johnny's younger sister and brother, or the Gruesome Twosome as he affectionately refers to them. They're calling for a free swim in the apartment block swimming-pool, which is supposed to be strictly for residents' use only. Johnny greets them by telling them that he's not going to offer them a cup of coffee. They wait while he searches in the kitchen for the swimming-pool pass. Lia is huddled beside you, with her finger held to her lips. She can be shy when there are strangers around. Both of you are out on the balcony, out of view of the Gruesome Twosome, who don't seem to realise just how poor the soundproofing in the apartment is. "Double income, no kids," the sister says. "It's the modern world we live in," the brother says. "Not a ring in sight." The sister sighs. "Isn't it shocking really." The brother sighs. "Well, at least they're sleeping in separate bedrooms." They both snigger. "Yes, I suppose we have to be thankful for small mercies." "Oh, we do indeed." You hear Johnny telling them that if they lose the swimming-pool pass he will force them to eat a dinner cooked by him. "Where's your flatmate?" the sister asks. The brother corrects her, "You mean, Where's your posh-apartment-avec-swimming-pool-mate?" "Disappear please," Johnny says in a weary voice. The Gruesome Twosome are hardly out the door when the intercom buzzer sounds again. Moments later, Anne enters the apartment and, as he always does, Johnny retreats to the bedroom with the newspaper. He's not supposed to be around when the children are here.

"I hope she was no trouble," Anne says.

"I is good girl." Lia is tugging out of her mama.

"Apart from burning down the apartment next door, she was well-behaved," you say.

"And what about his Lordship?"

"Not a peep out of him."

You step into the spare bedroom and watch while Anne lifts the baby from his cot. Three months old now, he's becoming aware of the world around him, and of the dangers posed by his older sister's bludgeoning attempts to monopolise attention.

"Will you have time for coffee?"

"No, Larry's waiting outside in the car."

There's an unspoken agreement between Larry and yourself. You avoid one another. It makes for easier living. So you go as far as the hallway and hold the heavy hall-door open to allow Anne to wheel the buggy out. Lia gives you a big wet kiss on the cheek and then waves up at the apartment window.

"Bye, bye Donny," she shouts.

"Bye, bye who?" Anne asks.

"Bye, bye Donny."

"Is he here?"

You blush.

"Him's in bedroom," Lia, the supergrass, announces.

Anne speaks in a low voice.

"What's he doing here?"

"His lectures were cancelled."

"Paul, you promised he wouldn't be here when the children were around. I mean, come on, what sort of example is it?"

"Oh yeah, like they're going to know what's going on."

"Never underestimate children. Especially not your daughter, she has all your secretiveness." This knocks the wind out of your sails.

Lia's had enough of this talking. She's dragging her mama towards the waiting car. It's almost a year now since Johnny and yourself moved into the third floor apartment. For two months, there was a complete freeze between Anne and yourself. And during that period, you had a regular daydream of her arriving to the door with either a .357 Magnum, or else a posse of the country's leading divorce lawyers. But then she met Larry and things began to thaw between you. One day, you ended up alone with her, and she asked the question she more than likely had been planning to ask for some time.

"Paul, why did you marry me?"

The words seemed to come out of nowhere, like there was an invisible third person in the room. The day of Great Pretence had flashed to mind and, in particular, the moment when the service was over and you were standing on the church porch, facing the barrage of photographers, and the swirling wind was blowing Anne's veil all over the place. Her pleading, distressed expression is frozen in your memory. All you had to do was utter a word of comfort, but something inside prevented you. Something inside you wanted to see her embarrassed, alone, isolated. Some irrational thought pattern resented her and wanted to teach her a lesson for agreeing to marry you. It wasn't the way you'd expect someone to treat a member of their family. The mind boggles.

There's still a fair bit you never mentioned to Dr Kelly.

But, when she asked why you had married her, it was your opportunity to make some sort of amends and you had said, "I don't know, I thought I'd change. I thought all those other desires would eventually vanish."

She had stared down at the floor. "I have to admit, that night I found out, I would've preferred if you had died rather than..."

"I wouldn't blame you." It felt strange. For the first time since you'd met her, you were being totally honest with her.

It was open season time, so you told her how you always felt as though you were floating about in a sea of lies. Everywhere you looked was false, every bone in your body felt false, so, to remain sane, you began to exist in a sort of parallel universe, and that this was all manageable until the day you met Johnny.

"You know, I sort of suspected that something might have been going on between Teresa and yourself."

You had smiled, somewhat pleased that you hadn't imagined everything. "Would I have been so predictable?"

She had emitted a snort. "I also thought that it might be that you just had a low sex drive."

That caused your eyebrows to lift in surprise.

She had leaned forward. "Paul, for Lia's sake, and for this one's sake," she had patted her bulging stomach, "I think we should stay in touch."

Your eyes were moist. "I'd like that."

"You can do your share of baby-sitting."

"Put old Tight Jeans out of a job."

Funnily enough, when you broke the news to your sister in Australia, she wasn't as surprised as you thought she would be. She admitted that, when you were younger, she did suspect that you might be gay. And when you asked her why she hadn't said anything, she laughed and asked what was she supposed to do? Halt the progress of your wedding by declaring that she had suspicions about the groom?

Johnny's parents give the impression that they believe that the pair of you are just two good friends sharing an apartment.

Whenever they call by, there's always something of a mad skirmish to make the spare bedroom appear inhabited. For the past year, Johnny's been working up the courage to tell them, and something tells you that, when he does, he's not going to surprise them in any way. You were there when he came out to his friends, the Wexford weekend friends, and while they gave the impression that they were surprised, you could see them thinking, Hey Johnny, tell us something we don't already know. Tell us news, not history.

Johnny is working with a landscaping company. The outdoor work suits him, and his green fingers have the apartment resembling a jungle. He went to America and only lasted a month there. Of course, during that month, you phoned him daily just to make sure he realised how homesick he was. The day you collected him from the airport still ranks as the day you finally shed your closet skin. The two of you snogged in front of everyone. Hugging and kissing usually goes unnoticed in airport arrival terminals, however, two men kissing mouth-to-mouth did attract a certain amount of attention. This was no pop video. This was real life. But no one said a word, and in fact, if anything, they seemed to silently approve of this spontaneous open display of affection. They seemed to like being reminded that this was a modern Ireland they were living in. That kiss broke all the rules you grew up with. It was a defining moment, the moment of release from the shackles of the past.

At Carney Textiles, once the dust settled, you realised that it wasn't such a big deal with people as you might have imagined it would be. Even on the factory floor, the occasional burst of sneering laughter, those nudges and winks you pretended not to notice, they soon faded away, and people grew to accept you for what you were. The fact that you were a director by then more than likely helped, but during that period, you understood the two lads you saw that night in the Chinese restaurant. When you're with the one you love, you can put up with almost anything. Like one night, you and Johnny popped into a pub for a drink after the pictures, and you ran straight into the Wax Hennessy and a group of college contemporaries you would have preferred to have avoided. Your initial instinct was to turn around and walk right out again. But then, you thought, why should I? So instead, you nodded to them, exchanged strained pleasantries, moved to the far side of the pub, where you were conscious that they were staring over at you like you were some sort of mutant. Even though you definitely would have preferred to have been elsewhere, it was important that you stayed there and let them know that you weren't going to let them make you feel in any way inferior. It was a difficult, but important, step to take.

Gradually, the overriding impression you got was that people were too concerned with their own lives to be bothered with anyone else's. The Phantom still pretends to know nothing of your present set-up, and something tells you that it'll take him another hundred years or so to change.

If someone were to have said to you a year before that you would be living life as an openly gay man in a year's time, it would have taken a remarkable stretch of the imagination to believe them. But now, you no longer feel the urge to stab anyone who delays you in the supermarket. The blood-pressure doesn't soar when you're stuck in traffic. The stress gauges no longer hit the ceiling whenever Kevin Daniels crosses your path. You no longer feel the urge to turn your head and ogle whenever a pretty woman passes by just in case someone might be watching. There's no longer any need to sneak up onto disused railway bridges or into toilet cubicles. You treat people better than you used to and, on Johnny's prompting, you even visit your parents' grave once a month. It's like a logjam has been cleared and the river is flowing along at the pace it ought to flow at. Your energy is no longer sapped up and wasted by the effort involved in leading that double-life. Now you know that you are finally moving on to wherever it is you are going.